The Bastard's Tale

The Bastard's Tale

MARGARET FRAZER

BERKLEY PRIME CRIME, NEW YORK

THE BASTARD'S TALE

A Berkley Prime Crime Book
Published by The Berkley Publishing Group,
a division of Penguin Putnam Inc.,
375 Hudson Street, New York, New York 10014.

Visit our website at
www.penguinputnam.com

First edition: January 2003

Library of Congress Cataloging-in-Publication Data

Frazer, Margaret.
The bastard's tale / Margaret Frazer.—1st ed.
p. cm.
ISBN 0-425-18649-0 (alk. paper)
1. Frevisse, Sister (Fictitious character)—Fiction. 2. Great Britain—
History—Lancaster and York, 1399–1485—Fiction. 3. Great Britain—
History—Henry VI, 1422–1461—Fiction. 4. Women detectives—
England—Fiction.5. Nuns—Fiction. I. Title.

PS3556.R3586 B37 2003
813'.54—dc21
2002027650

PRINTED IN THE UNITED STATES OF AMERICA

10 9 8 7 6 5 4 3 2 1

To Charlie. Just because.

To be a mordrere is an hateful name.

G. CHAUCER, *The Clerk's Tale*

Chapter 1

The Welsh wind moaned against the heavily shuttered windows and along the thickness of the tower's stone walls, giving the lamp-lighted, fire-shadowed room with its tapestries, carpets, cushions, and fire on the hearth even more than its usual sense of comfort from a winter's night, when dinner and most of the day's duties were done and there was quietness and talk through the while until bed. Curled down among cushions piled near the hearth with the rough-coated greyhound Gelert stretched out beside him, Arteys was trying to feel the ease he should, here in his father's Pembroke Castle, but all he had was more unease as he listened to what was being said around and above him by his father and the others—Gryffydd ap

Nicholas, Sir Richard Middelton, Yevan ap Jankyn, and ridden in yesterday from England, Sir Roger Chamberlain.

As usual, things had bettered when his father had come away into Wales, had come away from London, away from Westminster, away from the king and the men around him. If it were left to Arteys' choice, they would never go back. Once they were away, his father always remembered how to laugh again, took up his books with pleasure, sometimes even rode out hunting. Life became almost what it was until five years ago. Almost there was forgetting.

But not tonight. Arteys rubbed gently at the soft place behind Gelert's left ear, and deep in contentment, the greyhound sighed, its head sinking more heavily onto Arteys' thigh. Gelert's was the only contentment here tonight, Arteys thought, watching the breathing rise and fall of the dog's flank. He did not need to watch the men's faces in their half-circle facing the firelight around him. It was enough to listen to their intent and worried voices, uncertain—or with his father, too certain—what lay behind the letter Sir Roger had brought yesterday.

A month ago his father had replied to the official summons of all lords to Parliament that he would not come because of his health and the time of year. In truth, Arteys knew he had come into Wales particularly to have excuse not to go to Parliament, because among the things in which his father no longer took pleasure were the toil and tussle for power and favor around the king. He had lost his taste for it with Lady Eleanor's destruction. For five years now his wife had been imprisoned, kept from her husband and her friends, if any friends were left to her, and in that while Gloucester had grown further and further away from the ways of power that had once been his life.

Now this letter was come, sealed with the king's own privy seal, asking that the duke of Gloucester, the king's right well-beloved uncle, come to the present Parliament at Bury St. Edmunds, and Gloucester was of a sudden set on going, despite no one here trusted the summons except himself.

Gryffydd was putting it most bluntly, rolling the words like gravel in his displeasure. "You're mad if you go. Plead weather and winter. Plead your lungs are poorly and you don't dare trust them to the wind and days of riding. Nobody can quarrel with that if you say it strong enough and often. I care not half a jot what he hints he'll do. Don't risk it."

Occupied less with worry than with cracking a walnut from the broad silver dish beside him, Gloucester returned cheerfully, "Henry more than hints. He all but says he's ready to hear with mercy, finally, whatever I ask for Eleanor."

"There's a long way between 'all but' and an open promise," Gryffydd growled and no one disagreed with him.

Arteys kept silent. He was here because his father liked his company, not because he was anyone who would be listened to. Besides, he knew his father in this high humor—he would only half-hear whatever was said to him and heed none of it. These men knew it, too, but Sir Richard muttered, staring into the dark depths of wine in the goblet he held, "I don't even see it's certain King Henry signed it. It could come from anybody's hand for all we know."

Gloucester tossed the emptied walnut shells toward the fire carelessly. They scattered on the hearthstone and Arteys reached sideways from Gelert, picked them up, and tossed them the rest of the way into the flames while Gloucester said, "Of course he signed it. I know his hand as well as I know my own. And his privy seal. You think it's just wandering around for anyone to pick up and use?"

"But who told him to write it?" Gryffydd said.

"By St. Alban's grace, he's a grown man, Gryffydd." Gloucester laughed. "He doesn't have to be told to do things nor do what anyone tells him."

"What I want to know is why Parliament was moved from Cambridge to Bury," Yevan put in. "Why the change?"

They all looked to Sir Roger. He had been with the royal court less than a week ago and was most like to know, but he raised a shoulder to show he did not. "One day it was set for Cambridge. The next day it was shifted to Bury. That's all anyone told me and all I heard."

"Bury St. Edmunds is a bigger place, and there's the abbey," Gloucester said.

"Where King Henry is everybody's darling and he'll have all the abbot's power added to the rest," Sir Richard said. "You won't find allies there, Humphrey."

Gloucester shook his head, working at another walnut. "Lord almighty, but you're a glooming lot. Why not see it for what it is? A chance to have Eleanor free and with me again."

"It won't be that simple," Sir Richard said. "Mark my words."

"Of course it won't be," Gloucester agreed lightly. "I'll have to plead, agree to terms, probably swear to never let her come near the royal court again, and whatever else that dog Suffolk can devise and persuade Henry to. But if Henry's made up his mind she's been punished enough, if he's willing finally to let her go, then God forbid I hold back." He put a hand out over the carved arm of his chair to rumple Arteys' hair as if Arteys were still a little boy, rather than man-grown.

"Hai, Arteys. We'll be glad to have her back, won't we?"

Arteys looked up, making despite his misgivings the smile he knew his father wanted from him but his warmth unfeigned as he answered, "We will." Because if it ever happened, he *would* be glad. Lady Eleanor had been always kind to him, loving and giving and never grudging him a place in her husband's household despite he was her husband's bastard. Even after it had become certain she would never have any sons or daughters of her own to inherit Gloucester's royal dukedom, she had been good to him. Arteys had asked her once, at the surly end of his boyhood, if she would have been as good to him if he had been begotten after she had married Gloucester instead of before, and she had answered with her merry laugh, her eyes dancing with mirth and mischief, "Your begetting was none of your doing. Why should I hold it against you? Mind you, what I'd do to Gloucester is another matter."

She had said it easily, secure in her love. For all the feckless youth that Humphrey, duke of Gloucester, son and brother of kings, had led—and Arteys had heard stories in plenty over the years, including from Gloucester himself—only his follies in politics had continued into his middle years. Many people would include among those follies his marriage to Eleanor Cobham against the will, it seemed, of the whole realm of England, because a royal duke should marry for power and wealth, and all that Lady Eleanor, a mere knight's daughter, had been able to bring to their marriage had been her loveliness and love. But in return for those, Gloucester had given her his heart and faithfulness, and from everything Arteys had ever seen between them, they had been happy in each other. Only in two things had she ever failed Gloucester. First, in bearing him no children and then in seeking to learn unlawfully by sorcery whether he would succeed his childless nephew King Henry VI to the throne. She had been caught in the very act, and three of her accomplices had been hung, drawn, and quartered for their treason, the fourth burned for witchcraft, while she had been imprisoned, cut off from anyone ever dear to her for five years now, leaving Gloucester grieving at his own helplessness to help her.

Now here was come this letter, offering hope, and Arteys knew how little likely Gloucester would see trouble where he did not want to see it. Arteys had been brought into his father's household at eight years old, fetched from among the welter of small children being raised like a tumble of puppies in the household of one of Gryffydd's sons in a mountain-sided Welsh valley. All he had ever known about his mother was from the woman who had been his nurse—or keeper or whatever she might be best called—on the day his father's men had come for him, and all she had told him then as she bundled him into his cloak to be taken away was that his mother had been someone's younger daughter and her name Nan. "And if it ever matters who else she was, you'll be told. She had more lust than sense, God keep her soul, and an eye for a handsome man, for all the good that does her in her grave, and don't you go asking his grace your father anything more either. She was a long time ago and you can count yourself lucky he bothers to remember you're alive."

So Arteys had never asked and had found as the years went by, almost twenty of them now, that what mattered was not his never-known mother but that he had come to love his father and his father to love him; and if Gloucester was set on going to Bury St. Edmunds, then he would go with him.

Chapter 2

The high-walled, cobbled yard between the cloister and the guesthalls' gateway to the nunnery's outer yard was quiet and golden in the slant of late-afternoon sunlight. Looking down from the prioress' window into its sun-filled stillness, Dame Frevisse wished she believed in the sunlight's seeming warmth but cold was seeping in around the stone-framed window and she had her hands thrust well up either sleeve of her black Benedictine habit's wool outer gown and her arms crossed and pressed to her to keep to herself what warmth she had. This far across the parlor from the small hiss of flames among the careful coals on the prioress' hearth there was no pretense of anything but cold—the deep February cold that through these past weeks in this year of God's grace 1447, the twenty-fifth of King Henry VI's reign, had crept deep into everything and everyone not near a fire.

Not that anyone in St. Frideswide's lingered away from a fire if they could help it. For most of most days the soft tread and sweep of skirts along the cloister walk came only when the Offices of prayer called the nuns to the church, to huddle in clouds of their own breath over the prayer books.

Frevisse wished she was there now, in her own choir seat or kneeling below the altar, lost in prayer and quietness. Better to be there and cold rather than here with no quietness in her at all, only a strangled urge to curse his reverend grace the bishop of Winchester, while Domina Elisabeth stood waiting, beside the fire, for her answer. Because an answer could not be avoided, Frevisse set her face to show nothing of her race of thoughts and feelings and turned from the window toward her prioress, dressed like herself in black, from the long veils down their backs to their floor-reaching gowns and undergowns, relieved only by the white wimples encircling their faces and necks. With sleeves to hide the hands and layers of cloth to conceal the body, only face and voice were left to betray what was thought or felt, and very careful to betray nothing, Frevisse asked, "You want that I should go?"

Domina Elisabeth lifted the letter she held in her hand. "I want that St. Frideswide's not lose this chance."

Frevisse understood all too well Domina Elisabeth's barely held-in eagerness. St. Frideswide's was too small a nunnery with too many troubles and debts left from the last prioress' ill-managing even to think of refusing what the letter offered. The messenger who had brought it less than an hour ago had probably been hardly settled beside the guesthall fire before Domina Elisabeth had summoned Frevisse to her, and now, reluctantly, Frevisse agreed, "No, we shouldn't lose this chance."

"Nor is it something we can well refuse," Domina Elisabeth said.

"No. It isn't." Much though Frevisse wanted to. Not that her refusal would be of any use. Obedience was among the vows she had taken upon becoming a nun. If she did not give agreement, Domina Elisabeth would surely order it. And with good reason. His lordship Bishop Beaufort of Winchester had favored St. Frideswide's with the grant of a very profitable property in Oxford town, its profits to be the nunnery's own forever. In return he asked the small favor of "your Dame Frevisse attending on her cousin, Lady Alice of Suffolk, at Bury St. Edmunds during this present Parliament, to note what passes and do such service there as may be asked of her by one of my people, should there be need."

His request was made pardonable by his gift of the property and acceptable because it had come by way of Domina Elisabeth's brother, Abbot Gilberd of St. Bartholomew's near Northampton. That had been skillful of the bishop, Frevisse granted; it saved Domina Elisabeth from need of any hesitating scrupleness and equally forestalled delay, since St. Frideswide's was merely a priory, not an abbey, and therefore officially under Abbot Gilberd's guidance. Distant though he usually kept his hand, his permission would have been needed for this, but as it was, the letter had come with his word added to Bishop Beaufort's.

Left without recourse and hoping her anger did not show in face or voice, Frevisse said evenly, "Of course I'll go, if you so will it, my lady."

Domina Elisabeth smiled her approval. "Very good. My thanks, dame."

For not making Domina Elisabeth order her to go,

Frevisse supposed, and asked, "Does my lord bishop say how to go about telling Lady Alice I want to 'attend' on her?"

"Oh, yes." Domina Elisabeth consulted the letter. "His messenger who brought this will go on your behalf to Lady Alice with your request." She frowned slightly. "Won't she wonder why it comes by way of Bishop Beaufort?"

Frevisse, moving to join her beside the fire, said dryly, "I suspect that by the time he reaches Lady Alice, he'll seem to have come from you or else from Abbot Gilberd on your behalf, with no sign he's ever had aught to do with Bishop Beaufort." Who was a man with whom she had had dealings before now and neither liked nor trusted, the king's great-uncle and a power in the government for something like thirty years but also a cousin to the man Frevisse had counted her greatest friend, which was how, unfortunately, she had come to his notice.

For the first time Domina Elisabeth looked other than happy. "Dame Frevisse, is this . . ." She hesitated. Frevisse did not help her. "Is this something I . . . should have doubt about?" Doubt she all too clearly did not want to have.

Frevisse held back from saying that anything to do with the bishop of Winchester was something about which to have doubt; if she could not have her own way, she could at least give way gracefully, and she said, "Would your brother agree to anything likely to be unseemly?"

Domina Elisabeth immediately said willingly to let go her worry, "Of course not."

Frevisse slipped her hands from her sleeves to hold one out toward the letter. "May I?"

Domina Elisabeth handed it to her without hesitation,

murmuring as Frevisse began to read it, "Still, it's an odd asking."

It was and only the more odd when Frevisse had read the letter itself, finding it more full of what Bishop Beaufort did not say than what he did. "At least he gives excuse why I'm asking Lady Alice to see her." It was possibly even true that the grant of property needed the king's seal to make it certain due to a long-past but resurrectable quarrel between heirs now dead but with descendents.

"We can make another use of your going there, too," Domina Elisabeth said. "St. Edmund's Abbey has a fine library. If I send Dame Perpetua with you, she might copy out some book or two as well as take note of others the abbey might loan to us later at our asking, if she persuades the librarian of our good intent. That should be possible, yes?"

As a way to increase their income at St. Frideswide's, Domina Elisabeth had seen to starting a small scrivening business among such of the nuns as had a fair enough hand to it, copying out books in a plain fashion to be sold at plain prices. They were doing well enough at it after these few years that, yes, to increase what they could offer made sense.

"Lady Alice would be persuaded to put in a good word toward that," Frevisse said. And since some nun would have to accompany her, come what may, Dame Perpetua was a far better companion than some in St. Frideswide's would be.

"All's settled then," Domina Elisabeth said, smiling, pleased, all doubts forgotten.

And perversely Frevisse was suddenly taken with a small, inward merriment at the foolishness of it all. In return for a substantial reward without explanation, she was to go on a cold journey to Bury St. Edmunds, impose on her cousin's favor, and wait for she knew not whom to ask her for help—or maybe not ask her; Bishop Beaufort only said "may." Considering that she had before now made clear to him how little she liked him or wanted anything to do with his plots, he was bold to ask it of her, even for such a bribe as he was offering.

Or else he was desperate.

That thought sobered her. Because what would it take to make a man as powerful as Henry Beaufort, Cardinal and Bishop of Winchester, desperate?

Chapter 3

The strong east wind had broken the morning's clouds and was streaming them white across the bright, scoured sky. To Frevisse, standing small in the wide courtyard below the long, high-windowed flank and thrusting towers of St. Edmund's Abbey church with her cloak and skirts shoved against her legs and veil fluttering over her shoulder, it was not the clouds but the church itself that looked a-drift toward the town beyond the abbey walls, like some great ship too vast to be troubled by any storm.

It unsettled her head and stomach and she lowered her gaze, but at her side small John de la Pole, holding to her hand, stood with his head flung back to sky and clouds and church and laughed aloud with delight. He was all of four years old and her cousin's son and heir, and Frevisse smiled at his pleasure with more pleasure than she usually had toward small children.

Still watching the church, he said, "It makes me . . ." He whirled one of his hands at his head.

Frevisse raised her free hand to hold her flapping veil back from her face and offered, "Confused?"

John tried the word and liked it. "Confused. Confused, confused." He was merry as a sparrow and bright as a finch in his cherry red cloak and hosen, short green gown, and blue roll-rimmed cap. He gave a small, hopeful tug on her hand. "Can we see where it all fell down?"

"It didn't all fall down," Frevisse corrected. "Only the west tower, and now they're building it up again."

"Build it up and fall it down. My fair laaydee," John sang with another hopeful tug and she gave way, letting him lead her toward his favorite place in all of St. Edmund's Abbey. His mother had suggested they had set out early to do just that anyway this afternoon. Accompanying him should have been his nurse's task, or maybe his schoolmaster's, but both were laid low with heavy rheums and sent to stay somewhere away from the household. "Because with all else there is, I don't need coughs and running noses added in for all of us," Alice had said.

For her part, Frevisse was glad enough of something different to do. Time had been hanging heavy on her these two idle days since she and Dame Perpetua had come to Bury. After a little trouble, Dame Perpetua had settled to work in the abbey's library, and Frevisse would contentedly have joined her, except that she could not well "observe" things while hid away among books and desks and inkpots, nor be readily found by Bishop Beaufort's person if she were needed. So she was here instead, going from the Great Court through the broad

Cellarer's Gate into the smaller guesthall yard toward the church, John skipping beside her, wanting to run but held back by stern order to keep hold on her hand while they were out. That was the only hinderance to his pleasure, though. From what Frevisse had so far seen of him, he was both a biddable child and, as the marquis of Suffolk's heir, always companioned, either by his nurse or his schoolmaster or else with his mother and her ladies. Therefore Frevisse suspected that much of his present joy was at being free from them all, nor did she feel like curbing him, happy herself to be out and away from too many people and so much talk.

Not that she was really away from people. Within its walls the abbey probably covered more acres than the whole village of Prior Byfield near St. Frideswide's. It was a warren of courtyards, gardens, and buildings ranging from stables to kitchens to halls to chambers to chapels, all crowded around and spread out from the great abbey church that towered above them all, hugely visible for miles whichever way someone might come to Bury. In the usual way of things, the place would be busy enough with the perhaps fifty monks of the monastery itself, all the household officials, craftsmen, and servants necessary to the abbey's life, the constantly shifting tide of pilgrims to St. Edmund's shrine, and the daily come and go of Bury St. Edmunds townsfolk in and out and around on business if not worship, but to all of that was presently added the royal household, with King Henry himself and his Queen Margaret—as yet not even glimpsed by Frevisse—with all the many attendants and officers necessary both to their comfort and such governing of the realm as daily needed the king's own hand upon it, with all the servants and attendants required by all those royal officers for their own care and comfort. And added to all of them was Parliament, a tidy name for an untidy gather and sprawl of not only the ninety and more royally summoned lords and high churchmen, Alice had said, and *their* servants and attendants but also the almost three hundred knights and commoners elected from counties, cities, towns, and boroughs through all of England and all *their* servants and advisors and even wives come with them.

The town had perforce taken the overflow of them, to the undoubted great joy of innkeepers, foodsellers, and merchants, but the abbey was swarming full, too, the hum and bustle remindful to Frevisse of a beehive as she and John passed out of the guesthall yard, between the octagonal bulk of the abbey church's northwest tower and the east end of St. James parish church that served the townsfolk, into the broad foreyard between the abbey church's west front and a stone-towered gateway to the town's marketplace. This was the way that pilgrims were supposed to come, entering through the gateway to be confronted across the open yard by the wide, high west front of the abbey church.

Unhappily, the west tower's fall more than ten years ago had brought down much of the west front with it, and presently the yard was crowded and cluttered by piles of worked and unworked stones, stacks of timber, and the sheds of the stonemasons and other craftsmen who were slowly rebuilding tower and front. Because there was no trusting mortar laid in freezing weather, the yard and scaffolding were empty of workmen until spring, only the clink and clunk of tools on stone from one of the sheds telling that some of the more finely carved stonework was being done, to be ready when the rest of the workers returned.

John cared about none of that. His delight was the great wooden tread wheel high and higher yet on the scaffolding. Large enough for a man to walk inside of it to make it turn, it served for the raising of stones and mortar and whatever else was needed from the yard to the high walkways around the unfinished tower, and he tugged Frevisse into the open middle of the yard to see it better.

"He wants one of his own," Alice had said to Frevisse.

"You'll surely not deny him?" Frevisse had solemnly mocked.

"And give him a few masons and a stock of stone and timber all his own to go with it?" Alice had mocked back, smiling. She mostly smiled when she talked of John, the son who had finally come to her after two barren marriages and several daughters. "I think not. What I've promised is that if he does just as he ought in the play and makes no trouble while we're here in Bury, he'll have a toy of it afterward. I've already sent word to the carpenter at Wingfield to start one for him." Fond of her daughters though she seemed to be—she spoke of them affectionately the few times she spoke of them at all—John was openly her joy and Frevisse thought that only Alice's prevailing strong good wit kept him from being unredeemably marred. Thus far.

While John happily pointed out one thing after another about how the tread wheel worked, Frevisse nodded and murmured, taking pleasure in his pleasure. Someone among the workers or guards left here must have been brought out into the cold to talk with him about it and he, clever child, seemed to have remembered it all, but his interest was insufficient to keep her thoughts away from worry about Alice. Everything about coming here had gone as simply as might be hoped. Alice had returned prompt word that she would be glad of Frevisse's company and that by this same messenger she was sending word to Thomas Stonor, one of Oxfordshire's members to Parliament, that he should offer Frevisse and Dame Perpetua escort to Bury. "Since after all he is, in some way, my son-in-law," Alice had written, "being married to my lord husband's daughter, and as you are my cousin, it is therefore a matter of family. Whether you will thank me for this, I do not know. Master Stonor is of somewhat a strong nature."

From that, Frevisse had sorted that Master Stonor's wife was Suffolk's illegitimate daughter since she was not Alice's child and Suffolk had had no other marriages, and was probably from Suffolk's bachelor days since she was old enough to be married. And Master Stonor had proved to be as Alice had said. Though he had welcomed her and Dame Perpetua to join with his company and been courteous throughout the days of riding to Bury St. Edmunds, there had been a grudging beneath his graciousness, coupled with far too much awareness that Frevisse was cousin to Lady Alice and therefore, possibly, important. At journey's end Frevisse had parted from him with thanks and promise of prayers on his behalf and the thought that very likely Mistress Stonor had stayed at home for the pleasure of being without his company.

Or perhaps Mistress Stonor had simply foreseen the trouble of where to stay plaguing almost everyone here. Even Alice, provided by Suffolk's high place in the realm with three rooms together in the buildings that closed in the east side of the Great Court, part of the abbot's palace, had been full of regret that she could not have Frevisse and Dame Perpetua with her there. "But we're already sleeping six in our own bedchamber as it is. My ladies and some of the servants share what serves during the day as Suffolk's council chamber and the men lie wall to wall in the outer room. There simply isn't anywhere."

Frevisse had answered that she and Dame Perpetua

had already supposed they would stay in the abbey's
guesthall kept especially for Benedictine monks and
nuns come to Bury St. Edmunds for pilgrimage or whatever other reason.

Alice had been relieved. "That's good, and I've be-
spoken you both a place there. Otherwise, I don't know
there'd be a bed even there. What's supposed to be the
nuns' dorter is full of the overflow of everyone's waiting
women and ladies. I only wish you could be here. I was
afraid you'd mind. I was afraid you'd be . . ." Alice had
hesitated.

"Foolish?" Frevisse had offered.

"Foolish," Alice had agreed, from the heart. "You
wouldn't believe the foolishness there is here over who
stays where and why and is it according to their dignity
and . . ."

Words failed her, and Frevisse had said, meaning it,
"There's no need to worry over us. Let me be what help
I can to you and otherwise we'll fend for ourselves very
well. You've enough and enough in hand without taking
us on, too."

"Enough and more than enough," Alice had said, trying to make a jest of it and almost succeeding but not
quite.

That had been when Frevisse's first unease had prick-
led awake. Alice's mother had been a champion at fussing, a misplaced thimble as great a matter for upset as
the need for new slates on the great hall's roof, but from
girlhood Alice had taken after her father, going at prob-
lems with thought beforehand, rarely unsettled by anything, even sudden troubles. It had driven her mother
frantic—"Don't you *care*? Don't you *understand*?"—
that a moth hole had been found in a tapestry or the
steward said they would run out of salted beef a week
sooner than expected. Alice's care, like her father's, had

been shown by quietly dealing with matters, neither fussing at things nor being fussed by them and surely not by so common a trouble as the overcrowding that always came to anywhere with royalty, let be a parliament added on.

Frevisse had put that first small prickle of worry aside, willing to forget it, but there had been other prickles since then, each small, each easily ignored if she tried, but . . .

John was going on happily about pulleys and ropes. If he was as attentive to his lessons as he had been to whoever had told him all that, he was going to be a very knowledgeable boy, Frevisse thought, and regretfully gave his hand a small tug to draw his attention, telling him, "We should be going, I'm afraid."

John's sigh was heavy as he obediently dropped his heed from the heights to present necessity.

As Alice had explained it, Abbot Babington had, among other entertainments to divert the present crowd of nobility in his abbey, provided that a play be presented. "Of course not simply a play," Alice had said and for a moment had sounded very like her father, wry over a jest most people would not see. "It's one of the good abbot's gifts to the king, you understand."

"Oh my," Frevisse had said, because something presented to the king and queen and royal court would probably be, at best, beset with strange beings, fantastical clothing, and over-long speeches. At worst it would be so tangled with allegory and other obscurities that no one would know or care what it was about.

"Oh my," Alice had agreed. She had nonetheless found a way to use the thing to her own ends. When Abbot Babington had consulted with Suffolk about the play, she had taken the chance to read it for herself, had found there was place in it for small children, and suggested John would suit well. "No one," she said to Frevisse, "is ever too young to be brought to the king's favorable notice."

So John was bound for practice with the players and it was Frevisse's duty to see him there, keep watch over him, and afterward take him back to whoever of Alice's ladies was waiting for him. For her own part, Frevisse was glad of something to do besides sit about, but John trudged beside her back to the guesthall yard with its crowd and rise of the abbey's cloister buildings on the right and, ahead, the gateway back to the Great Court and more buildings stretching leftward from that to enclose the yard around to St. James church that opened onto the marketplace outside the abbey's great gateway. Frevisse was so sorry for him that she took him aside from the flow of people and leaned down to ask, "Do you know where we go from here?" She was fairly sure she knew but she also knew how tedious it was, even at four years old, to be all the time told what to do without ever being asked, and indeed John brightened, pointed toward buildings leftward from the Cellarer's Gate, and said, sounding somewhat less unhappy, "It's there. One, two, three doors along."

He pulled on her hand, leading her now, toward the wide doorway set in a fine stone arch into what looked to be a great hall, the principal building along that side of the yard, telling her, "This isn't where we'll do the play for the king and everybody. We'll be in the King's Hall in the abbot's palace then. But we have to practice here and Master Wilde says that's a cracked crock because here is so different from there that nobody will know what to do when we're there instead of here and everything will go wrong. Noreys says not to worry, though. He says that two practices there will set us up fine. But he doesn't say it to Master Wilde because, he says, Master Wilde likes to worry."

"Does he?" Frevisse ventured.

"Yes." John seemed quite cheerful about it. "I like him."

Meaning Noreys rather than Master Wilde, Frevisse supposed.

As they neared the doorway, a man plainly dressed in doublet and hosen and dun-colored cloak straightened from his lounge against one side of the arch to bow to both of them and ask, "You've lost your nurse, then, Lord John?"

"She's caught a rheum," John said, openly pleased. "And Master Denham, too. Dame Frevisse is come instead."

"My lady," the man said. He made her another bow. "You go on in, my lord. You're not the last but Master Wilde means to start soon and you know how he is."

John nodded and led the way inside and along a wide, low-ceilinged, wooden-walled passage, saying over his shoulder to her as they went, "Toller keeps people out who shouldn't be here. Master Wilde doesn't want everybody knowing what we're going to do until we do it. You're not to talk about it either. Even to Mother."

Already warned of that by Alice, Frevisse said, "I won't."

"I'll show you where to sit, too, so you won't be in the way." Openly eager now he was here, he turned through a broad doorway on the right and Frevisse followed him into a high-roofed, open-raftered hall clearly meant for great gatherings of people, almost as broad as it was long and well-lighted by windows set far above head height down both sides of the white-plastered walls. It was, Frevisse knew from Alice, the place where law matters in the abbey's broad jurisdiction were heard and judged by abbey officials, but with abbey life enough confounded by the presence of king and Parliament, such matters were set by for the while and the hall given over to the players.

Even if she had not known beforehand, Frevisse could have guessed about the players when she saw the raw-wood tower at the hall's far end, like seven giant boxes, each one smaller than the one below it, with a narrow, rough-built stairway going up the middle of this side to a platform topped by a joint stool. It was nothing likely to be found anywhere in the ordinary way of things. Besides that, near where she stood, among a scatter of large hampers and chests two women were holding up a swathe of blue cloth spangled and clattery with gold-looking—but probably brass—stars, and a little farther off three men with papers clutched in their hands were talking at each other in low-voiced but rhythmed haste, while at the hall's far end, near the tower, a broad man with disarrayed hair was roaring at four other men, "It's going to work because I'm going to make it work, by god!"

Before her nunnery days, Frevisse had seen enough of players and their ways to recognize all of this and found she was starting to smile with pleasure as John took her hand again and led her aside from the doorway and chests, hampers, women, and talking men to a bench along the wall where a somewhat older boy was sitting, his legs crossed tailor-fashion under him and a white satin shoe in his hands. He would have risen courteously to his feet but John said, "Don't," and Frevisse said, "Keep at whatever you're doing."

The boy smiled his thanks, then held up the shoe and said darkly to John, "For Lady Soul. Father wants it to have spangles all over it, and because they're horrible little things Mum says my fingers are small enough to do better at gluing them on than hers. I can't wait to grow up."

"Your father will have you do other things instead," John said, hitching himself onto the bench beside him.

"But when I'm big and clumsy like Ned, then I won't have to do this trifling anymore. I'm Giles Wilde," he added to Frevisse. "My father is Master Wilde. That's him raving away over there. My mother is there with Joane, deciding how many more stars they can put on the heaven-cloth that will hang behind the tower, and everybody else here are our company, except my brother Ned isn't here yet. He's late and going to be yelled at, sure as anything."

"He's not late yet," John said, swinging his heels. "It's not gone one o'clock yet."

As he said it, a bell from the abbey church's massive center tower boomed once, the stroke heavy as lead over the rooftops.

"Now he is," said Giles.

Frevisse had not yet sat down and behind her a man said, "Well, Lord John, what have you done with your nurse? Something terrible, I suppose?"

She knew his voice and turned. The fair-haired young man began a bow with, "My lady . . ." to her but paused, as if momentarily puzzled, then took a quick step backward for space to sweep her a very low bow, saying as he straightened from it, "Dame Frevisse of St. Frideswide's, yes?"

"Yes," Frevisse said and would have said more but he interrupted her, bending in another, quicker bow, saying, "You won't remember me so well as I do you, my lady. We met once when you were hosteler at St. Frideswide's and I a grateful guest of your nunnery's kindness. Master Noreys."

"I remember you very well," Frevisse said, matching him grace for grace. They had indeed met and almost in the way he had said, but she had known him only as

Joliffe, not Master Noreys, and had learned both to be wary of him and yet trust him and now said only, "Master Noreys," and nothing more, letting him turn his heed back to John, who finished explaining about the rheum-doomed nurse and schoolmaster just before Giles, watching the door, said, "Here's Ned finally come," and then with dismay, "Oh, no, that's why he's late. Old Lydgate had him and has come, too."

Frevisse and Joliffe both swung around toward the hall's broad doorway where a slender young man in a bright russet cloak and feathered cap was just come in, accompanied by a busily talking older man plump in the black robe of a Benedictine monk, his shiny forehead balded back into his tonsure and his smooth face round from years of indulgent living.

"Lydgate?" Frevisse asked with something of Giles' dismay. "As in John Lydgate, monk and poet?"

"Exactly as in 'monk and poet,' " Joliffe said.

For three reigns now, Lydgate's writings had made him known far beyond St. Edmund's Abbey walls and he had often gone out into the world to keep his reputation company, willingly writing anything he was asked and paid for, from a lengthy Life of the Virgin to farces to be performed at the royal court and all of it in what Frevisse had always found to be singularly lame-footed verse. With no attempt to hide her dismay, she demanded, "Is this play you're doing by him?"

"It will be if he has his way," Joliffe answered. He bowed toward both her and John. "I pray you, pardon me, I have to go save our playmaster from apoplexy."

Chapter 4

Arteys stood at the gateway into St. Saviour's Hospital, cloak-wrapped and a shoulder leaned against the gatepost, tired of his own company and considering what he could do besides watch the world go by.

Being among England's great pilgrimage sites, Bury St. Edmunds did not lack lodgings for travelers. There were the abbey's guesthalls, inns in plenty and, for the sick of body, church-endowed hospitals on all the main roads into town. The hospitals' first purpose had been the care of wayfarers and pilgrims either come to St. Edmund's shrine in hope of healing or else fallen ill on their journeying, but over the years they had begun to provide, as well, a comfortable living and lodging not

only for their wardens but for guests neither aged nor
infirm, merely sufficiently important to warrant hospi-
tality, and of Bury's six hospitals the richest was St.
Saviour's outside Northgate. Everywhere in and around
the town and abbey was crowded full with those come
to Parliament, those come to serve them, and those come
to make money off them all. Gloucester, coming late and
knowing St. Saviour's from other times, had sent Sir
Richard ahead with Arteys and two squires to claim
place for him. They had, though it meant Master Grene
the warden had to turn out the abbot of St. Mary's and
the earl of Salisbury. Their displeased lordships had removed farther out from town, to the Franciscan friary
that was already overcrowded with the duke of York and
his men and—as Sir Richard said—if ever Gloucester
needed help anytime soon, he had best not ask it of the
abbot of St. Mary's or the earl of Salisbury.

That had been four days ago and neither Gloucester
nor any word why he was late had come, so that yesterday Sir Richard had ridden out to find him, leaving
Arteys, Tom Herbert, and Hal Chicheley with the two
large chambers to rattle around in like three dried peas
in a bushel box until Gloucester arrived with men
enough to fill St. Saviour's lofts and corners and the
warden's hall, too. "A hundred men," Gloucester had
said. "I'm not going with less. I'm the king's uncle. You
want I should ride in looking like some beggar?"

Sir Roger had talked him down to eighty by the time
Arteys left, with Arteys hoping he had talked him down
more by now, wherever they were.

"Gloucester not sending word is only a bother, not a
worry," Sir Richard had said while readying to ride out.
"You know that as well as I do." And Sir Richard should
know. As he often said, he had been in Gloucester's
service since the year Gloucester's brother, King Henry

of blessed memory, "took us all to France and we beat the French into the mud at Agincourt. We were both striplings then, your father and I. You should have seen him then, him and his brother standing together, a matched pair all in scarlet and blue and gold. When your father went down in the middle of the fight, King Henry, God keep his soul, fought forward and stood over him until he could be carried off. St. Michael, but that was a day worth the remembering."

But King Henry V had died too soon and years of quarreling had followed between Gloucester and his uncle Bishop Beaufort of Winchester over who would govern England until their infant nephew King Henry VI came of age to rule for himself. As Sir Richard said, "If the damned bishop had choked on his bags of gold and died, we'd all be happier today." But he had not and through these past ten years Gloucester had been shoved steadily out of power, though not by Bishop Beaufort, who was grown old—"But not dead yet, damn him." Instead, it was by the men risen to power and favor around young King Henry now he had the government in his own hands. "And a bandy-brained lot they are," Sir Richard had said to Arteys in the stableyard yesterday when he had been tightening his saddle's cinch and no one else was close enough to hear him. "They're handing France back to the French with all but a thank-you for taking it off our hands, and all because they can't turn a penny from it fast enough to suit them. With them it's all give-me and profit and be damned to anything or anyone that gets in their way. It's what they've had against your father all this time. Against him and his." Meaning Lady Eleanor. "So watch yourself here. For all that Gloucester thinks everything is changing to the good for him, there's some of us . . ." Sir Richard had paused again, made up his mind to something, and went on,

"There's *many* of us have our doubts. So you be careful, Master Arteys. If it were me, I might choose to lie low these few days and not get noticed." He had gathered his reins and swung up into his saddle, then sat looking down at Arteys for another moment before adding, "If you've need, you might ask his grace the duke of York for help. He's sound, from all I know of him, and not much liked by those that least like your father either." He had smiled then. "But better you just stay out of trouble, yes?"

Arteys had smiled back and said, "We'll see." Which was a jest because he was never one for being in trouble and Sir Richard, knowing it, had nodded and ridden away satisfied.

In truth, Arteys had not intended to go out of St. Saviour's at all but with little to do now Gloucester's rooms were readied, he was restlessly considering it. Yesterday he had simply wandered in St. Saviour itself, finding nothing out-of-the-ordinary interesting. Stretched narrowly along Northgate Road, its walls on three sides and the River Lark on the fourth enclosed the hospital ward for the bodily care of the sick and the chapel for the comfort of their souls; the necessary kitchens, bakehouse, barns, byres, stables, and gardens with yards and paths among them; and the warden's hall with its cluster of private chambers and own small courtyard off the main yard and an outside stairway to what would be Gloucester's bedchamber when he came and was presently Arteys' way in and out, to be as little bother to anyone as possible. To see it all had taken hardly the morning and Arteys had spent the rest of the day alone, beside the fire in Gloucester's bedchamber, rereading John Lydgate's *The Fall of Princes*, found in the prior's library.

He had thought to spend today reading, too, but now

regretted he had refused Tom and Hal's offer to go into Bury with them. They had come back well after dark yesterday, a-light with ale and merriment, and Arteys did not think they minded he had turned down their company. They had possibly even been glad, being—like many people—unsure how to behave toward him.

That was something to which Arteys was used. In any household, from peasant to merchant to gentry to noble, everyone from kitchen scullion to duke had their named and particular place, knew the duties and rights that went with it. When everyone knew where they fit into the shape of things, dealings among them were, on the whole, straightforward. Arteys had no place. He was the duke of Gloucester's son and yet was nobody, with no named place or given rights and "What, exactly, are we?" his equally bastard half-sister Antigone had once demanded angrily at him. "Are we his dear children? Are we here because he 'loves' us? Or out of charity— hangers on at his royal cloak tail, better than beggars but not by much?"

Arteys had tried, "All of that together?"

"All of that together, yes," Antigone had flung back at him, "and it adds up to our being *nothing*."

When he would neither argue with her or grow angry, too, she had stormed away. Antigone was always fierce, and finally her fierceness had burned a place for herself in the world. At her demand, Gloucester had found her a marriage. She had become Lady Powys, with rank and husband and household of her own, and had not, so far as Arteys knew, ever looked back at her father since then.

Arteys lacked both her fierceness and her anger at Gloucester nor understood them. "He has the most generous heart," Lady Eleanor had once said, "but he doesn't see things, Arteys. You must ask for what you

want. Or tell me and I'll ask him for you." But soon
after that she was gone, and since then Gloucester had
been too alone and in pain for Arteys either to leave him
or ask anything, and things went on as they were, with
people not knowing what to make of him.

But come to that, Arteys supposed he didn't know
what to make of himself either. That was why, so far,
he had made nothing, and therefore times like this one
came on him, when all he had was idleness and no one
to spend it with, and so was standing in St. Saviour's
gateway, uncertain what to do.

Yesterday's weather yet held but without the wind.
The sky was bare and blue, with sunlight glinting off
the smooth-frozen ice in the deep ditch between St. Saviour's wall and the road, and none of the scattered crowd
passing by on the road on foot or horseback or with the
steady flow of carts going loaded toward Bury and
empty from it was lingering. It was cold enough that
Arteys had to cease lingering, too. Fur-lined though his
cloak was—being a duke's son, illegitimate or not, had
advantages, and a fur-lined cloak was one of them—he
was beginning to chill from the feet upward and must
either go out or else back. A pair of monks passed him,
crossing the bridge over the ditch and turning toward
town, swathed heads to heels in black hoods and cloaks
and complaining to each other of the cold as they went.
For no good reason, Arteys straightened from the gatepost and followed them, thinking plague take it, he'd see
what there was to see in Bury St. Edmunds.

He was not far along the road when the bright-edged
call of a trumpet, crisp in the cold air, warned of riders
coming behind him. Along with everyone else, he
moved as aside on the road as possible, on his part pressing back to a head-high fence with the sound of chickens
about their day's work on its other side, to clear the way

for whatever lord and company were riding into town.
Bury St. Edmunds was rife with lords and their people
these days. Some of the highest, including the archbish-
ops of Canterbury and York and the marquis of Suffolk,
were quartered in the abbey itself, in the abbot's palace
and other of the abbey's rich lodgings, and could stroll
to their parliament meetings without much display,
having no one to impress but each other except when
they mingled their lordly selves with the Commons in
some joint gathering. Other lords, without sufficient rank
or influence or, like Gloucester, simply preferring to stay
elsewhere, had found their own lodgings in and around
the town, not only in St. Saviour's and other hospitals
but wealthy merchants' homes whose comforts would
equal the abbey's despite every citizen of Bury St. Edmunds' unending tussle over their rights and freedoms
and fees with the abbey because it owned their town.

Arteys therefore had no surprise when he turned with
everyone else to see the perhaps dozen riders with the
duke of York's banner above them. Quartered scarlet
and azure, with gold lions and gold lilies shining in the
winter sun, it was almost the same as Gloucester's banner that was almost the same as the king's because
Gloucester as King Henry's uncle and York as a cousin
to them both were all of the blood royal. That made York
his something-cousin, too, Arteys thought, watching the
men ride past. They were hatted, with the fashionable
padded headrolls with a sweep of cloth down and around
their shoulders, but for the short ride into Bury from the
friary none of them had bothered with cloaks and their
richly made houppelandes and doublets were a glad
splash of many colors against the gray-brown February
world. Arteys knew York from other times and had brief
sight of him, clad in murrey-purple on a tall bay palfrey
with its harness hung with bells and white-enameled

roses, a man in his early middle years with a quiet face and something apart about him, even here, riding with probably the closest of his household around him. Arteys had often seen that same apartness in Gloucester, an awareness—except when he was with Lady Eleanor or nearest friends, with no one else there to see him—of being unceasingly watched by others who knew far more of him than he did of them.

Once Arteys had asked, "Why?" And Gloucester had answered with a slight, accepting lift of his shoulders, "Because I'm me." The duke of Gloucester, son and brother and uncle of kings and heir to England's crown until such time as King Henry had a son. And after him in claim to the crown came York.

And that, Arteys had thought more than once, was one thing to the good about his bastardy. No claim to any crown had claim on him. If that meant he did not, like York and Gloucester, go richly clad on fine horses with a knight bearing a banner over him to let the world and all know who he was, he did not care. There were things not worth their price and to Arteys' mind being royal was one of them.

The thought, unsought, came into his mind that he was afraid for his father.

More than worried. Afraid.

Around him, now that York and his men were past, everyone was reclaiming the road and going on their ways. Arteys hardly noted them. He had been worried how Gloucester would be if things did not go his way here in Bury but, "It's Suffolk and Dorset and the others crowded in around young Henry," Gloucester had said bitterly when last he had attempted pardon for Lady Eleanor. "They're after power, but there's only so much power to be had and so they grab and scramble for it like piglets at a sow. It's a foul game." A game Gloucester had played as readily as anyone for more years of his life than not, until he had been shoved out of it, Arteys knew. Now King Henry had summoned him, and there were lords in plenty who might well fear how quickly Gloucester would take to the game again if given the chance. Lords with power enough to do something about their fear.

The cold coming through his wool-lined shoes reminded him to move on. Ahead, the last of York's riders were disappearing through stone-towered Northgate, but Arteys' own going was slowed by the clotting of carts and people who had had to wait and were now all trying to go through at once. Being a-foot and unburdened, Arteys threaded his way through the crowd and the gateway's dimness, coming out between two carts piled with firewood and a man with a basket smelling strongly of fish strapped on his back into town. From when he had been here a few years ago with Gloucester, staying overnight on way to Our Lady's shrine at Walsingham, he knew going ahead from the gateway would bring him to the long marketplace in front of the abbey gates, but the lords and their people would be thickest there, he supposed, and he turned right at the first street beyond the gate, following its curve up and around to come out from between the houses into the Great Market.

He didn't remember if today was one of the town's usual market days or not but it hardly mattered. With king and Parliament in town and the overflow of people that came with them, anyone with anything to sell was come to Bury from a score of miles around and probably farther—neither Cambridge nor Norwich merchants would miss a chance like this—and the wide market was crowded full of booths and stalls and, by the sound and look of it, enough folk to people another town, all of them busy selling, buying, talking, eating, drinking.

With Shrovetide almost come—the four days or so of holidaying before Lent's austerity closed in on life—there would even more of everything in a day or so, spreading out through the town and even into the abbey, but there was plenty here as it was and for a time Arteys was happy with the noise and the crowd and simply looking while he wandered among the maze of booths and stalls where there looked to be everything for sale, from simply bright ribbons fluttering on a rack to swords and daggers laid out on crimson cloth to show off the sheen of their steel, to saddles gaudy with brass bosses over pommel and hindbow, to gloves both plain and fancy, high-cuffed and low, embroidered and not, to brooches and rings their seller swore were silver but Arteys doubted, to shoes and cloaks and skeins of colored wool, to a pig roasting over red coals, with slices of it for sale on thick slices of bread for a ha'penny, to maybe a dozen booths selling ale by the cup, bowl, or tankard with a bench to sit on while you drank . . .

It was while he was stopped to listen with half a dozen others to a minstrel trying to make himself and his lute heard amid it all that he began to hear ripples of sharper talk around him, eddies of voices excited not over sales but something else. As he tossed a penny in the minstrel's bowl, his ear caught Gloucester's name mixed into something being said angrily by a man behind him and he started to turn, was slowed by the shove of two housewives, brisk with baskets and their own talk passing by him, and heard next, ". . . means to seize the king, Suffolk says. That's why the council . . ."

Three men were moving away from him, talking. Arteys followed, able in the press and shift of people to come up close behind them and hear, ". . . has them mustering at Henow Heath. If there's need, see."

"How many is Gloucester supposed to be bringing?"

"A good three thousand, at the least."

The third man gave a low whistle. "There'll be . . ."

A man and woman, an arm tight around each other's waist and no heed of anyone else, cut between Arteys and what the men said next. Worse, they weren't the only ones talking in an angry, tight-gestured way. Arteys heard Gloucester's name from others around him now but closed on the three men again, following when they headed toward one of the shops surrounding the marketplace, a once green-leafed branch tied to an out-thrust pole above the door. What few leaves still clung there were brown and tattered but enough to tell it was an alehouse. The men went in, and because no one would think twice about one more man going in, Arteys did, too.

The long, narrow, low-raftered room was crowded, loud, and shadowy. Even with the streetward door and window standing open, daylight did not reach far along it but neither did the day's cold, since the benches behind narrow tables all down the length of one wall were full of men and some women, with just space in front of the tables for the aproned woman making her way with a tray, putting down full mugs of ale on tables as she came, scooping up coins in return, and all the while talking to one customer after another in a laughing voice louder than anyone's.

Reaching the newcomers paused at the doorway, she summed them up with a quick look and declared with a nod toward the far end of the room, "Down there, then, sirs, there's place. Just tell Kate to shift herself along and sit up a bit. You, too, love," she added to Arteys. "That's all there is and you won't find better ale in Bury today, so take it while you can."

The men, Arteys following, edged and shifted their way among the outstretched legs and feet to the far end of the room, to an almost empty bench beside the open doorway into a dark back room. Kate, with her head-kerchief askew and her brown gown muddled with spilled ale and other things, was somewhere between leaning on the table and sliding under it. She did not object when the men straightened her up, slid her over, and propped her into the corner of the wall but roused enough to smile at them, her smile as awry as her head-kerchief, and mumble something that made one of the men laugh and shake his head before she slipped back into her drunken slough and the men crowded onto the bench behind the table. With no room behind the table for him, Arteys fit himself into the gap left on the bench between them and the drinkers at the next table and tried to look at ease, ignored by the men, one of them saying now, "Better them than me, that's all I can say. It'll be devil's-arse cold out on a heath where the wind can get at them."

"Still, twopence a day for doing nothing."

"Nothing but freezing your ears off. No thanks."

"With maybe a fight at the end of it."

"There'll be no fighting. Not with that many against however many Gloucester is bringing."

"Three thousand, you said?"

"At the least. Maybe more. Depends on how much trouble he's expecting. He maybe doesn't know Suffolk is on to him, likely."

They were not making sense to Arteys. Gloucester was bringing nothing like three thousand men and what was this muster of men at Henow Heath, wherever it was? Suffolk at least was familiar from all Gloucester's talk against him—"If he were half so well-witted as he is charming, it wouldn't matter he runs both Henry and the government, but he's a short-seeing idiot and there's going to be trouble because of him, mark me."

The aproned woman passed by, headed to the back, gathering empties onto her tray as she went. Arteys leaned forward, elbows on knees, and turned his head as if watching her but using the chance, now the men had thrown back their cloaks in the alehouse's warmth, to see what lord's badges they wore on their doublets. Not Suffolk's ape with chain and manacle but the portcullis of Edmund Beaufort, marquis of Dorset. He was some-one else too powerful around the king, according to Gloucester "a mean-spirited, grabbing fool who'd just as soon kick you in the shins as not, to prove to himself he's the better man."

Arteys, his own cloak kept over Gloucester's white swan badge above his heart, was turning to join in the men's talk to find out what else he could, but a man making his way along the tables reached there at that moment and slid, hardly giving Arteys time to shift, into the gap that was barely there between Arteys and the nearest of Dorset's men. Wiggling to make space for himself, he said toward Arteys, "Packed in like salt fish in a barrel, aren't we? Keeps the draught off, though."

Arteys made a small, assenting sound because, yes, this far back in the room no draught had a chance; the air hung thick with the mingled smells of warm bodies and ale-laden breath, of which the man had both.

"Anything that keeps the cold off is welcome this time of year, though, isn't it?" the man went on. His eyes were too small and set too close to a thin nose above a mouth too full of teeth. He looked more as if he were in search of prey than talk and Arteys was trying to shift away from him when the aproned woman returned with a tray of new-filled tankards and a hand out for money.

Arteys and the other men perforce all elbowed each other while digging coins from their belt pouches, but before Arteys could lay his on the table, a fair-haired, lean-made man squeezed past the woman, said cheer-fully, "Here you are, then," laid coins on the tray, and took two tankards, handing one to Arteys while asking "Been waiting long?," adding to the small-eyed man, "You don't mind taking off, do you, since that's my place?"

The man rose, not as if he were happy about it, mut-tering what might have been "Sorry" or might not as he moved away. The newcomer sat, somehow crowding Dorset's men even more against each other without mak-ing an insult of it, and said with a smile at the woman and a nod at Arteys, "See to it he pays for the next ones, right?"

She laughed and moved on, leaving Arteys trying to remember if he knew him. He was well-spoken but wore no lord's badge and his plain clothing—dark green sur-coat over dark blue doublet and black hosen—gave nothing away except that he was no churchman. Arteys was puzzling out what was familiar about him as the man, frowning thoughtfully past him, said, "Why do they almost always look like that?"

"Who? Like what?" Arteys turned his head in time to see the small-eyed man going out the door.

"Like rats. Pointy faces and noses that almost twitch. Spies."

"Spies?" Arteys, startled, looked back to him.

"The bad ones, at least. I suppose there must be good ones."

"But we don't know them because they don't look like rats?" Arteys suggested, amused.

"You have it." The man drank from his mug and nod-ded appreciatively. "Good ale. You'd think Suffolk could afford better."

"Ale?"

"Spies. Or maybe the fellow was Dorset's." He twitched

his head slightly toward the men to whom he now mostly had his back. With his voice pitched under the alehouse's general noise, he was safe from being heard by them. "Dorset is the cheap-souled sort of bastard who'd hire a rat-faced spy instead of better. It was with that kind of idiot-wittedness he and his brother, God stomp his soul a bit before saving it, made fools of themselves all over France. You don't remember me, do you?"

Until that moment Arteys had not but said suddenly, "Joliffe. You were in my father's household awhile." About the time of Lady Eleanor's disgrace, and like much else from then, had disappeared soon afterward. "I don't remember your last name but you're a minstrel."

"Only when I can't survive as a player. That's why I'm here now. I'm one of the players doing Abbot Babington's play for the king."

Arteys, having given up hope of hearing anything more from Dorset's men, took a long drink, then asked, "That man just now, why do you say he's a spy?"

Joliffe leaned slightly toward him and half-whispered, as if giving away a deep secret, "Because he is."

That was so overplayed that Arteys laughed and remembered another thing about him—he had always been able to make Lady Eleanor laugh. But, "How do you know that?"

"Because he's a very poor spy. He's been hanging at people's elbows ever since the lords started gathering into Bury St. Edmunds, listening to talk or else saying things he hopes will lead someone into saying something he can go tale-telling back to his master, whoever that is. Someone in the little clot around the king who wants to be sure no one is a step ahead of them. It doesn't matter who. They're almost all against your father."

Arteys hadn't known ale could curdle in the belly.
"My father. What about my father?"

"Hold your voice down," Joliffe said evenly, his voice
still smiling but his eyes not. "Hold steady. Take a drink.
And if you're wearing a badge, go on keeping your cloak
over it."

Arteys drank without tasting the ale before he asked
with his voice down and the slightest nod at Dorset's
men, "They were saying something about a Henow
Heath."

"Our good marquis of Suffolk has gathered in a few
thousand men from his manors around here to Henow
Heath just north of Bury on the claim that Gloucester is
coming with an army against the king." Joliffe clamped
his free hand on Arteys' arm in a friendly-looking grip
hard enough to stop what Arteys had been going to protest while he went on, "By tomorrow, hopefully, someone will have pointed out to Suffolk how much a fool
he's going to look when Gloucester rides into Bury with
his eighty or so men. Then, before you know it, there'll
be a few thousand very displeased fellows making their
ways back home from Henow Heath."

Face and voice controlled, Arteys asked, "Why does
Suffolk have them there at all? He has to know Gloucester isn't coming with any army."

"He knows, but he's maybe thinking that if he yells
loud enough that the duke of Gloucester is dangerous,
no one will listen when Gloucester declares Suffolk's
sins aloud."

"Suffolk's sins?"

"Or however one sees his stupidities."

"Gloucester isn't coming against Suffolk. All he wants
is pardon for Lady Eleanor."

"And let's pray he gets it. But in the meanwhile you
might want to find somewhere else to be today besides
out and about in Bury St. Edmunds."

Chapter 5

Years ago Frevisse had chance to watch players at their rehearsing and had enjoyed it. Skilled craftsmen at work were almost always a pleasure to watch and at their best players were very skilled craftsmen, able to weave words and pretense into something that could bring their audience to laughter, anger, even grief. Since Master Wilde's company had been chosen to perform for the king, she had presumed they were not merely good but among the best and from watching them the past few days judged she was right; nor was she surprised that Joliffe was among the best of them.

But she had not been simply a looker-on for even the first day. When her presence was explained to Master

Wilde, he had warned her to keep secret anything she saw here and after that ignored her, but Mistress Wilde had come to where she sat and asked if she could sew. Frevisse had admitted to simple stitches and so this cold afternoon, with the thin sunlight through the hall's high windows giving light but no warmth, she was again on the bench along the hall's wall alternately breathing on her fingers and hemming a green gown, three yards around the hem and taking forever. The measure of Mistress Wilde's need was that, even after seeing Frevisse sew, she had let her go on with it, because the play was in two days' time and there were a great many hems and trimmings yet to be stitched if all the players—heavenly Wisdom and Lady Soul, the devil Lucifer, three Mights of Virtue, three Devils, and a pair of small demons who were John and Giles—were to be clothed by the night after tomorrow. The cost of it all was no trouble, even to Wisdom's grand robe of cloth-of-gold, since Abbot Babington was paying, and the hiring of sufficient seamstresses should have been no problem, except Master Wilde was determined to have as little as possible known about the play ahead of time.

"I won't have talk," he had said to Frevisse. "I want there to be surprise and wonder when we do it for the court. I won't have everything driveled away to the world and its cousin beforetime. So your promise, please you, my lady."

Frevisse had promised, more out of understanding for his passion than from belief in its necessity. Abbey and town were taken up with the business and bother that always encircled the king wherever he was. Lords, lawyers, officers, and clerks deep in trying to carry on the government and pursuing their own ends while they did were mixed in with the knights, gentry, and common men of Parliament all with ends of their own and far

more interested in making demands than agreeing to the
king's desires. There were undoubtedly cross-purposes
and dealings everywhere, made worse by the private pas-
sions and cares that people always had. The play when
it was performed would provide a welcome pleasure, but
until then Frevisse doubted that anyone not in it or of it
had more than a passing thought about it at all.

For Master Wilde, however, it was all and everything,
and so there was a desperate stitching by anyone with
hands to spare who could be trusted with a needle. At
least Wisdom and Lady Soul would be fully clothed and
surely splendid. Near to Frevisse now, the woman Joane
was sitting with her lap draped in fold upon fold of Lady
Soul's white cloth-of-gold gown, stitching gold-threaded
trim around its far more yards of hem than Frevisse presently worked at, while a little farther down the hall
Mistress Wilde had a little while ago folded Wisdom's
yards upon yards of gown away into a hamper and now
sat with small John standing for her to mark the sleeve-
length on his black demon's tunic.

But sewing was not the only work in hand in the hall.
Master Wilde was not yet come to start the afternoon's
practice but the six men who would be the Mights and
Devils were walking through their dance at the hall's
upper end to the tapping of a small drum by another of
Master Wilde's sons, in front of the tower that in two
days' time would be Heaven but was presently being
painted blue by young Giles and the older of the company's two musicians in grimy tunics and hosen, with
charcoal-burning braziers set around to hurry the paint's
drying because Master Wilde meant to run through the
whole play this afternoon. "From beginning to end without stopping no matter how rough it goes," he had said
yesterday. "We've need to see how the whole thing

hangs together, and woe to anyone who doesn't have his lines down pat by then."

Joliffe, standing next to small John sitting on the bench beside Frevisse, had leaned over and asked the boy, low-voiced in his ear, "You have your words all learned, haven't you?"

Swinging his feet happily, John had said back, "I know mine better than you know yours!" An ongoing jest between them because John had no lines. His part, with Giles, was to slither from beneath Lady Soul's be-fouled and ugly mantle after she had fallen prey to Lu-cifer's lures, dragging black, twisted ropes and dirty ribbons behind them and around her in an ugly little dance to show her vileness. He only had to know when to move and where, while Joliffe, as Lucifer tempting Lady Soul to her foolishness and sin, had a great many lines, and at John's challenge he had laid a tragical hand to his forehead, said, "Too true, my lord, too true. I'd best go practice," and after a bow to John and Frevisse, had taken himself away.

Frevisse had noted these past few days how good he was at taking himself away without much said to her. Though he sometimes came aside to talk with John, he had never spoken more to her at any one time than when they had first met here. Not that there was need he should, but neither was there reason why he should so avoid it as he seemed to, and she was therefore surprised, happening to look up, to see Joliffe was just come into the hall in company with a young man she did not know and was crossing toward her.

That they were coming to her was so clear that she laid her sewing in her lap and waited, watching them. Joliffe was tall but the newcomer somewhat taller, with a long-boned, well-featured face, dark gold hair, and an uncertain manner, as if he knew he shouldn't be there.

Nor should he be. What was in Joliffe's mind to bring him, and what was Master Wilde going to say?

Reaching her, they both bowed and Joliffe said, "My lady, a favor, if you will."

As formal as he was, she said back, "If it's within right and reason."

Joliffe's laughter glinted at her though he said evenly, "You know what my lord of Suffolk has been at? Mustering men north of town on Henow Heath against the duke of Gloucester and the supposed army he's bringing against the king?"

She knew. There had been talk about it all around Lady Alice this morning, though Alice herself had said not much before she went off to wait on the queen. "I've heard," Frevisse answered slowly, "though it seems to me that it would have served Suffolk better to muster his men south of town, between the king and Gloucester, rather than north of it."

"A well-taken point that seems to have escaped a great many people," Joliffe allowed lightly. "But however much we may question my lord of Suffolk's judgment, I thought myself that Arteys here might be better somewhere else than out and about." As he said it, Joliffe briefly lifted an edge of the young man's cloak, giving a glimpse of a white swan badge, and Frevisse said, "Ah."

"So may he keep you company this while?"

Arteys stood so carefully blank-faced, waiting for her answer, that Frevisse slightly smiled at him as she said, "Of course. But will Master Wilde allow it?"

"I asked him outside," Joliffe said. "He agreed, having more on his mind at the time. Brother Lydgate has him in talk."

"Again?" Frevisse said. Not only did Lydgate write lame verse, he had the unswerving opinion that anything

not written by himself was surely in need of mending
and it seemed he had been trying to mend this play ever
since the players had begun to practice it.

"He says the end needs something said between Lucifer and Lady Soul," Joliffe said cheerfully, "and a
longer speech from Wisdom that he's kindly penned for
us. He's trying to persuade Master Wilde to do it today."

"Two days before the play goes on? Blessed St. Jude
have mercy." The patron saint of desperate cases, because Brother Lydgate was undeniably a desperate case.

"Better add a prayer to St. Barbara against sudden
death, because that's what Master Wilde may have for
Brother Lydgate if he keeps at this."

With a grin at Arteys and a bow of his head to Frevisse, he headed away to where Ned Wilde was explaining to his brother Giles and the other painter how he
would have done the work faster and, of course, better
had he been there, and Giles was explaining back at him
how much he was in danger of having his kneecaps
painted.

"Don't even think of it!" their mother called from
where she was helping John take off his pin-perilous
tunic, and Joliffe added helpfully that, anyway, it would
be a waste of good paint.

Frevisse gestured at Arteys still standing uncertainly
beside the bench that he should sit. He did, somewhat
uneasily and on its edge, looking ready to leave at a
moment's notice. Returning to her sewing, she asked, as
much for curiosity as to put him at ease, "You've known
Joliffe long?"

The youth hesitated. "Off and on for a time." He hesitated again, then added, "Mostly off."

"How did he explain you to Master Wilde?"

"He said I had need lie low for the afternoon and
could I do it here? Master Wilde said he knew about

lying low, and if I promised to keep my mouth shut, I could stay."

"Joliffe didn't tell him you were one of the duke of Gloucester's men?"

"No." The hall was cool enough that no one would question why he still wore his cloak but Arteys pulled it closer around him as if to be sure Gloucester's badge stayed hidden.

"Come to that," Frevisse said, pretending she did not see his uneasy gesture, "I doubt Master Wilde, lost in the play as he is, even knows there's anything else happening."

"He didn't seem to."

"*Is* Gloucester bringing an army against the king?"

Arteys looked profoundly startled and answered more forcefully than he had yet said anything to her, "*No*. It's a flat lie. He's bringing less than a hundred men. Suffolk is a liar."

That was boldly said and Frevisse would have questioned him more, to find out what else he would say, but at that moment Master Wilde came into the hall, cap in hand, face furiously flushed, and hair ruffled into an angry crest. Behind him, almost treading on his heels, came Brother Lydgate, holding out papers toward his back and insisting, "Let me read it to you again. You'll surely hear . . ."

Master Wilde spun around, took the papers, and said with what sounded like a clenched jaw and the last bit of patience in him, "I'll read it and see what I can do. Right? Right. Now we have to get on with things. Toller will see you out. *Toller!*"

Toller appeared through the doorway at Brother Lydgate's back and, much like a shepherd's dog with a thick-headed sheep, ushered Lydgate backward from Master Wilde and out of the hall. No one else moved or spoke until there was the solid thud of the outer door closing. Then with a massive release of breath, Master Wilde spun around, declared, "Enough. Let's get on with this," and stalked up the hall, stripping off his cloak as he went and tossing it toward a lidded basket, not caring that he missed, ordering, "All of you to your places. Where you'll be when you enter at your turn. We're doing this all the way through, remember. No stopping. No help on lines. If you don't have them now, there's no hope anyway."

Ahead of him the paint and brushes were being hurriedly cleared to the side. The top and front of the stairs had sensibly been done this morning and hopefully were dry. Master Wilde started up them, turned around to give some order, Frevisse supposed, but instead roared toward the hall doorway, *"Now what?"*

Everyone looked. Even Joane, who had steadfastly gone on stitching through everything else, jerked up her head to see a man standing there, stopped by Master Wilde's roar. He was no one Frevisse knew; an older man quietly gowned in what was, although black and ankle-long, assuredly no monk's robe. Deeply pleated from yoke to belted waist, with full sleeves gathered to the wrists and high-standing collar, it bespoke a man of some position in the world, only its color and his closely fitted, plain black hat suggesting he was a churchman of some kind.

If he was, it presently carried no weight with Master Wilde, who demanded at full voice, "What do you want here?" And louder still, "Toller!"

Toller seemed to be absent but from a near corner of the steps Joliffe said something up to Master Wilde that Frevisse did not hear. It earned him a glare from Master Wilde, who then snapped, "If you say so," and to the man, only a little more graciously, "Come in if you will, my lord. Sit there, please you."

He pointed toward the bench where Frevisse and Arteys already were. The man bent his head to him, and while Master Wilde returned to dealing with his players, came up the hall. Frevisse and Arteys both rose to their feet as courtesy required and the man with equal courtesy nodded to them to sit, sat himself on Arteys' other side, and leaned forward to say past him to Frevisse, "My lady, you are . . . ?"

There was Oxford in his voice and something else that Frevisse could not immediately place as she answered him with the same graciousness as he had asked, "Dame Frevisse of St. Frideswide's priory in Oxfordshire, my lord. And you are . . . ?"

"Bishop Pecock of St. Asaph's."

That gave her pause. If that was what Joliffe had told Master Wilde, then Master Wilde had had small choice in "allowing" the bishop to stay because bishops, even of so small a bishopric as Frevisse knew St. Asaph's to be, were lords by virtue of their office and members of the royal council, not someone to be yelled at and ordered around by a common playmaster. But Bishop Pecock seemed to have taken no offense. Rather, his attention had shifted to Arteys. "And who are you, young man?"

"Arteys, my lord."

"A Welsh name," Bishop Pecock said promptly. "Often corrupted in English to 'Arthur,' a king of many legends and the subject of far more stories than can be true. A noble name nonetheless and better in the Welsh than in English. Are you Welsh?"

"On my mother's side."

Bishop Pecock leaned forward for a nearer look and asked, "What is the rest of your name, young Arteys?"

After a very motionless moment, Arteys answered, "FitzGloucester, my lord."

Bishop Pecock sat back with a single nod, as if satisfied of something, and veered his questioning back to Frevisse, asking courteously, "What do you here, Dame?"

It was a reasonable question, this being hardly a likely place for a nun, and Frevisse made brief explanation of how she came to accompany young John, leaving out everything about herself and why she was at Bury St. Edmunds at all. Then, deciding such questions could go both ways, she asked, "And you, my lord. Why are you here?"

Bishop Pecock smiled. "I'm avoiding one duty by claiming another. One might even say 'feigning' another. I should be with the lords in council at this very moment but found that my wits were at peril of curdling if I listened even another quarter hour to their talk. Therefore I determined to do something else and am here, where I doubt I'll be easily found even if someone is looking for me, which they are probably not."

That both a bishop and Arteys were here for the sake of not being somewhere else gave Frevisse an inward smile.

But Bishop Pecock still had questions and now asked, "This play, Dame, how much of it have you seen?"

"I don't know."

He raised his rather notable eyebrows, questioning her answer without need to say a word. Obligingly she added, "The few times I've been here, they've played it only in bits and pieces. Today is the first time they're to do it from start to end all at once. That's why Master Wilde is somewhat on edge."

She was surprised to hear herself excusing the playmaster; was equally surprised at Bishop Pecock's easy

nod accepting that. "Better honest irk than false courtesy," he said and probably would have said more—he
seemed to be a man with always more to say—but Master Wilde had finished with whatever last things he had
for the players and at that moment roared out to the hall
at large for silence and, when he had it, said, abruptly
calm, "Now we begin."

On the instant there was no movement or sound from
anyone in the hall. Even Mistress Wilde and Joane
paused their sewing, and because the curtains that would
back the playing place were not hung on their long
frames yet, all the players were in sight, too, grouped
here and there aside from Heaven's tower, wherever they
needed to be for when they would come into the play
on their turn. Even John, who was not needed until later,
was in his place, waiting solemnly, silently, beside Giles.
From partway up the stairs, Master Wilde looked at them
all, assessing their readiness, then went up the last steps
to the top, swung around, and sat down on the joint stool
in a way that made it, on the instant, no longer a joint
stool but Wisdom's throne and Master Wilde by the very
way he sat there no longer the harassed master of players
but Wisdom himself, all divine dignity and command as
he declared, as if to a vast multitude, "If you would
know the meaning of my name imperial, I am called, by
those that are on earth, Everlasting Wisdom . . ."

Chapter 6

hen Wisdom had finished his first speech, Lady Soul in the person of Ned Wilde wearing an old gown over his doublet and hosen, no longer a striding youth but all sweet womanliness, declared her love for Wisdom and Frevisse returned to her sewing, listening while they talked of the need to be rid of earthly sins. Beside her, Arteys was soon leaned forward, intently listening, and on his other side Bishop Pecock was sitting straightback with hands folded into his lap like someone accustomed to sitting for a long time listening to others, as undoubtedly he did in royal council meetings and his bishopric. As Lady Soul's Mights—Mind, Will, and Understanding—came on, likewise men a few minutes ago

but now sweet-spoken ladies, Frevisse finished the green hem but had no more than snipped the final thread than Mistress Wilde was silently taking the gown from her and handing her another, red this time, and the thread to go with it. Frevisse took them in equal silence and somewhat gratefully. Despite how little she liked sewing, neither did she like sitting idle and she was finding the sewing came more easily now she had the play to hold her mind.

It was better written than many of its kind. The verse was steady and what ribaldry there was, once the Devils came on, was never given the upper hand over the sense. King Henry, known to be adverse to ribaldry, would approve that, and yet there was enough wit that the play did not plod and for those lookers-on beyond anything else there would be splendid sights to divert them. If the players' garments were finished in time. Frevisse sewed on steadily.

Joliffe as Lucifer swaggered on, announcing in a smoothly rich voice, "For I am he that sin began," and set to wooing Lady Soul and her Mights to foolishness. While he spoke, Bishop Pecock leaned forward with a questioning tilt to his head, as if listening rather than looking, then he fumbled in the fine leather pouch at his belt and brought out and put on silver-rimmed spectacles, looping the black ribbons around his ears to hold them.

What had he heard to interest him that much in Joliffe? Frevisse wondered. It was perfectly possible for Joliffe to know him by sight—if, as the saying went, a cat might look at a king, a player might look at bishops—but what about Joliffe so particularly interested the bishop?

The play went on its way, sometimes unsteadily but never stopping. Partway through a long speech, Lady

Soul realized it was the wrong speech and had to sort
her words around. There was a brief, almost fatal confusion in the dance between the Mights and Lucifer's
Devils but with some quick-footedness they overcame it
and kept on. Arteys watched steadily, chin on hand, elbow on knee. Bishop Pecock soon sat back, but from
the corner of her eye Frevisse could see his interest was
still held. Lucifer's Devils sported with Mind, Will, and
Understanding. When Lady Soul, seduced by Lucifer
into worldly ways and corruption, came on again, her
beautiful gown replaced by black tatters, Frevisse
watched to see that John did not miss his time or mess
his part and was pleased when he carried it through
every bit as well as Giles did.

By then both the play and the red hem were nearly
done and she stopped her sewing to watch while Lady
Soul rejected Lucifer, reclaimed her Mind and Will and
Understanding, and returned, triumphantly welcomed, to
Heaven.

"And so to end with perfection. That is the Wisdom
we pursue. God grant it to those who do," Wisdom de-
claimed and it was over. Light clapping spattered from
the lookers-on, and grinning with satisfaction, the players made bows to them. Atop the steps, Master Wilde
ceased to be Wisdom, rose to his feet, and said, "Don't
fool yourselves, my fellows. They're clapping that you
finished, not that you did well at it."

This was greeted with laughter.

"You think I'm jesting?" He started down the steps.
"Come here then and listen."

From other afternoons Frevisse knew how it would go
then. He would spend a while detailing everything he
had liked and disliked about their performing, confirm-
ing one thing and another that had worked and changing
those that had not. Low-voiced, Frevisse explained this

to Bishop Pecock and Arteys, then asked how they had
liked it.

Arteys, his earlier stiff unease lost in momentary pleasure, actually smiled as he answered, "Very much."

More thoughtfully, Bishop Pecock said, "Traditional
though this portraying of wisdom, the soul, and so forth
is, I've never found to be either convincing or particularly satisfying. That said, I have to add that I found this
was both effective and affecting."

From his tangle of words, Frevisse sorted out he had
enjoyed it as with a small, thoughtful frown he went on,
"I understand, too, the playmaster's ire and irk before
they began and his impatience afterwards. He's seeking
to make a world in small, as it were, and knows it needs
to be sure in all its parts, great and small together, lest
it fail in its entirety. I daresay that God himself, what
with one thing and another, was perhaps a little ill-
humoured toward the end of creating the world. Though,
being all-knowing, he of course did not have to wonder
how it would all come out in the performance."

Frevisse quickly caught back an urge to laugh, then
saw that Bishop Pecock was widely smiling and she
smiled at him in return. A jest-making bishop was not
someone she had encountered before this.

Joliffe strolled over to them then, Master Wilde
having finished with him though not with anyone else,
it seemed. Frevisse saw him look sharply at all their
faces as he joined them though he said lightly enough,
with a bow to Bishop Pecock, "You all look merry. How
did you find it?"

Bishop Pecock, still smiling, said, "I found it far more
pleasurable than I'd expected to. Familiar figures presented in a new form or fashion can surprisingly refresh
them. Your play does it very well."

Joliffe bowed to him again. "We hope so, my lord."

"But when did you become player rather than clerk, young Joliffe?"

"When Fortune turned her wheel, which no man may escape."

"A come-down in the world, is it not?"

"No more than it might be said you're leaving off being a plain priest and master of Whittington College to become a bishop is a come-down in the world, my lord."

Smiles were pulling at both their faces but it was Bishop Pecock who laughed outright before he said, "I'll not argue that point, lest I lose. But about this play. Who wrote it?"

"Someone who wants to go unknown, I'm afraid."

"Not you?"

"Not me. I swear it."

"That's to the good, then. To find you were as shrewd at theology as you are at worldly matters would give me pause."

"My lord," Joliffe said and bowed.

But Bishop Pecock was away on another thought. "It's an interesting thing, though, that although all was pretense from first to last here, yet despite of that, some truths were most movingly conveyed."

"I'd suggest," Joliffe said, "those truths were conveyed 'because' rather than 'despite.' "

"A point to be considered," Bishop Pecock granted. "That truth can be conveyed by falseness." He peered intently at Joliffe. "On the other hand, my sometime clerk, I find it somewhat unsettling that you can be so convincingly Lucifer."

"My lord." Joliffe laid a hand earnestly over his heart. "I promise you I can play at being an angel equally well, given the chance."

" 'Play, being the word in question, I believe?"

"As surely as 'holy' goes with 'bishop,' my lord," Joliffe answered, hand still over heart. This time they both laughed aloud.

John joined them then, released and happy, taking Joliffe by the hand and saying to him and Frevisse both, "Master Wilde says if I decide not to be a lord, I can come be a player with him."

"I'd welcome you in any company of mine," Joliffe said before Frevisse could think of a discouraging answer. "You pay heed to what you're supposed to do and to what everyone is doing around you. I've known any number of players who are never good at that. Mind you, though, that's a useful skill for lords, too. You should give my lord Bishop Pecock of St. Asaph's greeting and Master Arteys, too."

John immediately did, bowing to both of them, saying correctly, "My lord," and, "Sir." They each bent their heads to him in return, but what was neglected, Frevisse noted, was any naming of him as Suffolk's son in return; nor did she. If Joliffe did not choose to tell them, she would likewise let it go.

Instead, Joliffe suggested, "John, why don't you take Bishop Pecock and Master Arteys to Master Wilde? It won't hurt him to hear from them that it's going well."

Done with his players for a while, the playmaster was standing alone, hands on hips, staring up the floor in front of him, and Bishop Pecock took up Joliffe's suggestion with, "I'd be pleased to tell him that, from what I've seen, I think the play will suit the king very well."

"And promise him again that we'll say nothing to anyone about it," said Arteys. He had been silent but smiling along with Frevisse at Joliffe's and Bishop Pecock's word-trading, with whatever had been taut in him when he had come here loosened, maybe even forgotten behind the pleasure he had had this past while. He held out his hand to John. "Would you take us to him, please you?"

John went willingly and Joliffe sat down on the bench, leaned back against the wall, and stretched his legs out in front of him, crossed at the ankles, like a man tired but satisfied with a task well done. Not believing in his apparent ease for even a moment, Frevisse took up her sewing again and said, to take advantage of this chance, finally, to talk with him, "I've known you as a player and a minstrel and a player again, and now it seems you've been a clerk to a bishop."

Toward the rafters rather to her, Joliffe answered, "He was merely master of a college of priests at St. Michael Paternoster in London when I knew him."

"What else have you been, I wonder?"

"A scholar but never a scullion. A poet but never a peddler. A vagabond but never a villein. A–"

Rather than find out how long he could keep that up, Frevisse interrupted, "I never even knew your last name until now, Master Noreys."

Joliffe made a small sideways tilt of his head. "That's me for now, anyway."

"For now?"

"Sometimes I'm . . . someone else."

Behind his lightness there was a challenge, and a thought Frevisse did not want to have stirred forward from the back of her mind. "And 'Joliffe'?" she asked. "Is that equally 'sometimes'?"

" 'Joliffe' is mostly. For simplicity's sake. But," he granted, "sometimes I'm not."

"Why?" She was sewing without heeding what she was doing, and although she kept her voice down, she was unable to curb its sharpness. "Why are you sometimes not Joliffe? Why are you Noreys for now but sometimes someone else?"

"Guess."

She stopped sewing and looked at him, the unwanted thought congealing into certainty. "Because you're Bishop Beaufort's man. The one he said would find me out if there was need."

Joliffe slightly bowed his head to her. "Even as you say, my lady."

The thought chilled her, the ugliness of it settling like lead into her mind and under her heart. Of all people, why Joliffe? And how? But her voice held steady, unrevealing, as she asked, "And now there's need?"

"Best you keep on with your stitchery, lest it seem I'm bothering you."

"You *are* bothering me." But she returned to sewing. "What is it you need?"

"You know Suffolk has gathered men to guard the king against Gloucester?"

"So it's being said among Suffolk's people. Though no one seems much concerned about it."

Joliffe's body gave no sign of anything but ease; only his voice sharpened as he asked, "No? No unease? No fears or alarm?"

"No." She had not heard much when she went for John, but enough. "Someone said they'd heard the men were mustered. Someone else said it was cold weather for it. Someone else said, well, they'd make hot work for Gloucester if it came to it. Then there was laughter. But no alarm, even among the women."

"And Lady Alice? Did she say anything?"

Frevisse nearly retorted she was not going to spy on her own cousin. But she already was, wasn't she, and said truthfully, "No. She didn't speak of it at all. What's being said in town?"

"The rumor is running everywhere that Gloucester is bringing an army to seize the king."

"An army? To seize the king? No one around Suffolk is saying that. *Is* Gloucester bringing an army to seize the king?"

"Gloucester is not," Joliffe said, flatly certain.

They traded long, level looks before she said, "I won't ask how you come to be so sure of that," and went back to sewing.

"Good. On the regrettable other hand, I'm going to ask you to keep as close an ear as possible on anything being said by Suffolk's people."

Frevisse slightly nodded to show that she would. Joliffe stood up and moved casually away to meet Bishop Pecock, John, and Arteys coming back toward the bench, and she found she had finished the hem and was started around again. Impatient at herself, she fastened off the thread, snipped it, and rose to take needle, thread, and gown to Mistress Wilde. That done, she called for John to come to her, well-wrapped him into his cloak, and left without more words to anyone except farewell to Toller at the door.

Not until she and John had gone outside, into the fading late afternoon light, did she have a thought she no more wanted than others she had lately had. "Fitz-Gloucester" was an old way of saying "Gloucester's son," a way—sometimes—of naming a bastard-born child, acknowledged by his father but without claim to his father's name. The duke of Gloucester had no legitimate son but . . . FitzGloucester. Gloucester's son. Was that who Arteys was? If so, no wonder Joliffe had thought it best he not be out and about in Bury St. Edmunds today. Nor wonder that Arteys had been so ill at ease.

Another thought came, equally unwanted.

For thirty years and more, there had been nothing but rivalry and hatred between Bishop Beaufort and

Gloucester. How did Joliffe—Bishop Beaufort's man—come to know someone who wore the duke of Gloucester's badge—whether his bastard son or not—well enough to offer him refuge and what looked much like friendship?

The cold wind, catching at cloaks and veil as she and John came through the Cellarer's Gateway into the shelterless open of abbey's Great Court, was less discomforting than the question that came next.

What was Joliffe playing at?

Chapter 7

rossing, with John's hand firmly in hers, among the ever-busyness of people coming and going in the abbey's Great Court toward the stone-built length of buildings that was partly the abbot's palace, partly wealthy guest rooms, partly offices for abbey officials, Frevisse's immediate want was to be done with her duty to John and then escape to prayer in one of the abbey's many chapels until time for Vespers.

What she also wanted was time to consider Joliffe. He had chosen to tell her who he was when she could not question him well, and she did not think for even half a breath that was by chance. She did think it was because of this Arteys, though. Why was Joliffe befriending him?

Or seeming to befriend him. Had Bishop Beaufort ordered that? Because if he had and Arteys was indeed
Gloucester's son, it was foul to use him unwittingly
against his father. Or was he unwitting? She knew nothing particularly good about Gloucester. Maybe his son
was willing to be used against him.

But more than her questions about Arteys were her
ones about Joliffe. How did he come to be working for
Bishop Beaufort? Had Bishop Beaufort known she and
Joliffe knew each other when he decided on her coming
here? If so, what else hadn't she been told, and wasn't
being told?

Questions and more questions and she doubted Joliffe
would give her any chance to ask them. She was to look,
to listen, to tell. That was what Bishop Beaufort had
written he wanted from her. But he had to know she
would also think. He had made use of her thinking before now and once she had even used it against him.

But what she most deeply wanted at this moment was
simply to be far away from all of this, at least in mind,
for a while. She wanted to kneel quietly in prayer, go to
Vespers, have supper in the guesthall's refectory, say
Compline's prayers with Dame Perpetua afterward, and
then, please God, go simply to bed.

The penticed walk running the length of the buildings
along the courtyard's east side gave welcome shelter
from the wind but even more welcome was escaping it
altogether as she and John went inside and up the stairs
to the rooms given over to Suffolk and his people. In
keeping with Suffolk's importance, they were among the
best the abbey could offer its guests. Large, with polished wooden floors, pattern-painted ceilings, a small
fireplace in the middle of the three, and windows overlooking the abbot's garden and the river, they were presently somewhat crowded with traveling chests lined along

the walls and the general clutter of too many people in too small a space, but at this hour of the day less full of people than they often were. As she and John passed through the first room, a few squires rose and bowed. In the second, John's nurse was sitting on a stool pulled near to the fire with a handkerchief to her nose and two ladies-in-waiting were busy with shaking out a dress that had crumpled while packed and debating whether it would need to be pressed or if hanging it up near the fire would be enough. They gave brief curtsies when Frevisse and John entered and Nurse made to rise but Frevisse said, "No, don't."

The woman gratefully didn't. Her rheum had bettered but, "That wind," she had said, snuffling, as she put John's cloak around him to go to the players today. "It would do my head no good."

Frevisse had agreed and now supposed she should encourage Nurse to nurse herself longer and said, taking off John's cloak and laying it aside on a chest, "You were wise to stay inside today, Nurse. Shall we plan for me to take him tomorrow, too? Even if the wind stops, you don't want to be out in the cold."

"If you would, my lady, I'd be so grateful." Nurse wiped at her red, raw, running nose with the tired handkerchief and told John, "You go play, dear," pointing him toward a corner and some of his playthings. "This rheum is just hanging on and on. Poor Master Denham is still in the infirmary."

"My lady asked to see you when you came in, my lady," one of the ladies interrupted. "If you will."

Nurse nodded toward the doorway into the next chamber. "She's there." And hastily pressed the handkerchief to her nose again, groaning, "I don't know. I just don't know . . ."

Leaving her not knowing, Frevisse crossed the room,

tapped lightly at the door already standing half-open, and entered the bedchamber. The high, curtained bed took up much of the room, a tree-trunk-long traveling trunk along one wall took up more, and at night when the truckle beds were pulled out from under the bed for John and the more favored servants, there was very little floor left open at all, but this afternoon the lesser beds were out of sight and way and so were the several waiting women usually attendant on Alice. Instead Alice was sitting with a woman Frevisse did not know on the cushioned bench under the window, and Alice greeted her with, "Frevisse. You're here. Good. Leave your cloak anywhere and come sit with us," then asked, while Frevisse laid the cloak on the chest and drew a small, curved-back chair to them, "How did it go with John?"

"He knows his part perfectly," Frevisse was glad to say. "You'll be pleased with him."

Smiling at that, Alice nodded toward the other woman. "Mistress Tresham, please you to meet my cousin Dame Frevisse of St. Frideswide's priory near Banbury." Frevisse and Mistress Tresham bent their heads to each other while Alice went on, "Mistress Isabella Tresham. Her husband is Speaker for the Commons this Parliament."

Both Alice and Mistress Tresham were lovely with all the grace and grooming that wealth and a high place in the world could give. Their elaborate headdresses framed their faces with padded cauls covered with figured satin, gold netting, and a froth of pale veiling so light it floated with the slightest movement of their heads. Their gowns—Alice's in her favored dark blue, Mistress Tresham's in rich brown—were both furred with sable around their deep-veed necklines and heaped in excessive yards of fine-woven cloth around their feet.

Frevisse's uncomplicated veiling of white wimple

around her face and a black veil over it and her outer
gown with its plain practicality and reasonable length—
although, by courtesy of Alice's gift, of fine black wool
and fur-lined—were severely plain, but it was a plain-
ness Frevisse had chosen and preferred, and matching
her cousin's graciousness, she said, "I believe I met your
husband once, Mistress Tresham. At dinner at Lady Alice's in London. He was to be Speaker then, too, as I
remember."

From that small ground a few mild exchanges were
made, Mistress Tresham asking about St. Frideswide's
and how long Frevisse had been a nun there. In return,
Frevisse learned the Treshams were from Northampton-
shire. "Not so far a ride to here as you had," Mistress
Tresham said. Alice said she had had the shortest ride
of the three of them, having come only from Wingfield,
perhaps thirty miles away. Then they all agreed that despite the rigors of winter travel, frozen roads were to be
preferred to muddy ones, and all the while Frevisse felt
that under the surface-seeming she was not the only one
uneasy in her thoughts. In both Alice and Mistress Tresham there was something else, and nonetheless she was
surprised when, after a pointless comment that spring
would be here before they knew it, Alice suddenly said,
"Isabella, let me ask her."

Mistress Tresham regarded Alice a quiet moment before saying, "Go on then."

Alice paused, troubled, then said, "Frevisse, you have
a chance to hear things we won't. What's being said
about the duke of Gloucester? Do people truly believe
he's coming with an army against the king?"

Frevisse was immediately somewhere she did not
want to be—in the middle of too many people wanting
to know what she knew, without being certain what she

should tell any of them. For gaining time she tried, "Shouldn't they believe it?"

Alice was her father's daughter, not to be turned aside that easily. "Frevisse, don't. Please. I . . . we need to know. Do people believe those some thousands of men on Henow Heath are called up because Gloucester is bringing an army against the king? What were the players saying?"

"The players are too bound up in their play to pay much heed, one way or the other." Frevisse hesitated, then asked anyway, "*Is* Gloucester bringing an army?"

"He may be. Everything is uncertain." Including Alice's voice as she said it.

Joliffe had it right, then, Frevisse thought. Gloucester was bringing no army. Alice's half-lie had been given unwillingly but was still a lie and Frevisse ventured, "But Suffolk has gathered those men. He must be expecting Gloucester will make trouble of some kind."

"Gloucester always makes trouble of some kind," Alice returned quickly. She stopped, turned her look to Mistress Tresham, then back to Frevisse and added, "But Suffolk has promised there won't be a battle. Otherwise we'd send John away."

"What will there be instead?" Frevisse pressed.

Alice shared a look with Mistress Tresham, asking her something. Mistress Tresham made a slight, refusing movement of her head, leaving whatever it was to Alice, who looked down at her lap a moment before raising her gaze to Frevisse and saying, "We don't know what there will be. That's what has us . . ." The word she wanted was *afraid*, Frevisse thought; but Alice finished, ". . . uneasy."

They were that and more, but all Frevisse could do was slightly lift her hands to show she had nothing to give.

Alice sighed and Mistress Tresham stood up. "It was worth asking, anyway," she said. "I'd best leave now. By your leave, my ladies. There's this evening to ready for."

Alice and Frevisse likewise rose, but Frevisse stayed where she was while Alice saw Mistress Tresham to the door. Low words passed between them and Mistress Tresham briefly touched Alice's arm before Alice called one of her ladies to see her out, then returned to Frevisse at the window. Frevisse sat again but Alice stayed standing, silently looking out, until after a few moments she turned and sat down, her face quiet with what looked to be worry to which she saw no end. "The pity is that Isabella and I like one another," she said, "but must needs watch everything we say together, unless it's about our children or our gowns, because . . ." She broke off and made a helpless gesture.

"Because of who your husbands are," Frevisse said. The king's chief lord in the royal government and the Speaker for the Commons of England. Two men whose interests might sometimes run together and much of the time would not.

Alice nodded weary agreement.

Sorry for her, Frevisse asked gently, "What is it, Alice? You must have some thought of what's making you . . . uneasy."

"Of what's frightening me, you mean. All I know is that something is deeply wrong and I don't know what it is, nor will Suffolk tell me."

"You've asked him?"

"I've asked him." Alice's rare anger burned suddenly on her delicately boned cheeks. "He patted my shoulder and said I wasn't to worry. He said he has it all in hand, but he wouldn't say what it is." The bitter edge to Alice's voice shifted to barely in-held desperation. "All

that we've done this far we've done together. Why isn't
he telling me this?"

"Because he knows it's something you'll try to turn
him from," Frevisse said. When Alice did not refuse that,
she tried, carefully, "The talk has been that Gloucester
has hope of winning a pardon for his wife. Could it be
he's bringing men enough to force the matter?"

"I can't see him thinking he could force a pardon from
the king. No one would let him."

"Is he likely to get it without force?"

"No." Alice was flatly certain of that. "If he won
mercy for Lady Eleanor, it would mean he was returned
to the king's favor. Everyone who's against Suffolk
would join Gloucester and we'd be back to arguing end-
lessly over peace with France."

That was probably too true. Gloucester had opposed
ending the French war. Only after he was out of the way
had Suffolk been able to bargain a French marriage for
the king and make a truce. If Gloucester came from disgrace into any kind of favor, he would attack that truce
and maybe that marriage, and all those among the lords
and commons opposed to Suffolk would willingly join
him. Factions were inevitable around the king but each
needed a leader to be effective. Because no one had
moved into Gloucester's place with those against peace
with France, Suffolk had held almost unchallenged
power these past few years, and one of the things he
must want least in the world was Gloucester rising up
to challenge him again.

Alice seemed about to say something more, but the
slightest of taps at the door interrupted her. The daylight
had been falling away rapidly while they talked. Here at
the window they could still see each other's faces but
the lady-in-waiting who came in at Alice's bidding was

in shadows as she asked, "Would my lady like a lamp brought now?"

"What?" Alice answered distractedly. "Yes. Thank you."

The woman withdrew and the bells to Vespers began their calling from the abbey's tower, bold down the wind. Alice flinched her head up and toward the sound as if startled by an unexpected thing, although it sometimes seemed to Frevisse, used to St. Frideswide's lone, untuneful bell in the cloister garth, that church bells were as common here as air. That Alice flinched at them told her more of how far astray things must be for her, but she only said, "By your leave, Alice, I'm minded to go to Vespers."

Alice immediately stood up. "Yes. Of course I won't keep you from prayers."

Frevisse rose more slowly, wondering if she did right to leave Alice but not seeing what she could do for her by staying. The lady-in-waiting returned with a three-cupped oil lamp, its light sudden against the shadows, set it on the room's small table, curtsied, and went out. Frevisse made a slight curtsy of her own to Alice and started to draw back, but of a sudden Alice asked, "But come back here after supper. Please. We're having guests. Some men" she paused to choose her words— "allied with my lord husband and some others he hopes to at least work better with hereafter. It's only for talk. Wives will be here, too. If you could be here, listen to what's being said, tell me how things seem to you . . ." She stopped, her eyes rapidly searching Frevisse's face before she asked, "Will you?"

It was the kind of thing both Bishop Beaufort and Joliffe wanted her to do, but it was for Alice, not them, Frevisse said, "If you want me to, yes, I'll come. I should bring Dame Perpetua with me."

"Of course. Yes. Certainly. Thank you."

Frevisse briefly laid a hand over Alice's on her arm and they parted, Frevisse gathering up her cloak as she left. Alice would be readied now by her women and go to dine at the high table in the King's Hall with king and queen and whoever of the lords and Commons from Parliament were being favored tonight. For Frevisse there was the return into the cold and wind, and she hurried across the Great Court through the late afternoon's gathering shadows, wanting to reach the church before the bells had ceased to summon.

Because St. Edmund's Abbey was large, with its monks scattered to tasks all over it and needing time to reach the church, the bells were only beginning to ring down as she entered the vast nave with its twelve-bayed double line of stone columns rising far above a man's height into arches and more arches above those into finally gray-shadowed darkness under the almost impossibly distant roof. Stained glass windows, presently deserted by light and color though they were, and the glow of altar lamps and flicker of prayer candles in the many chapels aside in the transepts and around the curved far end of the church added to the certainty of St. Edmund's holiness as she made her way past other people toward the tall carven rood screen that separated the nave—open to everyone—from the monks' choir meant for those whose lives were sworn to God's service. The screen, with the cross atop it outlined from below by the golden glow of the candles along the monks' polished wooden seats in the choir behind it, served to divide the world of prayer, turned toward eternity, from the mortal world where all things changed and perished. How little at bay the mortal world was actually kept by even the grandest of rood screens Frevisse knew more than well enough, but it was not the failure that

counted with her, it was the attempt, because without a
reaching toward a greatness beyond the self, that self
would stay too small, never grow enough to be able to
look on the face of God in joy and freedom.
Unfortunately, here in St. Edmund's her place was not
there beyond the rood screen. While a last few black-
gowned, black-cowled monks passed through to their
places, she turned aside among the lay people standing
in the nave, some speaking hastily to each other before
the Office began, others with bowed heads beginning
their prayers, and went rightward along the choir and
into the south transept, to the farther, smaller of the two
chapels there, St. Nicholas' set in a curve of wall bright-
painted with pictures of his miracles, the saint himself
tall behind the altar, eyes kindly and hand raised in ben-
ediction on those who came to him in prayer.

Dame Perpetua was already there. She and Frevisse
had just time to trade nods before the last bell ceased
and the monks' deep voices began. After the opening
prayer came the Office's psalms, with today one that
Frevisse always especially pleasured in and took comfort
from. *Laudate Dominum, quoniam bonus, quoniam in
aeternum misericordia eius* . . . Praise the Lord, since he
is good, since forever is his mercy . . .

But today, less comforting, came the thought that before this matter of the duke of Gloucester was done,
there might be much need of mercy.

Chapter 8

s Frevisse had hoped, Vespers' prayers and psalms gave her respite from the day's tangle of thoughts. That was, after all, Vespers' purpose—to turn the mind toward God as the body turned toward its night's rest; to move the self out of a day's passing cares into remembrance of the All that lay beyond the World's brief importances.

Unhappily her day's end was farther off than she would have liked it to be. If she had been in St. Frideswide's, after Vespers would have come dinner, an hour's recreation with idle talk and small pastimes, and then Compline's prayers and bed. Here, there would not have been even a bed to which to go if Alice had not forethought to bespeak one for them and even then, with the overflow of ladies-in-waiting and waiting women from other households, one bed had been all even Alice could manage for Dame Perpetua and her. It made for narrow sleeping and little ease but Frevisse was grateful for it, and grateful, too, that Dame Perpetua was happy in her purpose here, now that the monk in charge of the library had grudgingly given her leave to work there.

It seemed that despite the library was open to citizens of Bury as well as monks, he did not hold with women reading. Only because another scholar working there had spoken on her behalf had Brother Adam given way and now Dame Perpetua was so settled in that she rarely left. After every morning's Mass, Frevisse saw her only at the Offices in St. Nicholas' chapel and sometimes at midday dinner. Their only time for much talk was between Vespers' end and Compline and today as they went from the church to the guesthall refectory for their supper, Frevisse said under the general talk of the crowd around them, "I pray your pardon but we've been asked to spend the evening at a gathering in my lord of Suffolk's chambers."

Dame Perpetua smiled mildly. "You mean you've been asked and I'm needed for seemliness' sake." Frevisse granted that, smiling, too, and Dame Perpetua asked, "How does our business go? No trouble, I hope?"

"Lady Alice only needs to find when best to ask the queen's help and that's difficult, with everything presently so over-busy."

"Besides, she probably enjoys your company, and isn't eager to lose you."

In the refectory they gave over talking, crowded elbow to elbow on the benches with other people all talking to be heard over one another and the clatter of dishes, the din rising to the raftered roof and only falling away as servants passed along the tables, ladling goodly portions of thick-gravied stew onto the thick bread trenchers set at each place. With the stew there was fresh-baked bread, heavy cheese, new-brewed ale and, as hungers eased and talk began to take up again, a dried-apple pudding at the end, leaving everyone filled and, unless they were greedy, satisfied. It being far more food than they would have at St. Frideswide's and taking longer to eat, Frevisse and Dame Perpetua went directly from it to Compline and afterward out into the cold twilight where sunset was a fading pale orange in the west and overhead stars were showing sharply bright between more clouds than had been there earlier. Dame Perpetua shuddered and huddled her cloak high toward her ears as they made haste across the Great Court toward the torch-lighted walk along the eastward buildings but asked as they went, "Do you think the king and queen may be there tonight?"

"I fear not," Frevisse had to answer. "I'm sorry." Though she was not. Thus far they had had no sight of either the king or queen. They went to Mass in the abbot's chapel, Frevisse understood, and had not been out and about to be seen. She knew Dame Perpetua was thinking how pleased everyone at St. Frideswide's would be to have report of what they looked like and she offered, "There's the play. We'll see them at that, surely."

"Are we going to that? I thought it was for . . . well, not for us."

"We're going," Frevisse said firmly. She had not sat through all those rehearsals not to see how it played at the end.

That left Dame Perpetua content until, as they neared the penticed walkway, she said hopefully, "Anyway, there'll be good wine tonight."

Frevisse felt an unseemly rise in her spirits at having one thing to which she could look forward. For the rest, she meant to listen long enough to feel she had done her duty to Alice and Bishop Beaufort then, as soon as might be, leave. Good wine along the way would be some compensation for being here doing what she did not want to do.

She and Dame Perpetua reached the lighted doorway at the foot of Suffolk's stairs almost together with three cloak-wrapped men likewise hurrying to be out of the cold, who nonetheless paused and bowed for them to go ahead. Frevisse and Dame Perpetua acknowledged their courtesy by a simple bending of their heads, went in and up the stairs, and only at the top, when a servant had taken their cloaks and they had gone into the first warm, brightly lighted, already crowded room, turned back to give the men better thanks, finding that uncumbered of their own cloaks, the men were all too clearly someone to whom she and Dame Perpetua should have given way. Their clothing, if nothing else, showed their nobility, their full-sleeved, thickly pleated doublets of wool so fine it had a sheen almost to satin, two of them darkly blue, the third man's a deep-dyed murrey—a costly red-purple—that set off the wide chain of gold and enameled white roses he wore around his shoulders.

Frevisse, taking in all that and the heraldic badge of a falcon displayed in the arch of a fetterlock hanging from the middle of the chain, realized whom she was thanking just as Alice swept up to them, a froth of transparent veils floating from her high-cauled headdress and an emerald necklace at her throat that matched her velvet gown, holding her hand out to the dark-haired, quiet-faced man with all the smiling pleasure of a hostess greeting a treasured guest, saying, "My lord of York. You've been missed."

He said, "My lady," took her hand, bowed, and kissed it as she curtsied to him.

She made a graceful sideways gesture, saying, "Dame Frevisse, my cousin, and Dame Perpetua of St. Frideswide's Priory. My ladies, please you to meet my lord Richard, duke of York. And Lord Bourchier and Sir William Oldhall."

Frevisse and Dame Perpetua made deep courtesies to York's slight bow and the somewhat deeper bows of Lord Bourchier and Sir William, all carefully matched to their differences in place, with York's royal blood and dukedom putting him well beyond any of them, even Alice, who was already moving him away, his two companions with him, toward the next room.

Frevisse did not mind being left behind. If she was to hear anything Alice did not, she should be where Alice wasn't, and was satisfied to look around the room, taking in the perhaps dozen finely dressed men and half as many women standing about in mannered talk, wine goblets in hand, voices rising over one another. She did not know any of them. Even if she heard something of use, she'd not be able to say who said it.

Beside her, with no such concerns, Dame Perpetua breathed in wonder, "The duke of York. The king's own cousin." She turned to Frevisse. "He's fought in France. He was governor there. His wife is a Neville. Her brother is the earl of Salisbury. They have five children now, I think. Or did one of them die? Anyway, there's almost no one nearer in blood to the king than he is. After the duke of Gloucester, he's—"

"Dame," Frevisse said quietly but enough to stop her. That York was next heir to the crown after Gloucester was probably a thing best unsaid in this place and company.

Dame Perpetua stopped and after a moment said quietly, "Oh. Yes. What with one thing and another. Yes." She leaned closer and asked in a much-lowered voice,

"What's he doing here at all?" Because it was no secret anywhere, even in so removed a place as St. Frideswide's, that those closest around the king, including Suffolk, were at odds with York and he with them.

With a firmly placed smile, Frevisse said, "I don't know. Maybe he was asked because this is a gathering simply for pleasure, not politic dealings."

Dame Perpetua was becoming unawed enough to ask, "Is that possible here and now and in the midst of Parliament?"

"No," Frevisse said flatly.

Dame Perpetua smothered a small laugh. Happily for her, politic dealings were something other people did and nothing to her. Unhappily for Frevisse, they were presently otherwise and she said, "Let's find our wine." With goblet in hand they could stand or wander and seem to belong, but no wine was being served in this room and they moved to the next, where at a table set out with small cakes, thin, crisp wafers, sugared fruits, and nuts, several servants were standing with tall, worked-silver pitchers of wine, one cooled, the other warm and spiced, Dame Perpetua and Frevisse were told when they approached.

The room being crowded and warm, they chose the cooled and, filled goblet in hand, Frevisse edged with Dame Perpetua toward a corner where Dame Perpetua said, low in Frevisse's ear, "We're so out of place here."

They were, and for more reasons than their plain black gowns and simple veils among all the brightly fashionable folk around them; but Frevisse said, deliberately sententious, "Everywhere is God's place, and as God's servants we have as much right here as anyone." As hoped, Dame Perpetua softly laughed, and Frevisse added, "Besides, when we've returned to St. Frideswide's, you can tell how you saw the duke of York, the marquis of Suffolk, the earl of this, the lord and lady of that, and too many bishops to bother counting. There's one of them now."

With a small beck of her head, she directed Dame Perpetua's gaze to a stout, loud man a few people away from them, gowned to the floor in ample purple velvet furred with ermine at the throat and a large cross of gold set with amethysts hanging on his chest from a heavy gold chain.

"Who is he?" Dame Perpetua asked with mingled awe and dismay.

"I've no thought." Frevisse slightly pointed toward a man more quietly dressed than many in the room but far from poorly nonetheless. "But over there is Master William Tresham, presently Speaker of Parliament. I met him once, that time we were in London, years ago. That's his wife beside him." Who presently showed nothing of this afternoon's worry as she listened smiling to a heavily beringed gentleman saying something to her husband.

"Why, there's someone *I* know," said Dame Perpetua with surprise.

She made a small movement with her free hand toward a man standing alone a little way along the wall from them, a goblet in one hand, a wafer in the other, gazing tranquilly around the room from behind thick, silver-rimmed spectacles. His long black gown was of simple cut, without the excess of cloth that showed wealth but of fine wool and banded with dark fur at neck and sleeves, while the plain gold cross he wore was a modest one among so much other display. "He's the man who took the librarian aside and talked him into letting me work in the library without trouble," Dame Perpetua said. "He's there himself most days, but usually for only little whiles. We haven't spoken since I thanked him that first day. I don't know his name or who he is but . . ."

"He's Bishop Pecock of St. Asaph's," Frevisse said.

"He's never a bishop!" Dame Perpetua protested. "How do you know?"

"He was at the players' practice this afternoon, hiding out, he said."

"Hiding out? Why would a bishop have to 'hide out'?"

"To avoid a meeting of the lords, he said."

Dame Perpetua seemed to find that reasonable. "There was someone came looking through the library for someone this afternoon," she mused. "People must know he goes there."

As she said it, she began to ease her way behind people and toward him. Frevisse went with her, not unwilling to meet him again, and Bishop Pecock, seeing them, slightly bowed his head in welcome. They bowed their heads in return, low curtsies difficult in the crowding.

"Well met again," he said to Frevisse, and to Dame Perpetua, "How goes your work, my lady?"

"Very well, your grace. Please, take my thanks again for helping me to it."

"One scholar should always help another."

"And please, my deep apologies for that day. I didn't know who you were."

"Nor was there reason why you should. No one told you, and though a lion may know a prince by instinct, as the old belief is, there's nothing says a nun should know a bishop thus."

"And most bishops make instinct in the matter unnecessary," said Frevisse with a sideways look toward the purple-clad one now in the middle of the room.

"My lord bishop of Chichester," Bishop Pecock said. "Indeed, one is never left unknowing he's a bishop." A thoughtful frown lined his brow. "Though I sometimes wonder if God is perhaps a little doubtful, there being so little besides the gorgeous robes to show it."

"Who else is here?" Dame Perpetua asked. "Dame Frevisse has pointed out the Speaker of Parliament and his wife and we met the duke of York as we came in. Otherwise, save for you and now the bishop of Chichester, we don't know anyone. Except Dame Frevisse's cousin, of course."

"Your cousin?" Bishop Pecock inquired politely of Frevisse.

"Lady Alice of Suffolk," Frevisse said evenly.

Bishop Pecock's look sharpened. "Young Joliffe didn't mention that."

"Joliffe?" Dame Perpetua asked.

"One of the players," Frevisse said. "He's particularly befriended John these past few days." Though probably for other reasons than kindness to a child, she added bitterly to herself. To forestall other questions, she added, "Our priory received a grant of property and we were advised to have it as strongly confirmed as might be. Our prioress therefore sent me, with Dame Perpetua, to my cousin for her help in having it done."

Said easily, it sounded probable. A servant threading his way through the crowd with one of the silver pitchers refilled their goblets, and as Bishop Pecock began to oblige Dame Perpetua with telling her such of the guests as he knew, they joined in the slow shift and drift of people around the room. They met Alice passing among her guests, gracefully making certain all was well. She only nodded to Bishop Pecock, Frevisse, and Dame Perpetua as she passed, going on to pause with the Treshams and the several men now in talk with them before moving on again, taking Mistress Tresham with her. Behind her, Master Tresham said something to the two men with him, there were nods all around, and he left them, moving away toward the bedchamber.

Thus far, listening aside while Bishop Pecock talked, all Frevisse had overheard was the nothing-talk usual to an evening gathering of people variously acquainted, newly acquainted, or unaquainted. The only mention of Gloucester had been someone saying he was a fool but Frevisse had not heard why. The one thing certain was that there seemed to be no alarm that he would soon be here. People seemed more taken up with a bill in Parliament to reaffirm some old statutes against certain Welsh freedoms in North Wales, and with her curiosity getting the better of her, she drifted in Master Tresham's wake toward the one remaining room, Bishop Pecock and Dame Perpetua drifting with her.

The bedchamber proved to be the least crowded of the rooms, with half a dozen men and one woman in quiet talk among themselves. The bedcurtains were closed, the traveling chest was gone away somewhere, and tall oil lamps stood in every corner, casting warm light over the sheen of pattern-woven damasks and cut velvets and the glitter and glint of jewelried gems and gold worn around every neck and on every hand. If nothing else, that would have told Frevisse that here were people among the wealthiest and probably most powerful of the realm and that this was not somewhere she or Dame Perpetua should be nor company she wanted to keep.

Half-thinking of retreat, she stopped where she was, but Bishop Pecock went past her to where Master Tresham was standing a few paces from the doorway, looking as if he had expected some sort of greeting from someone and not received it. They exchanged bows of greeting and he asked Bishop Pecock, "Were you sent for, too, my lord?"

"I've only come to breathe a little less crowded air, I fear."

"Well, Suffolk sent for me and I daresay he'll notice me when he's made his point."

"Made his point?" Bishop Pecock asked, sounding as if he could not imagine what Master Tresham meant.

"That I'm his to bid and unbid, and that I'd best remember it when the time comes he tells me which way I'm to lead the Commons. No," he amended quickly, "I didn't say that."

"No, you did not, sir," Bishop Pecock agreed. "May I present to you Dame Perpetua and Dame Frevisse of St. Frideswide's priory."

Frevisse could see that Master Tresham had no memory of ever having met her, nor was there reason he should or reason to remind him of it, and she merely bowed her head to him as he bowed his to her and then to Dame Perpetua, saying, "My ladies."

"They've come to see our various and sundry lords, so they'll have tales to tell when they return to their nunnery," Bishop Pecock said.

"If that's what you want, we've lords in plenty here," Master Tresham said.

Dame Perpetua had been looking quickly all around the room and now made bold to half-whisper, "I know my lord of Suffolk and the duke of York but nobody else."

"To begin," Bishop Pecock promptly answered, "in talk with my lord of Suffolk is Edmund Beaufort, marquis of Dorset and nephew to Bishop Beaufort of Winchester."

Frevisse, hiding her interest, asked, "I suppose the bishop favors him?"

"The bishop of Winchester," Bishop Pecock blandly observed, "has been heard to say that his great-nephew is among the greatest asses of Christendom." He paused, then added thoughtfully, "Of course his grace was angry at the time."

Master Tresham passed a hand downward over his mouth, wiping out a smile.

Suffolk was the older, somewhere in his early fifties, Frevisse knew, but his figure still trim as a youth's, suiting well his present sable-black velvet doublet drawn tightly in at his waist, the sleeves puffed widely out at the shoulders, the thickly pleated skirts coming down to only his midthigh, to show a great length of smooth-hosened legs, the left one circled below the knee by the blue and gold band of the Order of Knights of the Garter. A gold chain in the double S pattern of the king's House of Lancaster heavily circled his shoulders, matched by a gold-linked belt around his waist, hung with a thin, sheathed, gold-pommeled dagger. He looked entirely what he was: the most powerful man in the realm after the king.

The marquis of Dorset was younger, possibly forty, and dressed likewise in black velvet with likewise the gold double-S chain, and stood with the somewhat arrogant assurance of a man possessed of wealth and power and the certainty that he knew how to use them well. Unfortunately he was a more thickly made man than Suffolk and sallow-skinned. Neither the tight-waisted shape of the doublet nor black velvet suited him but he did not look like a man who would take well to being told so—or to anything else he did not want to hear.

"That's my lord of Dorset's lady in talk with the bishop of Salisbury near the window," Bishop Pecock went on, "and Lord Saye talking with his grace of York. Except he and York now seem to be coming our way. Or more likely, your way, Master Tresham."

"Very possibly," Master Tresham said. "If you'll pardon me?"

As he moved away, Frevisse took the chance to say, with what she hoped sounded like innocent curiosity, "My lord bishop, I've heard my lord of York and Suffolk were at odds. Is that ended?"

Bishop Pecock regarded her with a benevolent mildness that she was coming to regard as warily as she did Joliffe's mockeries. "Not unless one of them or the other completely changes from the man he is."

"Then why is York here?"

"He was invited, I daresay."

Frevisse fixed the bishop with a hard stare and, smiling, he gave way and said seriously enough, "Very possibly York is here so Suffolk knows he's not elsewhere, such as with the king while Suffolk is not. Or they may be feeling their way toward a marriage alliance between one of York's sons and a Suffolk daughter. Suffolk has the wardship of the young Beaufort heiress and intends, so it's said, to marry her to his son and heir. If so, a marriage with York would—"

Alice had said nothing about a marriage for John, and Frevisse interrupted, "What Beaufort heiress?"

"Little Margaret Beaufort. The only child of the late duke of Somerset, my lord of Dorset's older brother."

"The Beauforts are related to King Henry," she said.

"They are," Bishop Pecock agreed. "And never think they have forgotten it."

"Could it be argued then," Frevisse said slowly, sorting the pieces around in her mind as she spoke, "that they have some claim to the throne? After the dukes of Gloucester and York? Or before York, if things are looked at a certain way."

Bishop Pecock beamed on her. "Concisely and precisely put."

"But the Beaufort line is illegitimate," Dame Perpetua protested.

It was, being sprung from the lust of a royal duke of Lancaster and his mistress more than seventy years ago, with Bishop Beaufort the last living of their children and the present marquis of Dorset their grandson, but, "King Richard the Second, God assoil his soul, legitimated the Beauforts fifty years or so ago," Bishop Pecock said.

"But their half-brother King Henry the Fourth directly barred them from inheriting in the royal line by an act of Parliament," Frevisse responded.

"He did, but of course acts of Parliament can be reversed if a man with sufficient power is interested in so doing."

Frevisse looked toward Suffolk. He had, she supposed, that kind of power. Therefore, if he married John to this Margaret Beaufort who could possibly be made heir to the throne should King Henry and the duke of Gloucester die as childless as they presently were, and also married a daughter to a son of York, then he would have a foot on both branches of the royal tree. The possibilities of power that would come from that were frightening, and quietly Frevisse asked, "Is his grace of York interested in an alliance with Suffolk?"

"Unfortunately for Suffolk," Bishop Pecock said, "the duke of York is *not* an ass."

ChapteR 9

uffolk and Dorset were moving, with no obvious haste but open intent, toward York and Master Tresham now, and Dame Perpetua whispered with both eagerness and unease, "They're coming this way."

Bishop Pecock murmured, "Probably because they don't want York in much private talk with Master Tresham. It's always better that like-minded men be kept apart if you don't like the like of their minds. And here comes the bishop of Salisbury to join the fray. My, my. Perhaps I should go and annoy him. Pardon me."

With a small bow of his head to them, he moved away, into Salisbury's course, leaving Frevisse somewhat discomfited by how much alike his mind ran to

Joliffe's. That their wry, slightly awry way of seeing things was much like her own only discomfited her the more.

"I think we should go," Dame Perpetua whispered. "We don't belong here." She began to ease away but Frevisse held where she was, agreeing with her but watching Bishop Pecock talk at the scowling bishop of Salisbury, who openly lacked interest in what he was saying and the grace to hide it, while Suffolk said to York by way of greeting, "You'll have a cold ride back to the friary tonight."

York answered smilingly, "There'll be a warm bed at the end of it. Better than those men on Henow Heath have."

Dorset, looking as if he disliked York's smile, said irritably, "It's Gloucester's fault they're there and let them remember it. He was supposed to be here before now. If he'd come when we thought he would . . ."

Across that, Suffolk said smoothly to Master Tresham, "You're staying at that man Baret's place, aren't you? I wanted to ask you . . ."

Frevisse saw Dorset's wife was headed toward her. Not wanting to explain herself and why she was there, she faded through the doorway into the crowd and noise of talk in the other room, catching up to Dame Perpetua, who asked, "Why was it so unpleasant in there?"

"Because too many people disliked each other."

"They did that. Did you see Suffolk look at the duke of York when York went to talk to Master Tresham? If a look could strike a man down, York would be dead. My head is beginning to ache. Can we go?"

The heavy warmth, unaccustomed wine, and too much talk around her were making Frevisse's head ache, too. She had promised to be here and she was, and had had enough and said, "We can go, surely. There's just the matter of making our way out. You go on and find our cloaks and I'll give our thanks and farewell to Lady Alice."

Dame Perpetua immediately headed away, threading her way around people toward the doorway. Frevisse, after pausing to be sure Alice was not in this room, followed her into the next and immediately met Alice in an eddy between one swirl of people and another. In what would have to pass for privacy, Alice said quickly, "You're leaving. I saw Dame Perpetua go out. Did you learn anything?"

"Nothing. But doesn't *anyone* believe that Gloucester is coming with an army against the king?"

Alice's smile neither wavered nor reached her eyes. "Not anyone around the king, anyway. Not anyone here."

"Then why . . ." Why was word that he was being spread all over Bury St. Edmunds and some several thousand men freezing on Henow Heath?

She didn't finish the question but Alice answered it. "Because the common people favor Gloucester. They always have. The only person they care for more is King Henry. The rest of us . . ." She made a dismissing gesture.

And therefore Suffolk hoped to turn the people against Gloucester by saying Gloucester was become a danger to the king. Did Suffolk also hope that if the people turned against Gloucester, they would turn toward him?

For a long moment Frevisse and Alice looked into each other's eyes, neither speaking what they were both thinking. Then Alice broke away, said openly, cheerful to anyone who heard her, "Thank you for coming, dear cousin. Good night and, again, my thanks."

Frevisse said courteous things back to her and, thankfully, left.

*   *   *

The next day went, outwardly, much the way of others lately. Frevisse and Dame Perpetua attended Prime's prayers as usual, shivering in St. Nicholas' chapel, went to a crowded, hurried breakfast in the guesthall refectory, and after that to Mass in the abbey church before Dame Perpetua went off happily to the library and Frevisse, far less eagerly, went to fulfill a promise made to help Mistress Wilde with the sewing this morning. The day was too early yet for the players to be at work, but when Frevisse entered the hall Mistress Wilde, Joane still with Lady Soul's gown, and the wife of one of the Mights were already seated around a lighted brazier, stitching rapidly. They welcomed her with hardly a pause from their sewing. Frevisse, given a yellow gown to hem, briefly warmed her fingers at the brazier and joined them.

The other women's talk was of how comfortable or not were the places they were staying and that there was a cookshop in Bernewell Street where a good but uncostly supper was to be had but the ale was better at a tavern near Risbygate. Not part of that, Frevisse would have been content to let her mind go quiet over the sewing, but found her thoughts ranging back to last night and ahead to when she would next speak with Joliffe.

What else besides a headache had she brought away from that gathering of supposed greatness? A continued dislike of Suffolk, unfortunately. Some grasp of the politic games he was playing with his children's hoped-for marriages. The knowledge that Bishop Beaufort thought his great-nephew the marquis of Dorset was an ass. A curiosity about the duke of York, who had quietly stood there goading Suffolk and was not an ass, according to Bishop Pecock.

None of that looked likely to be particularly useful.

What about the blunt fact that no one among those positioned to know best had any fear that Gloucester was bringing an army? Indeed, rather than any fear, Suffolk and Dorset had seemed to be both very pleased and sure of themselves. Which might mean nothing; most of the other times she had seen Suffolk, he had seemed pleased with himself.

So she was nowhere. She had not helped Alice. She had nothing of any worth to tell Joliffe. She doubted she would ever get anything of any worth to anybody, and she was tired of people hoping she would. She wanted to be done with this nonsense and go back to St. Frideswide's in peace.

When dinnertime brought the sewing to a pause, Joane had finished at last with Lady Soul's gown and among them Frevisse, Mistress Wilde, and the other woman had everything else nearly done. Thread, needles, and scissors were tidied away and the four of them rose to go their separate ways, but Mistress Wilde drew Frevisse a little aside, letting the other women go ahead while she said with mild concern, "One thing. I've seen Joliffe Noreys talking at you. Much though I like him, I doubt he's above plaguing a nun for a pastime when he's in one of his fey humours. If he's a bother, just tell me and I'll see to him."

"He's been no bother," Frevisse answered. At least not in the way Mistress Wilde meant. "And Master John likes him."

"Children always like Joliffe and he likes them. He has a good heart under his jesting ways," Mistress Wilde said warmly. "Until this afternoon, then."

With the comfort that maybe Joliffe's friendship to John had not been merely expedient after all, Frevisse went off to dinner and after it fetched John, relieved when a maidservant told her that Lady Alice was, as usual, gone to companion the queen. No message had been left either and Frevisse chose to think that meant Alice had no new trouble to share with her. That was as well, because John proved to be trouble enough. Crossing the Great Court, he pulled loose from her hand and galloped around her like a colt freed to pasture, into her way and other people's until she caught hard hold on him, ordering him to walk beside her, whereon he turned gloomy and outside the hall pulled loose from her again and ran inside by himself, past Master Wilde and Toller talking together at the door. With nothing more than sewing and probably Joliffe awaiting her, Frevisse made no such haste and as she approached heard Master Wilde say, "I've avoided Lydgate all day so far. If he shows up . . ." He paused to give Frevisse a quick bow of his head. "My lady."

"Master Wilde," she returned passing by.

". . . do whatever it takes to keep him out and away from me, short of maiming or killing him," Master Wilde went on. "Maim him and we'll have the abbot on us. Kill him, we'll have the crowner."

"Though, mind you," Frevisse said over her shoulder, "there's good likelihood the jury would find it was manslaughter rather than murder, being done under provocation. To prove it, you could read out some of his poems to them."

She went inside to the sound of Toller laughing. Her quick look around the hall told her Joliffe was not there and that John was busy sorting shoes out of a basket with Giles. Mistress Wilde gave her another doublet to hem and she went to sit alone in her usual place on the bench along the wall, barely started before Joliffe strolled in and over to her. She looked up and he pointed at John across the hall as if asking about him but said,

"Did you hear anything of interest last night among the lords?"

Looking at John, too, she answered, "Nothing, except no one there seemed worried about this army Gloucester is said to be bringing."

"Because they know he isn't," Joliffe said. "So you don't think he's sickening for anything?" he asked, not about Gloucester but because the player who would be the Might of Understanding when the time came but was now merely a young man in need of a shave, was going past them.

"No. He had that little cough, but it's gone," Frevisse said unhesitantly. "He's fine."

Joliffe stood up. "Good then. I'll—"

The other player was away and no one else near and Frevisse said quickly, "They expected Gloucester to be here sooner than he is."

"They who?"

"Dorset said it. He said it was Gloucester's fault the men were cold on Henow Heath. 'If he'd come when we thought he would' is what he said before Suffolk interrupted him."

"That's Dorset. Whatever is wrong is always someone else's fault."

"What do you think is going to happen?"

"I don't know, but my guess is that it's going to happen *to* Gloucester, rather than by him."

"Are you supposed to . . . what did Bishop Beaufort intend you do?"

"Only find out as much as possible about what's being planned against Gloucester. Because something is. 'What' is the question, and the more Bishop Beaufort knows, the more he'll have to work with if he wants to counter it."

"Why . . ." Why would Bishop Beaufort want to counter

anything done against his old enemy, Frevisse meant to ask, but Ned Wilde and another player were passing close by and Joliffe said lightly, "Do you know, I tried to persuade Master Wilde that Lucifer should be in a black churchman's gown, but he said that would be unwise here and now."

"Considering who is paying for the play and all," said Frevisse dryly, "yes, I can see his point."

Joliffe gave the deep sigh of the gravely misunderstood. "Ah, well."

Master Wilde was calling the players to him from the steps of Heaven, but before Joliffe started to move away, Frevisse took the chance to ask, "How would you have found a way to talk with me if I'd not been bringing John to these practices?"

"If nothing else, I'd have lain in wait for you at prayers in the church." Joliffe smiled with all Lucifer's charm. "That's always a good way to meet a nun."

There wasn't time to ask him any of the many other things she had in mind. About Arteys, for one. Was he indeed Gloucester's bastard son? How did Joliffe come to know him? And Bishop Pecock. How were he and Joliffe known so well to one another? More immediately, how much more than what he was telling her did Joliffe know?

Joane came to take the doublet from her, unfinished though it was. "Master Wilde means to run it with the garments as well as music this afternoon," she said. "He says if Ned is going to break his leg tripping over the skirts in Lady Soul's gown, let him do it now so everyone can forget the whole thing and have a rest."

"Is Ned likely—"

Joane smile widely. "Not him. You'll see."

Since Arteys had not come with Joliffe today, she presumed he would not come at all, nor did he, or Bishop

Pecock either, though she had half-hoped he would. But
Brother Lydgate did not appear either and that was just
as well; there were troubles enough without him even
before they began the play. One of the Devil's shoes
pinched cripplingly and had to be stretched. Another Devil complained his doublet was too small in the waist,
would not go around him, until Mistress Wilde pointed
out he had Rob's doublet and Rob had his. Among the
Mights there was laughter and grumbling as they fixed
and fastened on their womanly long wigs of flaxen hair
and then much stumbling and fumbling as they tried out
their gowns' trailing skirts, fuller than the ones they had
practiced in. Ned in Lady Soul's far more full-skirted
gown was all-graceful from almost the first and he and
Joliffe—sleek in a short, black-damask doublet and
crimson hat and hosen—set to showing them what to do
and shortly had them sweeping back and forth across the
playing place. Master Wilde meanwhile was occupied,
first, with setting up the new musicians come to join the
company's piper and drummer, then with practicing the
lift and shift of God's heavy cloth-of-gold robes because
although he would be seated throughout the play, at the
beginning he had to reach his throne—as yet still the
joint stool, not yet replaced by Abbot Babington's best
chair—and at the end come down from it, quickly and
gracefully.

John and Giles sensibly came to sit beside Frevisse,
out of the way, until Master Wilde called everyone to
their places and began. With her sewing taken away,
Frevisse was free to watch as well as listen and was
surprised, as always when she had watched players at
their work, how whatever seeming confusion there had
been fell away once the play began. There might still be
confusions—as when Lady Soul crossed to a place she
should not be until two speeches later, and Lucifer had

to shift his own movements to match hers without losing
his lines—but it was a contained confusion and the play
went forward despite it, with Master Wilde brooding
from above, sometimes forgetting to be Wisdom, especially when the Devils in their dance with the seduced
Mights added undignified hops and skips to avoid skirts
that had not been there before. By Master Wilde's down-
drawn brows, Frevisse knew *that* would be rehearsed
again.

Despite of everything they made it to the end without
stopping and on the whole more smoothly than yesterday
had gone, with time to run through it all again before it
was time for Master Wilde to let them go to their suppers. The second time was even better, with little for
Master Wilde to say at the end and even a little praise
before he went on to remind them to meet in the King's
Hall after supper, to practice tonight where tomorrow
they would perform. That was met with a general groaning, even from John and Giles, though more for the form
of protest than otherwise, Frevisse thought, because they
had all known this was to come.

Master Wilde, ignoring the groans, went on, "It will
be double work tonight, mind you, because besides it
being our next-to-only chance to get a feel for the place
and see how we fit it, we'll as well be trying out the
smoke and Devil's stink and everything suchlike for the
first time, to find if they're going to work at all."

Giles gave a glad whoop and John, who had been
drooping, sat up, instantly no longer tired. Frevisse
wished she felt the same.

Chapter 10

Long before today Arteys had determined that patience was the greater part of being attendant on any lord or lady. It had assuredly been among his earliest lessons in his father's household. Beyond being taught to read not only English but French and Latin and the reckoning of accounts, he had likewise learned the manners and graces of a gentleman and the duties that came with them, including to be where your lord needed you, when he needed you, ready to do whatever he needed done, and today that meant riding horseback for a cold two hours southward out of Bury St. Edmunds between winter-plowed and fallow fields under a gray and lowering sky with four grumbling men and a chill wind for company, hoping to meet with

Gloucester riding northward before too many more miles.

Yesterday Sir Richard had come back with word that Duke Humphrey would spend the night half a day's ride away and come on in the morning, to be in Bury St. Edmunds for dinner. Master Grene, warden of St. Saviour's, had been told and orders accordingly passed to the kitchen for readying the welcome feast that even now had people at bustle in St. Saviour's warm and crowded kitchen—*warm* being the word on which Arteys particularly dwelled as the cold fingered across the back of his neck and he shifted in the saddle to hitch the cloak higher toward his ears and ease his seat at the same time. His horse shook its head in answer, bored after too many days of being shut up in a stall and wanting to gallop. Arteys ran a hand along its neck to say he felt much the same.

Behind him Tom and Hal were passing the time playing at knife-parchment-stone, with smothered laughter and slaps at each other's hands depending on who had won or lost. Ahead, Sir Richard was in talk with Master Needham about Parliament's present dealings. Master Needham was member of Parliament for Dover but also Duke Humphrey's receiver of rents in Kent and eastern Sussex and therefore doing his duty today as the duke's man, come out with the rest of them to join Gloucester's retinue for its ride through Bury St. Edmunds. Even half-listening as he was, Arteys could hear how wary they were in their talk together. Not of each other, he thought, but of something neither wanted to say straight on.

It was like the unease Arteys had brought back from his venture into Bury St. Edmunds two days ago. After the players' practice Joliffe had offered, lightly enough, to walk with him back to St. Saviour's. Another time Arteys would have welcomed his company but that day he had not known whether he wanted Joliffe's company for itself or because he was afraid, and if he had accepted, he would never afterward know for certain why he did. So he had refused with thanks and gone out alone into the waning afternoon and the crowd and hurry of homeward-bound people and carts.

He had had no trouble, but Tom Herbert had been waiting at St. Saviour's gateway for him, demanding, "Where have you been?" as Arteys came over the bridge.

He had sounded so much like Arteys' foster mother when he had come home late from playing in the stream beyond the orchard that Arteys had nearly laughed, as much with his own relief as anything, but only said, "Just into Bury. Why not? You and Hal were."

"Hal and I were back here at midday. Do you know what's being said about Gloucester? Didn't you hear it?"

"Yes, I—"

"Then where have you *been*?"

Arteys had seen then, while they were crossing the yard toward the warden's small, walled garden and the outer stairs to Gloucester's room, since he had the key to there and it was shorter than going around, that Tom was afraid and had felt better about his own fear, finding he was not alone in it. While they went up the stairs, he explained how he had spent the afternoon, unlocked the door and been greeted by Hal with, "Where've you been? We'd have been out looking for you if we'd thought we could find you!"

Arteys had demanded back at him, "Why didn't you tell me what was going on? All this about Suffolk mustering men and Gloucester coming with an army didn't come out of nowhere this morning. You've been into town enough these past days to have heard it!"

"Two days ago there wasn't a word about any of it anywhere," Hal protested.

"Yesterday then?" Arteys challenged.

Tom and Hal had traded looks compounded of guilt and smothered laughter before Tom said, "Um, yesterday, yes. There's this house outside the east gate, see . . ." and Hal had finished, "The thing is, we didn't spend time in Bury yesterday."

And this afternoon they had been waiting for him to come back before they did anything. By then it had been too close to dark for anyone to set off with word to Gloucester but they had decided that, come morning, Hal would go south by the way he was expected to come, and Arteys and Tom would spend the day in Bury, learning what they could. So Hal had ridden out at first light and Arteys and Tom had spent the forenoon going together from tavern to tavern, alehouse to alehouse, cookstall to cookstall, and back and forth from end to end of Bury's two marketplaces until they were swilled full of ale and footsore with walking and not much better knowledged than when they had started. Word was still running that Gloucester was coming with an army, that the men on Henow Heath had been summoned to protect the king against him, that the town gates might need to be shut at any time.

"A pointless move, given the state of the town wall in most places," Tom had said glumly.

Then, at midday, word had started to spread, with much head-shaking and disgruntled laughter, that the men on Henow Heath had been unmustered at midmorning.

"Told to go home," one man was saying to another at the cookstall where Arteys and Tom were sharing a meat pie. "Just like that. Told there was no more need of them, to clear out."

"Daft they were there at all," his companion had said. "Only half as much paid them as promised, too, I heard."

"Why?" Arteys had said to Tom as they moved on. "Why send them all away before Gloucester even comes?"

"Maybe Suffolk saw how idiot he was going to look, all those men at his back, when Gloucester rides in with only eighty or so?"

"Why call them up at all?"

"To scare people and turn them against Gloucester? Who knows? Come on. I want to sit down and let my feet pretend today didn't happen."

They had been almost back to St. Saviour's when Sir Richard and Hal had ridden up beside them. They had met on the road, and although Hal had wanted him to turn back to warn Gloucester of what was happening at Bury, Sir Richard had wanted to see for himself how things were before he stirred up alarm and, "Now there's no need," he had said, sitting with his feet toward the fire in Gloucester's bedchamber, where they could all talk privately together. "This kind of nonsense is what makes Suffolk a problem. His wits are quicker than his good sense. He thinks a thing and does it before he thinks it through. Leaps at the pretty bird before he sees there's a thorn bush under it."

"How does he have so much power from the king then?" Tom had grumbled.

"King Henry became king when he was nine months old and was brought up being told what to do by whatever men were nearest around him. He's used to it." Sir Richard had been more blunt about it than Arteys had ever heard anyone dare to be. "Now Suffolk is nearest to him, and however poorly he *thinks*, Suffolk *talks* beyond ordinarily well. He's talked himself into favor and no one's been able to have him out of it. We can just be glad his latest idiot's trick fell apart before it did harm. When he thinks straight, he knows he can't touch

Gloucester. Gloucester is the king's uncle and heir. Now, where's pen and ink? I have to send a message to Needham about tomorrow."

He had, and this morning when they had ridden into Bury as the abbey bells were ringing to Prime, they had accordingly found Master Needham waiting for them outside the abbey gates and they had all ridden south together, in no haste about it because the farther out they rode, the farther back they would have to come after meeting Gloucester.

Arteys' horse pulled at the reins, suggesting they could do more than amble. Arteys wished they could but returned the pull, telling there'd be no galloping this morning. Their duty was to come as gleaming-groomed as possible back into Bury St. Edmunds as part of Gloucester's retinue, for everyone to see that Gloucester might be out of royal favor but still had power of his own and the royal pride of blood that was his right despite however many upstarts challenged it. Ahead, speaking of exactly that, Master Needham was asking Sir Richard, "Do you think a quieter in-coming might have been better advised, given the way things stand?"

Sir Richard shook his head against that. "I wouldn't say so to Gloucester for any price. On the way from Wales he's been saying he's as royal as his nephew and why should he pretend he isn't, just to satisfy ravens and kites like Beaufort, Suffolk, Dorset, Chichester, and Salisbury."

"He said that?" Master Needham's open dismay matched Arteys' silent own. "Not for anyone else but you to hear, I hope."

"For half the household in hall to hear."

"Blessed St. Edmund. If he's coming with that turn of mind, we're in for it."

"We are," Sir Richard agreed grimly.

But his father's humours could shift with the wind, Arteys told himself. By today, please God, he might well be ready again to be a humble petitioner of King Henry's mercy for Lady Eleanor. Not that it would help him if whatever spies were in the household—and other lords had spies in Gloucester's household as surely as he had spies in theirs—had sent word of his rashness on to whoever was paying them—Bishop Beaufort and Suffolk surely, Dorset very probably, and any other lords who saw Gloucester's royal blood as a threat.

Arteys had sometimes—maybe, he suspected, more often than he admitted to himself—looked on his own share of royal blood as an ill jest, bastard as it was. But at least it was not—as his father's was—a danger. In truth, looked at from one way, Arteys suddenly thought, his bastardy was his safety.

"There!" said Tom, from behind but more forward-looking than any of them just then. "Foreriders!"

Indeed, ahead where the road curved into sight around a low-rolled shoulder of hill, three men in Gloucester's livery colors were just riding into sight, a flare of scarlet against the winter-drab fields, one of them raising a thin traveling trumpet from where he had been carrying it poised like a baton on his hip to sound a frilled ta-rah as warning to clear the way.

In answer, Sir Richard rose in his stirrups and waved. Another of the foreriders waved back while behind him more of Gloucester's men were coming into sight with the ducal banner of quartered scarlet and azure with gold lions and lilies and white border bold even under the dull sky. The knights and squires riding behind it matched it for colors in their reds, russets, yellows, greens, and blues, their horses as gaily harnessed, but Gloucester on his tall white palfrey outdoing them all in his ankle-long, full-cut, deep-pleated houpelande of the same strong azure as his royal banner, with miniver at collar, cuffs, and hem, and sleeves hanging halfway to the ground, his horse's harness of scarlet-dyed leather hung with small, gold-shining bells.

"Jesus have mercy," Master Needham breathed. "There's going to be nothing humble about his entry into Bury, is there?"

"Not a thing," Sir Richard replied.

Gloucester, glowing-faced with the wind, greeted them warmly when they met, shaking hands with Sir Richard and Master Needham, saying, "Sir Richard. You didn't freeze on the way, then?"

"Not yet, my lord."

"Master Needham. I take it Bury St. Edmunds still stands?"

"It still stands," Master Needham answered. "But Suffolk has been making trouble."

Gloucester dismissed Suffolk with a wave of his hand. "Suffolk is always making trouble. Let him wait until I have the king's ear again and then we'll see. Arteys." He reached out in the same moment Arteys reached toward him, clasping each other's right arm in greeting, Arteys surprised both at his own gladness and Gloucester's open pleasure at seeing him. This was Gloucester as he had been in the best days Arteys had known him, warm with affection, wearing pride and confidence as familiarly as he wore a cloak.

They rode on, Gloucester keeping Master Needham with him to tell how Parliament was going, Arteys and the others dropping back among the other riders, who all seemed to share their lord's high spirits. Sir Richard, Tom, and Hal fell in with friends but Arteys dropped farther back until almost at the company's end, keeping enough aside that no one tried to talk with him, his momentary gladness fading as abruptly as it had come. He

wanted to believe with Gloucester that everything would
go his way the next few days but a darkling feeling told
him it would not. The feeling was so strong that when
they were almost into Bury St. Edmunds, with the abbey's sky-tall spire sharp against the gray-clouded sky
above the low spread of houses outside of Southgate and
Gloucester's trumpeter ta-rahing their approach, a flurry
of horsemen riding out through the gateway made him
lay hand to his dagger hilt before he thought about it.

Immediately, glad his cloak had hidden the gesture,
he let go again. Alertness rippled through the rest of the
company but no alarm. There were only six mounted
men coming toward them, and four of them, Arteys
judged by their plainer clothing, were attendant on the
other two, who wore surcoats parti-colored with King
Henry's livery of white and green and were mounted on
horses too good for merely servants. They drew rein beside Gloucester's foreriders and Gloucester drew rein
where he was, stopping the riders behind him while his
herald rode forward to meet the newcomers. Arteys
would have ridden forward to Gloucester but the street
was narrow between houses and people were beginning
to gather, an excited running of Gloucester's name
among them and growing louder as more folk came out
to join them, happy for a diversion.

Ahead of Arteys, a woman with a market basket on
her arm called a question to Jenkin ap Rhys. Arteys
heard neither what she said nor what Jenkin answered,
but it was more probably his voice than his words that
made her step hurriedly back from him and say something to the woman next to her and the people beyond
her, because the next moment there was a rush of rising
voices along the street. Arteys caught the words "Welsh"
and "Wales," saw a man spit at the ground, and remem-

bered Sir Roger had advised Gloucester to take no Welshmen with him to Bury.

"I've had more loyalty and better service out of them than from most Englishmen," Gloucester had said, stubborn.

Sir Roger had ignored that enlarging of the truth. "You know how the Welsh are looked on in England. They're supposed to be half wild and wholly treacherous. It'll do you no good with anyone to have an array of Welshmen with you."

Arteys, used to it, had not thought about that until now but over half the riders were indeed Welsh and people were drawing back and pointing, heads coming together in quick talk. Even this far from Wales, where the Welsh wars had never come, there was dislike and distrust of Welshmen, and Sir Roger had been right. Gloucester would have been wiser not to bring them, or at least not so many.

The herald turned his horse and came back with the two surcoated riders to Gloucester. Arteys recognized them now, Sir John Stourton and Sir Thomas Stanley, both of King Henry's household and, according to Gloucester, self-servers of the deepest sort. "They'd serve a bunion if they thought there was profit in it for them," he had said once. "Well, maybe not Stourton. He has some honor in him. But Stanley? The most I'd trust him with is a rabid dog and then only if it promised to bite him."

But Gloucester, when he was in the midst of a dislike, was given to over stating things that later he either unsaid or, more often, forgot he'd ever said at all. Presently he seemed, from what Arteys could see, to greet both knights cordially enough while they bowed deeply from their saddles to him. Nor did he seem disturbed by whatever they then told him but nodded to it and answered with no sign of anger about him. Then, with more bows, they parted from him and rode back toward town, their four men parting to let them pass and falling in behind them while Gloucester signaled with a raised hand for his own men to ride on.

With the way already cleared for them, they rode into Southgate Street. More people were coming out to see them pass, the riders jostled into an even longer line along the narrowed way, with "Welsh" and "Wales" still running through the crowd but Gloucester's name being said more strongly, more excitedly. Despite people might well be tired of lords after all the days of them displaying through the streets, people were leaning out at upper windows into the cold, waving and calling to Gloucester as he rode by, and he was raising a hand first to one side, then to the other, acknowledging them. He would be smiling, Arteys knew, pleased and loving the people back as strongly as they loved him. Whatever his quarrels with other nobles over the years, no one had forgotten he was still the last of the great King Henry the Fifth's brothers and part of the days of glory in France.

The column rode into the marketplace outside the abbey gates where Arteys and the others had met Master Needham at dawn. In late morning it was far more full of people, most of them leaving off whatever they were doing to watch Gloucester ride past. More people were crowding full the abbey's gateways, and although here among the followers of so many other lords the cheering had fallen away, a few bold voices called out, "God bless the duke!" in despite of all, and maybe in godly answer, as the head of the retinue passed the abbey's great gateway, a narrow streak of sunlight broke slantwise through the wind-driven clouds. Pale and moving swiftly across the marketplace, it caught the lions and lilies of Gloucester's banner to sudden gold fire before it was as suddenly gone, swept over the abbey wall and away on the sharp gray wind.

"There's some would say that was a sign of some saint's favor on his grace," Sir Roger Chamberlain said at Arteys' side.

He had been riding back along the column, closing up the line into better order, and now swung his horse around to ride beside Arteys, who was glad of it and answered, "St. Edmund himself, maybe."

"May be, God willing. How have things been here?"

That might have been an ordinary asking but a tightness in his voice suggested otherwise and Arteys, glad to be able to say it, answered, "Not good. Have you heard what Suffolk was at?"

"Sir Richard was telling me of it just now. If I understand a-right, it came out of nowhere and went away as quickly?"

"Yes. We think maybe Suffolk found out Gloucester was only bringing eighty men and saw how foolish he would look, meeting him with an army."

"The question is, why did Suffolk ever think Gloucester was bringing an army? Or was he just trying to raise dread in people?" Sir Roger shook his head. "Either way, he misplanned again. I wonder what else he's maybe misplanned?"

"What did Stourton and Stanley want?"

"They brought King Henry's word that, the day being so bitter cold, Gloucester need not attend on him now but should ride on to St. Saviour's and his dinner and come to him later, at better leisure."

"That was graciously done."

"I just hope gracious is all it was," Sir Roger said, then ruefully half-smiled and added, "No. There's no fault in the king that way. It was gracious. I'm uneasy

but probably for no good reason. How have you been?"
Arteys thought about it before echoing, "Uneasy."

They rode on side by side in companionable silence
the few minutes more to St. Saviour's, where Gloucester
was met by Master Grene with word that dinner was
ready, if it so pleased his grace. Gloucester declared it
pleased him very well, horses were hurriedly given over
to scurrying stablehands, and Arteys sped with other
squires to scrub their hands and smooth their hair and
race to the great hall while Gloucester and the rest were
yet being sorted to their places.

Gloucester was at the high table on the dais, of course,
with Sir John Cheney and Sir Roger to his right, and
Master Needham and Master Grene to his left. The rest
of the company had place at the two long tables facing
each other down the hall's length and, to begin, squires
and servitors with linen towels over one arm carried ba-
sins of warmed rose water from man to man, for them
to wash and dry their hands. Arteys' place was at the
high table and Gloucester smiled at him over the basin
and made a little flip of the fingers to spatter water
lightly at his face. Arteys grinned and slightly shifted
the basin, as if threatening to slosh its water over the
edge at him, an old game between them, then straightened his face and moved to Sir John.

After that came the ceremony of serving the meal,
something Arteys always enjoyed because however har-
ried and harassed things might be in the kitchen, butlery,
and pantry, with dishes being served forth and orders
flying as to who should take what to where—and why
wasn't the venison ready—and where were the pears in
wine syrup—and had someone taken the fish tart to the
high table, they shouldn't have yet—the moment he
stepped over the threshold into the great hall bearing the
broad serving platter or deep bowl or whatever was in

his charge for each remove, everything took on order and grace, from his walk up the hall to the setting of the food before Gloucester to the serving of it to his withdrawal down the hall to bring whatever came next. For that while, everything he needed to do and be was ordered and certain, his place among everyone without question or doubt.

Today the meal went its way through its three removes of four dishes each, with wine in plenty along the way and Gloucester's pleasure in it so open that his laughter spread merriment along the high table to either side of him. The final dish—a petypernaunt of ginger, dates, and raisins in sweet pastry—had been served and eaten and Arteys was at one end of the high table, refilling Sir Roger's goblet with a red wine, when a sudden rise of voices from the screens passage to the outer door to the foreyard turned everyone's heed toward the far end of the hall, without even time to begin asking each other what was happening before perhaps a dozen men in royal livery shoved past servants and into the hall. Moving swiftly, they made a double line between the tables the hall's length, from the door almost to the dais, ignoring the babble of questions and demands rising all around them.

Arteys, clutching the wine pitcher to him, looked quickly to Gloucester, risen to his feet to stand straightly upright, his head lifted and eyes widened with question and wariness and the beginning of anger.

Sir Roger clamped a hand on Arteys' arm. "Get behind me," he whispered harshly. "Get your back to the door there." Meaning the one at this rear corner of the dais, leading to the master's parlor and the stairs up to Gloucester's rooms.

The sharpness of Sir Roger's order made Arteys set down the pitcher and back up just as four more men entered the far end of the hall, not liveried men this time but the duke of Buckingham, the marquis of Dorset, the earl of Salisbury, and Lord Sudeley. Arteys knew them all. With the swift certainty of authority, they came up the hall to stand below the dais two by two, with room between them for one more lord—John, Viscount Beaumont, High Constable of England—to come striding past them.

Arteys' stomach clenched hard with plain fear, even before Viscount Beaumont stopped with only the table between him and Gloucester and, facing him, declared in a voice raised to be heard throughout the hall, his words deliberate as hammer strokes, "Humphrey, duke of Gloucester, in the king's name I arrest you here on charges of high treason against his grace King Henry the Sixth of England, France, and Ireland. Submit you . . ."

Without turning his head, Sir Roger said, low under the shouting beginning to break out from one end of the hall to the other, "Arteys, get out of here."

Arteys took a forward pace. "I—"

"Gloucester would rather have you safe than here. You can't help. *Go.*"

Arteys took a backward step. He understood what Sir Roger was telling him. There was nothing he could do here and now, but there might be later, if he got clear. Pushed by that thought and Sir Roger's order, he took another step, felt the door's handle against his hip, groped one-handed behind him for it but was looking at Gloucester still standing behind the table with shoulders back and head proudly lifted, saying something at Beaumont with red-faced contempt, the words lost under the general shouting.

Still looking at him, Arteys opened the door as slightly as might be and slid out of the hall's bright warmth into shadows and cold.

Chapter 11

ot needed for more sewing nor by Alice who was, as usual, with the queen, Frevisse spent much of that gray-skied morning in the abbey's library. The elderly, somewhat deaf monk in charge accepted her presence with ill-grace but no refusal, and at Dame Perpetua's suggestion, she searched the list of books that were supposed to be in the library for any that might be profitably copied for St. Frideswide's. Then, when she and Dame Perpetua returned from Tierce, she began to look for them through the library's shelves and chests, unexpectedly finding after Sext a copy of *Boece*, Geoffrey Chaucer's translation of the ancient philosopher Boethius' *Consolation of Philosophy*. The list made no mention of it, but she forgot

the life of St. Bartholomew for which she had been looking when she realized what she held.

The *Boece* she had first read, in her uncle's library
when she was a half-grown girl, had been on fine parchment, bound in crimson-dyed leather, the first initial of
each part flourished in red and blue ink. The copy she
now held had been written out in a fair enough hand but
on cheap paper with never a colored letter anywhere nor
even bound, the pages merely stitched together, but Boethius' worth was in his words, not in their binding. He
had written that Evil was not a reality but only a mis-
perception by the human mind, flawed as that mind was
by sin. Frevisse remembered being both discomfited and
comforted by the thought that there was vast difference
between the world's seeming-real and Reality, but as
Boethius said, in the person of Lady Philosophy, "With-
stand then and give over your vices; worship and love
your virtues; raise your courage to rightful hopes; yield
your humble prayers to God on high."

She took the book to Dame Perpetua, who exclaimed
in a delighted whisper, "I read that before ever I came
into St. Frideswide's. Yes, let's copy it out. Can you
begin while I finish these poems I have in hand?"

Frevisse was willing but the bell began to ring for
Nones and they had to leave their work and hurry. The
library was above the monastery's novice school in the
prior's courtyard, close to the abbey church's east end,
and the short way from library to church was through
the cloister, forbidden to women, so they had to go the
opposite way, along the back of buildings and into the
abbot's garden to a passage through the buildings into
the Great Court, across which they went at a long angle
to the gateway into the guesthall yard and from there, at
last, into the church, then up the nave with its pairs of
massive pillars to the south transept and St. Nicholas'

chapel, with barely time to catch their breath and open their breviaries before the Office began.

They had the chapel to themselves and to judge by the sparse chanting from the choir the monks had not flocked to the Office either, nor had there been many worshippers in the nave. At the Office's end she and Dame Pepetua sat silently for a few moments, listening to the monks hurry away, before Frevisse said, "It's hardly worth the while for me to go back to the library before dinner since I have to take Lord John to the players afterward. There's chance I might talk to Lady Alice about our business if I go now, if you don't mind."

"I was already thinking I might stay and pray awhile," Dame Perpetua said. "And rest my eyes. I'll start Boethius myself this afternoon if I can."

Content that Dame Perpetua seemed not to mind, Frevisse left her, wishing she could stay to pray, too, but needing to take this chance to ask if Alice had learned more last night. Crossing the Great Court, keeping tight hold on her cloak against the whipping wind, she was giving small heed to the general hurry of people around her until, from somewhere beyond the abbey's outer wall, there was the cry of a trumpet, bold in the cold air, and the next moment the word *Gloucester* was running across the yard. Heads turned, people stopped, then began to move toward the great gateway all at once.

Frevisse paused, resisting her curiosity, before giving way and going with the crowd toward and into the long arch of the abbey's gateway tower leading to the marketplace outside the abbey walls. The push of people crowded her forward and sideways and without particularly trying she was against the leftward pillars of the outer archway when scarlet-clad foreriders rode by, but all heads on both sides of the way were turned and craning to see Gloucester and by leaning forward Frevisse saw him, too, a tall man with the good looks of his youth not gone from his long-boned Plantagenet face, straight-backed in the saddle as his tall white palfrey played to the crowd, prancing with high-arched neck under a shining fall of mane, hoofs light and quick on the paving stones, the small bells hung from its harness chiming and jinging.

There was little cheering, here among the followers of so many other lords, but Gloucester was acknowledging what there was with a raised hand and a smile to one side and the other. He was not as Frevisse had seen him in her mind these past twenty and more years of hearing what trouble he made around the king with his demands and angry wrangling for more power than other lords were willing to give him. Rather than a face harsh with failed greed, bitter with loss, taut with the verjuice of thwarted ambition, he looked simply a hale man in middle age, openly pleased by those in the crowd who were pleased to see him.

Did he also see how many men in lords' liveries or wearing lords' badges were there and not cheering, Frevisse wondered.

A streak of sunlight through a sudden, wind-torn rift in the clouds swept across the marketplace, caught bright for an instant on the gold lions and lilies of Gloucester's banner wind-shifting above him, then was gone, fled away over the abbey wall, and Gloucester was gone, too, riding on with his men behind him, all wearing his white swan badge on their shoulder. The crowd, not interested in them, began to disperse but Frevisse held where she was. Curious to see if Arteys was there, she found him among the last riders. He did not see her nor had she thought he would but neither did she see what she had thought she might—some likeness to the duke of Gloucester. Arteys was simply a tall young man with golden hair riding among many other men.

When he was past, she turned away, back into the abbey, putting thought of him aside. She was somewhat looking forward to today's last rehearsal of *Wisdom*. Last night's work had mostly been feeling out how voices and gestures played in the different space of the King's Hall and with another practice of the dances and everything interrupted as they went along by Toller trying out his smokes and stenches. It seemed Toller not only kept watch out the door during rehearsals but was likewise adept at what could be done with gunpowder and other things to—as Joliffe had put it—"confound a play."

"And please a crowd," Master Wilde had said, overhearing.

"One might hope," Joliffe had answered, sententious as preacher in pulpit, "a crowd such as this would be above such things." But added with instant grin and in chorus with Master Wilde, "But a crowd is a crowd is a crowd. They'll love it!"

From all Frevisse had seen of it, she agreed. The play itself dealt with solemn enough matter to please the piety of anyone inclined that way including King Henry himself, given to prayers as he was said to be, while the gorgeous garments, the bright-musiced dancing, and Toller's surprises would satisfy the rest.

She found the outer of Alice's three rooms unexpectedly empty save for several clerks scribbling rapidly away at small, easily shifted desks near the window, too in haste at their work to give her even a glance. A scatter of Alice's women were more attentive in the middle room, lifting or turning their heads from their work or talk as she entered, one of them saying, "My lady thought she'd be here but the queen kept her after all. I don't know when she'll be back."

"Lord John?" Frevisse asked.

"With his nurse. In there."

Frevisse went into the last room, to be greeted by John looking up from a scatter of bright-painted blocks on the floor to ask eagerly, "Can we go now?"

"Not yet, my lord," his nurse said from where she sat at the window with sewing in her lap. "You must needs first eat and so must Dame Frevisse and I."

She asked then about the trumpet they had heard, and Frevisse filled in the time with telling what she had seen of the duke of Gloucester's going by until a servant came with the light meal supposed to suffice for two women and a child. For Frevisse, used to nunnery fare, it was more than good enough—rabbit in a plain wine sauce and a cheese tart—but Nurse complained, cutting up John's meat for him, "This isn't what one expects, I have to say, nor how it is when my lord and my lady are properly at home, I promise you. We dine very well then, from hall to nursery. But with so many crowded together here and it being winter, well, there's not so much to go around as should be, I suppose, and what there is goes elsewhere first, I daresay."

Frevisse agreed it very likely did and kept up her side of the conversation with telling she had heard in the guesthall refectory that the abbey's brewhouse was barely keeping ahead of the demands for ale but the wine merchants at least seemed to have unstinted supply of their wares.

"My lord and lady bring their own wine with them," Nurse sniffed.

When it was time to go, Frevisse wished her well and bundled John into his cloak and away. The clerks were still scribbling in the outer room but an older clerk had come in, was standing beside one of the desks with one hand full of papers and the other out to take another as soon as it was done and dried. He gave her and John a brief look and then a bow and Frevisse forgot him, helping John down the stairs too steep and deep for his short legs until, safe at the stairfoot, John said, "They've been doing that all day."

"What?" Frevisse asked, busy with tucking his cloak more closely around his throat.

"Writing, and that man coming for everything. He's the king's clerk." Because she was bent over, dealing with his cloak, her ear was near him and he leaned closer to whisper, "Momma is angry about it."

Frevisse straightened and looked down at him. "Angry? Why?"

"Just angry. You know." He took hold of her hand and tugged, dismissing the strangeness of parents and other creatures. "Can we go?"

They went but not far. King's Hall was only a little way along the penticed walk toward the abbey church. Because the abbot's rooms were at present mostly given over to royal use, there was much coming and going of servants, clerks, churchmen, lords, and others along the walkway, and Frevisse took herself and John aside from it, into the yard where the cobbles made the going no worse and they were in fewer people's way. The clouds had tattered a little since Gloucester had ridden by. Gray shadows and bright sunlight were fleeting across the Great Court on a wind that flapped at any loose cloak edge and made reaching the shelter of the doorway to the King's Hall a pleasure.

Toller was keeping the door again, sitting inside away from the worst draught but where he could stop anyone well before they saw through the inner doorway into the great hall. He was working a thick cord through his hands and John immediately wanted to know about it.

"I'm checking it over, my lord, to be sure it'll burn true come tonight."

"Boom!" said John joyfully.

"Fizz and smoke," Toller responded. "That's what we're after this time. No booms. But maybe later, when the play's done, we'll find a far corner of a field and have a go at some booms."

He winked at Frevisse, who smiled back and privately thought she might do well to forewarn Alice. But Toller was saying to her, with a sideways nod of his head toward the hall and his voice dropping to a conspiratorial whisper, "You'll want to keep your head down in there today. Master Wilde has his hair on end and his tail twitching."

Frevisse had already been warned by Mistress Wilde that Master Wilde tended to be over wrought in the hours before a play was finally performed and she promised easily, "I'll mind that. Thank you."

Behind her, the outer door was flung open, then slammed by someone in haste. "Whoops, young Ned," Toller said. "Caught the wind in your cloak, did you, coming in like that?"

Frevisse looked over her shoulder to see Ned Wilde coming toward them, looking indeed as if the wind and something worse had caught him, his cloak thrown back from his shoulders, his hat in his hands and his hair tossed about. Forgetting any greeting or respect nor even slowing his pace, he burst out, "The duke of Gloucester has been arrested!" and hurried past, into the great hall.

Frevisse stared after him. Toller, shaking his head, said with heavy regret, "Master Wilde isn't going to like that."

"For what?" Frevisse asked at the empty air. "For *what* was he arrested?"

"*Treason?*" roared Master Wilde from the hall.

"Seven devils out of hell! What do you mean—*treason*?"
Keeping firm hold on John, Frevisse went in and aside
to where Mistress Wilde and Joane were seated among
the garment baskets, both of them paused at darning
someone's hose while at the head of the hall Master
Wilde was going up much like one of Toller's "effects,"
loud and fuming, pacing distracted back and forth in
front of the Heaven steps with hands gripping his head
as if to keep it from bursting while he cried out against
idiot lords bent on ruining him.

Around him such players as were already there were
demanding more from Ned, who was exclaiming back
at them that all he knew was that word was running
everywhere that half a score of lords or more had gone
with men to arrest the duke of Gloucester for treason.
That was what he'd heard and that was all he knew and
did his father want him to go out again to find out more?

"No!" Master Wilde roared at him. "I want everybody
here. Where is everybody? There's only half of you
here . . ."

Giles, with a solid sense of when to be out of the way,
slipped between the baskets to his mother's side. She
smiled comfortingly at him without ceasing her sewing
and Frevisse went with John to join them. She was taking John's cloak from him a moment later when Master
Wilde came raging down the hall, crying out at his wife,
"The play will never go on now. Not tonight, not tomorrow. Not with all this . . ."

Mistress Wilde smiled at him just as she had at Giles.
"Of course it will go on. The abbot isn't going to let his
money go to waste."

Master Wilde stopped, face blank, mouth open, then
said, "Oh," stood frowning but thinking and finally said,
"Right. The king will want distracting, that's certain, and

here we are, ready to hand. Or almost ready. Right."
Thunder and storm vanished, he swung around with a
loud clap of his hands, and called at full voice, "That's
enough, then. Dukes can come and dukes can go but
we've a play to do. Get your garments on. We haven't
all day. You!" He pointed an accusing finger at two of
the players just coming in. "Where've you been?"

A monastery bell was just striking the hour, telling
they were on time, not late, and Master Wilde waved
away whatever they started to say, saying, "Get on with
things, then. Go. Go."

Mistress Wilde snipped her thread, said, "There.
Done. Lord John, Giles, come. I'll help you dress," and
went calmly away, a boy on either side of her.

Frevisse, left to herself, stayed where she was,
thoughts racing. No matter how out of favor and out of
power Gloucester had been these past years, he was still
heir to the throne. Could he even be brought to trial?
Whether he was or not, every political balance must already be shifting. Remove him as someone to be considered in the pattern of things and what happened? She
didn't know. And perhaps more to the immediate point
was the question, Who was removing him? Who had laid
this charge of treason against him?

She realized she was thinking about it as if the charge
was false. What if it was not? But why, after almost
twenty-five years of loyalty, would Gloucester try treason now? And if it wasn't treason, who had prompted
King Henry to such a dark move?

Unwillingly she remembered the clerks scribbling
away in Suffolk's outer room where there had never
been scribes before and John saying his mother was angry.

The players were nearly done dressing, save for Lady
Soul being helped by Giles to find her hands' way

through her gown's elaborate, floor-trailing sleeves, but of a sudden Master Wilde, long-bearded and wigged in gold now, holding a scepter and standing at the foot of Heaven in Wisdom's spreading robes, bellowed, "Where in all Hell's rings is Joliffe?"

Frevisse was just wondering that, looking around for him while the questions rushed through her mind. Despite his well-kept air of fecklessness, feckless was probably the last thing Joliffe was—at least with his work, she amended. Why wasn't he here?

"And my crown," Master Wilde said angrily. "Someone has stolen my crown." Mistress Wilde went calmly to open a basket sitting along the wall, lifted out the tall, tiered hat with its rising series of brass crowns circling the cloth-of-gold covering the buckrammed form made to fit firmly to Wisdom's head, and carried it to her husband. Grumbling that if people would just put things where they belonged, he wouldn't have to worry about it, Master Wilde let her put it on him, and by the time she stepped back, the change that usually came over the best players when the time came was coming over him. From being a hard-driven master of players, he lifted his head, set back his shoulders, and seemed to grow taller with taking on the massive dignity and certainty of Creation's Wisdom. Even Joliffe finally entering the hall did not stir him. He only pointed the scepter at him and demanded in Wisdom's deep voice, "You. Where have you been?"

A little breathlessly, throwing off his cloak while he answered, Joliffe said, "The streets are madness. Everyone is thronging and talking. You've heard?"

"About the duke? Yes." But the duke of Gloucester was clearly irrelevant to Master Wilde at the moment. "Get clothed. We're going to start. Everyone, take your places. Let's get on with it."

Joliffe disappeared behind the frame-hung blue curtains with their spangling of stars now flanking the heavenly stairs, the musicians signaled the play's beginning, Wisdom and Lady Soul set to their talk together in Heaven, and from the very first something was wrong. Even Wisdom's speeches lacked their usual force, and Lady Soul stumbled twice on her words and once on her skirts and, further on, the Mights and Devils were not vigorously, only flatly, sinful, and their dance a shambling disaster. Even Joliffe drove forward at his lines as if to have them done as soon as might be. Only John and Giles played their parts well, without stumble or shambling, but the play was nearly done by then and, somehow never having to stop but never rising above painful to watch, it limped and bobbled through to its end.

When at last it was over and the actors came straggling from behind the curtains to stand before Heaven with shamed, discouraged faces, Master Wilde, taking off Wisdom's crown and wig and beard, simply gazed down at them with a sorrow too deep for any trace of anger before he pointed at John and Giles and said, "You. You two were good. The rest of you . . ." He shook his head. "The rest of you were unspeakably bad. Go away. All of you. Be back here when the bell calls to Vespers. By then we'll know if we're—St. Genesius, take pity on us—to perform tonight. In the mean time, do *not* get drunk. Do not fall to brawling. Eat something. Pray St. Genesius gives us better wits than we showed this afternoon. Now go away. I want to weep."

Subdued and mostly silent, the players set about getting out of their garments. Frevisse in equal silence helped John back into his own clothing, wrapped him well into his cloak and herself into hers, and left before anyone else was ready to go, since there was no chance she could talk to Joliffe here.

The walkway was more crowded than before, men and some women standing in clusters talking intensely, shifting from one group to another to talk more and sometimes one or another of them going off across the yard to other clustered, talking groups. Frevisse skirted as close as she could to them along her way but overheard nothing of any use or interest. What was known—and apparently all that was known for certain—was that the duke of Gloucester was accused of treason, arrested, and under guard at St. Saviour's. But not any of his men, despite many of them were said to be Welsh.

Unsurprisingly, Alice was not returned. Frevisse gave John back into his nurse's keeping and immediately left, could have gone to the church to pray, she supposed, but equally supposed she would not pray well, her mind twisting around the question of Gloucester and wanting to talk to Joliffe. Instead, she went to the library, with the hope she might distract herself by being of some use to Dame Perpetua until supper and time to face the play again.

The abbey library was a long room with all along one side high-set windows above shelves, closed aumbries, and chests of books. Facing them across the room were taller windows spaced so that daylight fell on the desks set endwise to the wall between each one, with each desk almost a small room in itself, enclosed on three sides, open to the room only on the fourth and raised on a dais half a step up from the floor to protect against feet-chilling draughts. In front of each desk was a slanted shelf for resting books at an angle best for reading and copying, with another slant-backed shelf above that upon which to lean other open or closed books and along the wall and below the desk flat shelves for piling more. For good measure, each desk had a smaller slanted desktop mounted on a swivel arm that the scholar could position to the light as best suited him and a cushion on each chair for better sitting through hours of work. Because of each study stall's head-high walls, Frevisse standing in the doorway could not tell if Dame Perpetua was at her desk or not—or for that matter, whether anyone else was in the library save for the elderly monk bent over an open book at the table beside the door, his cowl pulled up against draughts and his hands tucked into his sleeves. Resigned to nuns in his library and too deaf to bother with idle talk, he hardly looked up and said nothing as she passed him.

As she had expected, Dame Perpetua was at her desk, writing briskly. She paused when Frevisse softly said her name, her pen ready over her work, and said, "I've started the Boethius. You haven't come to say all's done and we're to go home soon?"

"No," Frevisse said, much though she wished that were true and despite it would hardly have suited Bishop Beaufort's purpose to have her lose her excuse and leave.

"I'll work on, then. Unless you need me for something?"

"No. I don't. I just thought . . ."

Frevisse momentarily forgot what she thought because at the far end of the line of study stalls Bishop Pecock had leaned into sight and was beckoning to her. She blinked, as if seeing him were a mistake and he might go away, but he did not and she regathered her thoughts enough to say, a little faintly, to Dame Perpetua, "I thought I'd read awhile here. Where it's quiet."

Dame Perpetua, dipping pen into inkpot and bending to her work again, nodded and probably within three words forgot she had been there at all.

Quiet-footed past empty desks, Frevisse went toward where Bishop Pecock had now retreated from sight. Save for the faint scritch of Dame Perpetua's pen and the faint crackle of a parchment page being turned by the monk, the library was deep in book-kept silence, no sign that anyone else was there until she came level with the last desk and saw not only Bishop Pecock but, standing behind him, Arteys.

Chapter 12

Forgetful of any respectful greeting or curtsy, Frevisse joined them out of sight in the stall, saying in a forceful whisper, "*Arteys*. What are you doing here?"

"You know who he is?" Bishop Pecock asked back in lowered voice before Arteys could answer.

Keeping her guess at who Arteys was, she said, "I know he's one of the duke of Gloucester's men. The word running is that Gloucester is arrested but none of his men. That's true then?"

"He's arrested. I don't know the rest," Arteys whispered. He had the look of someone who, having taken a hard blow, was trying to hide the afterpain. "I ran."

"One of the knights told him to take the chance to

leave while it was happening," Bishop Pecock said. "Arteys, having common sense, did, since there was no knowing what else was going to be done or to whom."

"I ran," Arteys said bitterly.

"You left where you could do Gloucester no good, on the hope you could do him good elsewhere," Bishop Pecock answered.

"I left him. I . . ."

Bishop Pecock raised an admonitory hand. "You were ordered to it by one of your father's knights, a man with the right to give you orders, yes? By obeying, you did your duty as it was at that moment. To twist and turn about it afterwards is a waste of wit and time, neither of which you—or in truth anyone else but you most especially just now—should waste, however plentiful both or either may be."

Arteys shook his head, probably as lost as Frevisse was among so many words, but she had managed to hold to one thing and asked, "One of your father's knights?"

"Sir Roger. He . . ." Arteys started to answer, then saw the real point of her question and froze for a moment before lifting his head and saying, in defiance or pride or maybe only with the tired relief of admitting it, "My father's knight. I'm the duke of Gloucester's bastard son."

Frevisse would have asked more, beginning with why he had gone to Bishop Pecock for help and why Bishop Pecock had brought her into it when he could have left her out, but there was a soft footfall behind her, both Bishop Pecock's and Arteys' heed went past her, and she turned as Joliffe sighed and said, in the same low voice they had been using, "So much for my plan of where to hide you, Arteys."

"It was a quite reasonable plan," Bishop Pecock replied, "made as it must have been with hardly time to think about it and not intending it to be for long." He moved aside and backward to make room for Joliffe to join them in the now crowded shelter the stall's high walls still gave. "I came here myself for respite from all the talk and goings-on and happened on him, that's all. Joliffe, the chair is going to waste, all of us standing here. Make use of it. You look as if you need it."

Joliffe did not argue the point but edged past Frevisse, turned the chair from the desk, and sat with a wry, "My thanks, my lord."

Since there was nothing she could do for his tiredness, Frevisse asked, still trying to put together what had happened, "Arteys came to you for help?"

"It was more that we happened on each other while he was trying to get out of St. Saviour's after Gloucester's arrest."

"You were in St. Saviour's when Gloucester was arrested?"

"As it happens, yes."

"Why?"

Joliffe pulled a slight face at her. "Does it matter?"

"You've made me part of this whether I wanted it or no. If I've no way out of it, I at least want to know more than I do."

"I didn't make you part of this."

"Your good Cardinal Bishop Beaufort of Winchester did, then," she snapped, "but he's not here and you are."

Arteys, who had been leaning back against the bookshelf at the desk's end, straightened. "Bishop Beaufort?" he repeated in a strained voice.

"That tears it," Joliffe said to no one in particular.

"You're here for Bishop Beaufort?" Arteys demanded at them both.

Frevisse made a sharp nod at Joliffe. "He's here for Bishop Beaufort. I'm here because my prioress was bribed to 'give me leave' to serve the bishop's 'request' for my help."

"Bribed?" Bishop Pecock asked.

"With promise of a gift of property our nunnery sorely needs, if I'd come to Bury St. Edmunds and see whatever might be happening. I was to watch and listen and give the use of my wits, if asked, to someone else the bishop would have here." She turned an unfriendly look on Joliffe. "Him."

Arteys' look at him was as unfriendly as hers. "She was forced to it, but you weren't, were you? You've been looking how to make use of me against my father, haven't you?" His eyes widened with a sudden thought. "That day in the tavern you knew how many men he was bringing with him. When all the rumors said thousands, you knew it was only eighty. I've been a fool!"

At least briefly his fury was greater than his fear or shame and he jerked forward as if to shove past Bishop Pecock and leave, but Bishop Pecock put out a hand to stop him while asking Joliffe, "Well?"

Joliffe hesitated, for once without even a glint of mockery, before he said, "Bishop Beaufort is dying. He likely won't live to see the summer and he knows it."

Bishop Pecock and Frevisse made the sign of the cross. Unwillingly, belatedly, Arteys followed them.

"You're certain?" Bishop Pecock asked.

"Certain enough. He says it and he had death's look on him when I last saw him, a month ago."

Bishop Pecock shook his head. "I hadn't heard. I didn't know."

"No one is supposed to know except the few in his household who have to. He's given out he took a chill before Christmas and is having trouble being rid of it, nothing more."

"Believable enough at his age," Bishop Pecock granted. "Not that there won't be guessing going on by some. He's had lessening power in England's governance these few years past, but still . . ." He shook his head again with the worried wonder of someone watching the world change shape. "There'll be a different balance to things when he's gone, that's sure."

Bitterly Arteys thrust in, "If he's going to die, he wants my father dead with him. That's what's brought this on, isn't it?"

"Go at it the other way," Joliffe said. "He *doesn't* want Gloucester dead."

"They've been enemies for thirty years and more and suddenly, dying, he has a care for my father?" Arteys mocked savagely.

"I doubt he cares for Gloucester any better than he ever did," Joliffe said back. "But he cares even less for what he's seen of Suffolk and his little pack of lords."

"Disliking Suffolk and wanting to help Gloucester are two different things."

"Except where they meet in Bishop Beaufort's worry over what's going to happen when he's gone and there's no one left around the king of royal blood save Gloucester and the duke of York to be any check on Suffolk."

"The more so," Bishop Pecock put in, "when neither Gloucester nor York are in any kind of favor or have much influence with King Henry and against Suffolk."

"They both have their royal blood, though, which counts for something, however far out of power they are," Joliffe returned. "And two of them alive and well are a better guard against Suffolk having all his own way than if there's only one of them."

"You're watching York, too, then?" Bishop Pecock asked.

"I'm here because Bishop Beaufort told me to find out

what I could about everything. If Gloucester was at peril, as Bishop Beaufort had half-heard he was, he wanted to have some thought of what was going to happen, on the hope he could do something against it."

"Only they moved too fast or sooner than he expected," Bishop Pecock said. "Not that there's likely much could have been done to stop them, even if he'd known."

"None of you seem to suppose Gloucester might be actually guilty of treason," Frevisse said.

"He isn't," Arteys said fiercely. "The one thing, the only thing he had in mind, coming here, was hope he could plead pardon for Lady Eleanor."

"Did he think he had any better hope of it than he's had these past five years?" Bishop Pecock asked.

"Yes. He'd been told . . ." Arteys briefly stopped, then went on more slowly, "He was told there was finally a chance of it, he said." He looked from Joliffe to Bishop Pecock. "There was never any hope of her being pardoned, was there? He was baited to come here. It's been a trap all along, hasn't it?"

"I would judge so," Bishop Pecock said.

Joliffe looked to Frevisse. "You were supposed to be picking up what you could in Suffolk's household. Has there been anything?" Before she could answer, he shifted to Arteys and said, "You may as well know she's cousin to Suffolk's wife."

"That's why Bishop Beaufort was able to make use of me," Frevisse said to forestall whatever Arteys might say to that. "But I care as little for Suffolk as any of you do. And to your question, Joliffe—Suffolk and Dorset seem to be riding high on glee over something and all this morning there were clerks writing madly at something in the outer chamber of his rooms but I've found out nothing else." Alice's unease she kept to herself.

Joliffe switched to Bishop Pecock. "Among the lords? In parliament? Talk from your servants? Anything?"

"Nothing. No. You've surely noted by now that Bury St. Edmunds is presently full of a large number of people who talk much but know nothing?"

"Why were you at St. Saviour's?" Arteys demanded at Joliffe, his voice heavy with distrust. "How did you come to be there then?"

Level-voiced, Joliffe answered, "I was there because I'd seen the duke of Buckingham and his gaggle of nobles and royal-liveried men going that way. I followed them because I thought they looked like trouble."

Bishop Pecock peered at him. "Curiosity and the cat. I keep thinking of that when I'm around you, Joliffe. Presuming that his grace the duke of Buckingham was not so slack as to leave no guards at the gateways into St. Saviour's, may one be told how you got yourself in and Arteys out?"

Joliffe inclined his head to him as if conferring a favor, the small curve of a smile at his mouth's corners. "But of course, my lord. Scholar, priest, and bishop as you are, you've likely never had reason to note that servants like to keep their comings and goings to themselves if they can."

"Oddly enough," Bishop Pecock returned, matching his dryness, "I have occasionally noted such a thing, yes."

"Then perhaps you've likewise noted that if there's another way out of somewhere besides the usual, it will be the servants who know of it. At St. Saviour's the way happens to be a slight gap in the wellyard's wall at the stables' far end where a board swings loose to the side when pushed, enough for someone of no great bulk to slip through."

"And how did you happen to know that?" Frevisse asked.

Joliffe shrugged. "One sees things if one looks."

"And you'd been looking before today, I take it?" she said.

"One never knows," Bishop Pecock put in, "what stray bits of knowledge may prove of use in the fullness of time. Arteys, he found you trying to leave but balked by Buckingham's men, I take it?"

"I'd escaped the hall but couldn't go out any gateway and was circling the yard behind the outbuildings, trying to find another way out or a place to hide." Something of the hopelessness and fear from then was still in his voice. "I met him there."

"And here was the best I could think of for him for the while," Joliffe said. "Now, since you can't stay here forever—"

"Now," Arteys interrupted, "I'll see to myself."

"You have money and a way to leave Bury St. Edmunds?" Bishop Pecock asked mildly. "Or somewhere to hide while you find money and a way to leave?"

"I don't mean to leave!"

"Then you know someone else here in Bury St. Edmunds you can go to for help? You have friends here? Or someone who'll do it for the sake of your father?"

Arteys' silence was answer enough.

"Then by removing the impossible and unlikely, it will have to be our help," Bishop Pecock said.

Arteys pointed angrily at Joliffe. "Not his."

"Since I think we can well assume he was not in St. Saviour's on the supposition of your escape, it can be argued that his willingness to help you then says something to his favor, don't you think?"

"Come to that," Arteys said, ignoring the question, "why are *you* willing to help me?"

"A very sound question," Bishop Pecock said approvingly, "to which, unfortunately, I lack a sound answer. Will it be enough to say that I'm among those who don't much care for what I see of Suffolk and those around him and therefore have no reason to refuse help to someone in need of it when that someone has done no wrong of which I know?"

"Put simply," Joliffe said, "he'd rather help you than Suffolk."

"And you?" Arteys demanded. He gestured at Joliffe and Frevisse together. "Why would you help me?"

Frevisse winced inwardly at being lumped so unquestioningly with Joliffe, but he answered straightly, "For the same reason."

"How do I even know I need help?" Sharp with confused anger, Arteys' voice started to rise but he caught it down again to say at Bishop Pecock, "Maybe I didn't even need to run. Maybe I should just go back. What good am I doing my father here?"

"What good can you do him there?" Bishop Pecock returned. "Moreover—and this is a thing you'd best not forget—your father's greatest danger comes from his royal blood. Without that, he'd not be such a desperate problem to Suffolk and the others, and it may well occur to them, while they're about it, that you're royal blooded, too, and may likewise be worth being rid of. It's no secret, I believe, that you're his son."

"It's not, but I hardly matter. I'm bastard-born."

"So is Bishop Beaufort and so was his brother, whose son is now marquis of Dorset and likely, in due course, to be earl of Somerset," Bishop Pecock said serenely and, leaving Arteys to make what he would of that thought, went on, "As for your accepting help not only from me but from Dame Frevisse and Joliffe, I have to say that, taken all in all, their reasons for giving it are creditable and that so long as things hold as they are, I believe they can be depended on."

Joliffe silently mouthed a mocking "thank you" while Arteys, intent on Bishop Pecock, asked, "But if things change?"

"Not 'if' they change but 'when,' " Bishop Pecock said. "The world is mutable and always changing."

"And because it is," Joliffe said, "the best you can do is play the game as it stands now." He leaned back in the chair and crossed his arms on his chest, somewhat insultingly at ease and more as if he were watching an entertainment than something real and dangerous. "And like it or not, as it stands now, you have no likelihood of help from anyone but the three of us, who are willing to help you because it's against Suffolk. So what will it be? Striking out on your own with nowhere to go and no way to get there even if there was? Or our help, such as it is?"

That was blunt to the point of brutal and Arteys, standing stiffly at bay against them all, flushed a strong red before snapping back, his in-held desperation flaring to defiance, "There's hardly choice, is there?"

"No, there isn't," Joliffe returned, "so you'd better take what's offered."

Arteys turned his back as far as might be on Joliffe and asked Bishop Pecock, "How can you help me?"

"A place to stay until we know better what's happening. An advantage of being a lesser bishop is that I can stay in lesser places, rather than here in the abbey. I have rooms somewhat out of the way at St. Petronilla's hospital outside Southgate. My people will say nothing about you if I tell them not to, nor is anyone likely to take particular note you're there because no one takes particular note of me. If you're willing to this, then by your leave I think we should go now."

Arteys hesitated, then gave a tight-lipped nod of agreement. Bishop Pecock nodded back, bent his head to Frevisse with, "My lady," and to Joliffe with, "Master Joliffe," and left. With neither word nor nod to either of them, Arteys followed and in silence Frevisse and Joliffe waited, listening while Bishop Pecock passed a few words with the monk at the door, then waited longer in the library's quiet before Frevisse said, still remembering to keep her voice low, "You were harsh with him."

Joliffe sighed heavily, rubbed with both hands at his face, and drew himself up in the chair. "I had to move him. Otherwise we might have stayed here arguing forever."

"I know. It was well done," Frevisse said quietly.

Joliffe looked up at her in surprise. "Thank you."

"On the other hand, you didn't give his grace the bishop an actual answer when he asked if you were set to watch the duke of York as well as Gloucester."

Maybe remembering that by rights he should not be sitting while she stood, Joliffe rose to his feet. "I serve Bishop Beaufort at present, not the bishop of St. Asaph."

"Which still is not a straight answer."

"No," he agreed. "It's not."

He met her look long and level, with laughter in his but none in hers as she asked, "How long have you been Bishop Beaufort's man?"

"I'm not. I'm merely someone he sometimes hires for one reason or another."

"How long," Frevisse said, letting her forced patience show, "has he been sometimes hiring you?"

"For rather longer than I think I'll admit to."

"Joliffe."

His laughter faded. He regarded her in silence for a moment, then said, simply serious for once, "You don't like me much, do you?"

She was tired of word gaming and snapped, "I like you very much. It's one of the things about you that irks me. What I don't is trust you."

That caught him off balance but with an inward twist that she almost did not see, he shrugged and said with a one-sided smile, "Come to that, why should you trust me? Why should anyone ever trust anyone else? Unless they're forced to it by necessity and lack of choice. Like Arteys just now. So trust be damned. Can't it suffice for you that Bishop Beaufort values your wits and likewise mine and will pay us for the use of them?"

"I don't like being used toward ends I don't know."

"Isn't most of life lived toward ends we don't know?"

"Don't," she warned, "go clever on me, Joliffe."

He spread his hands as if to show he had no weapons. "I offer, simply, what comforts I can, poor though they are. Praise and philosophy—"

"Your philosophy is suspect and I'd rather be left alone than praised, so if you think either one is going to help, you'd best think again."

Joliffe grinned. "I always think again."

"Another thing about you that irks me."

Behind her, hesitantly, Dame Perpetua asked, "Dame Frevisse? Is something wrong?"

Frevisse turned with alarm to find her standing beside the desk with pen still in hand and a worried frown. "Dame Perpetua," she said quickly. "We forgot our voices. I'm sorry."

Dame Perpetua's doubtful look went from her to Joliffe and back again. "But something's wrong?" she persisted.

"My manners, my lady," said Joliffe. He gave her a deep bow and a far-too-winning smile. "Bishop Pecock— you saw him leave just now?—and I were consulting over what play he might hire our company to give as his gift to where he's staying. I fear I drew Dame Frevisse into debate with me afterwards on whether it's better to perform John Lydgate's plays or burn them. I say that no matter how base or badly done the work itself—and I grant that much of Lydgate's work is badly done"— he made a half-bow to Frevisse—"yet nonetheless and so long as they please those willing to pay to hear them, they should be played. Dame Frevisse, to the contrary, holds that there can be no excuse for playing anything so poorly made. But that's the easier for her to say since she does not need to make her living by such paltry means, if I may say so, praying your pardons, my ladies, for my boldness."

It was an excess of words worthy of Bishop Pecock himself and done just lightly enough that Dame Perpetua was smiling by the end of it, worry forgotten. "But what—" she started to ask, only to be interrupted by the monastery bells beginning to ring to Vespers.

Joliffe bowed to them both. "Until the play tonight, then, my ladies," he said, slipped past Dame Perpetua, and was gone.

Chapter 13

t Vespers' end, a servant in Suffolk's livery was waiting outside St. Nicholas' chapel to ask that Frevisse and Dame Perpetua come to Lady Alice.

"Both of us?" Dame Perpetua asked in surprise.

"Both, if it please you," the man said, certain.

"Our supper?" Dame Perpetua asked of Frevisse.

"That will be seen to, please you," the man said. "If you would come, my ladies?"

They went, following him across the nave and outside into twilight and a few snowflakes swirling down from the thickened clouds. Not many people were still in the yard or along the penticed walk, but while passing the second or third clot of them, Dame Perpetua caught enough words that she asked of Frevisse, "What are they saying about the duke of Gloucester?"

Taken up with her own worries, Frevisse had forgotten how very away from everything Dame Perpetua had been in the library. "He's been arrested," she answered. "Not long after he arrived today. For treason, it's said."

"For treason? He's the king's uncle. What's he done, to be arrested for treason?"

"I don't know." Too aware of Suffolk's servant close ahead of them, Frevisse added, "I was with the players all afternoon. I've heard almost nothing."

"The players. Oh my! Will the play even be done, do you think?"

The man looked back. "It's going to be, my lady. I've heard that's sure."

"What about the duke of Gloucester?" Dame Perpetua asked.

"He won't be there." The man took open pleasure in his own wit. "He's under guard in St. Saviour's and all his men potted in with him. There'll be no trouble."

"What's Gloucester supposed to have done?" Dame Perpetua persisted.

"He brought a pack of Welshmen with him and was going to throw out the lords around the king and take over for himself. That's what's being said."

"Yesterday," Frevisse pointed out tartly, "it was being said he was bringing thousands of men with him."

"It was, wasn't it?" the man agreed, cheerful about it. "Good thing he wasn't. Or bad for him, as it's turned out. Damn Welsh."

The man was openly untroubled that one day's report jarred so completely against the other's, and while Dame Perpetua tried to learn more from him, Frevisse held silent. Considering everything into which she had somehow slipped—here for Bishop Beaufort's purposes;

asked for help by Alice; now somehow part of hiding an arrested traitor's bastard son—silent seemed the best thing she could be.

Only one clerk was left writing away in the outer room, with men and servants around him readying for the evening. The middle room was likewise busy with women but in the bedchamber beyond it there were only two women tending to Alice, who said to Frevisse over the head of the one fussing at the front folds of her crimson damask gown, "Don't even look like you're going to mention Gloucester to me."

Frevisse closed her mouth with a deliberate snap.

Alice laughed. "Yes, well, all right. Go on. Everyone else is. Dame Perpetua, if you will, there's supper laid out on that table by the window. Help yourself, I pray you. And you, too, cousin."

Dame Perpetua went to the table but Frevisse stopped, well clear of the busyness around Alice, to ask, "Exactly what treason was Gloucester planning? Is it true his men are arrested with him?"

"No, they're not arrested. They've been told not to go anywhere until this is sorted out but they're not arrested. As for what Gloucester meant to do . . ." Alice turned away to nod acceptance of the topaz-hung necklace being held out to her by one of her ladies, then turned back to Frevisse, her voice light but her gaze not as it met Frevisse's. ". . . no one has made it very clear to me what he meant to do."

And she was not happy about that.

But with too many other ears to hear there was little they could say outright to each other, and Frevisse had to be satisfied with asking, "But the play is to go on tonight anyway?"

Head bent forward for her lady to fasten the necklace, Alice said, "Everything is to go on. The king is distressed, and the thought among the lords is that the more like usual we keep things, the easier it will be for him."

Easier to what? Grow used to the thought that the uncle who had had the keeping of him and his crown since he was a baby was now accused of treason against him?

Alice's look, raised to meet Frevisse's, said their thoughts were matched as she asked, "What's being said among people? You've been out and about. What have you heard?"

"Very little. Much of the afternoon I was with John and the players at their practice and then with Dame Perpetua in the library." Frevisse framed her answer carefully, trying for balance among the different footholds she had to keep. "Mostly I've only heard the same thing over and over. There seems to be a great deal of . . . surprise."

"Yes. Surprise. Many of us are surprised." Alice nodded toward the bed with its drawn curtains. "John is asleep there. Considering how late he'll be up tonight, a nap seemed best, but Nurse took to coughing again and I've sent her off to rest. That's partly why I sent for you so well ahead of time, for you to see to him because you'll know better than anyone about how soon or late to ready him for the play and I can't stay. Since your play has the hall for now, the abbot is giving a feast tonight in the monks' refectory for king and queen and lords and commons. Where the monks will eat I don't know. Yes, it's time, I know," she added to one of her ladies come to stand beside her, ready with a tall, jeweled headdress fluttered with veils. With what seemed more resignation than pleasure, Alice went to sit on a chair for the thing to be put on, hiding her fair hair and framing her face.

Considering the hours Alice would have to wear it,

Frevisse hoped it was as light as it looked to be and was glad all over again for her own plain gown that did not require two hands to manage its skirts, the way Alice needed for hers as she rose and turned to say, the veils wafting on the gentle air of her movement, "With all of this, I hope this play is going to be worth our while. Is it?"

Frevisse hesitated, thinking of this afternoon, then offered, "With God's grace."

"Oh dear," said Alice and left, her ladies taking up their cloaks and hers from a chest and following, leaving Frevisse regretfully wondering if Alice was keeping as much from her as she was keeping from Alice.

Her regrets were still with her when she and Dame Perpetua brought John—eager and wide awake—to the King's Hall. The two men in royal livery on guard at the outer door did not question John's assertion that he was part of the play or hinder her and Dame Perpetua from going in with him. Since afternoon the hall had been cleared of all the players' clutter, leaving Heaven rising splendidly alone at the hall's far end, Wisdom's throne half lost in shadows at the top now that there was no daylight through the hall's tall windows, only shutters closed over the black night outside. Light for the play would come from two candlestands flanking the playing place in front of Heaven; round and tiered and taller than a man, they held dozens of candles each, all unlighted for now. It was by the lesser light of smaller candlestands set along the hall that servants were presently setting the last of several paired rows of benches in front of the playing place, a wide gap left between the pairs for three tall-backed, ornately carved chairs set side by side directly in front of the playing place. Looking at them, Dame Perpetua asked a little breathlessly, "For the king and queen?"

"And Abbot Babington," Frevisse said. She had been keeping tight hold on John and with, "Wait here for me," to Dame Perpetua, she let him pull her away, around and behind the nearest frame-hung curtain to the doorway to the room beyond it. Whatever its usual use, it had been given over to the players for tonight and was crowded full with all the hampers, baskets, and boxes moved out of the hall and with the players themselves, loud with talk and taut laughter and all in various stages of dress and undress, with Joane crouched on a stool stitching swiftly at something that had torn and Mistress Wilde handing a pair of red-and-purple-striped hosen toward one of the Vices. Frevisse, before someone found something for her to do, pushed John in and took herself away.

In the hall Dame Perpetua had gone aside to stand near the wall not far from the playing place's right side where few heads were likely to come between them and the play. Frevisse joined her and they waited together while a man bearing a staff that marked him for a household officer paced the hall, checking what had been done, then went behind the curtains, shortly came out, gave an order to the servants, and left. The servants immediately hurried to light all the candles in the great candlestands beside the playing place, making a warm bloom of light that sent shadows away to the rafters, shone on Heaven's stairs, and glinted across the brass stars on the hangings.

The servants finished and were withdrawing to stand beside the lesser candlestands along the hall as a tide of lords and ladies bright with rich gowns, jewels, and talk swept into the hall, spreading through it on the wave of their own excited pleasure. Behind them came men and women more quietly dressed only by contrast, with rich fabrics and glint of gold enough among them—the members of Parliament and their wives and some of the more important citizens of Bury St. Edmunds, Frevisse supposed.

She had found Alice among those first in, when Dame Perpetua said, hushed with wonder, "There's the king." He was mere yards away, his Plantagenet height making him taller than almost everyone around him, a thin, dark-haired man looking younger than his twenty-five years—hardly older than the girl beside him, her golden-fair hair loose to below her waist. They wore matching narrow circlets of gold around their heads and were both dressed in green velvet patterned on purple silk, his houpelande three-quarter length and furred with ermine at throat and hem, her gown trailing on the floor behind her, its ermined collar plunging to her high-belted waist to show an underdress of blue damask.

"And Queen Margaret," Dame Perpetua breathed. "Oh, isn't she lovely?"

Frevisse murmured agreement, able to see why a man might think her worth the cost of no dowry and a weak truce when so much more should have been had for a king's marriage. But yes, at seventeen years old, with the grace of girlhood still on her, she was lovely, Frevisse acknowledged. God grant she was also fertile, and soon.

Abbot Babington, a gray-haired man in dark, elaborate robes, bowed the royal couple to their chairs, then sat himself in the chair at King Henry's right hand and leaned over to say something to him. Meanwhile, two staff-bearing household officers were sorting favored lords and ladies to their places on the benches, leaving everyone else to spread through the hall as they would. A lady of some girth made to crowd in on Frevisse, who braced an elbow sideways, holding her off while watching the duke of York be ushered to a place on the bench on Abbot Babington's other side from the king. That would have been Gloucester's place if he had been there, Frevisse supposed, and briefly she wondered what was in York's mind as he took it. It was no one's secret that he was as unfavored by the lords around the king as Gloucester was, and if the king's own uncle could be falsely charged with treason, why not his cousin?

Frevisse stopped that thought short and looked at it. When had she turned from only assuming the charge against Gloucester was false to fully believing it was? She did not know. Another question then: Why had she?

Straightly asked, the question had straight answer: because she disliked Suffolk.

Disliked and, more to the point, distrusted him. Or even more to the point, disliked him *because* she distrusted him.

Dame Perpetua was craning from side to side, looking around heads to watch the king and queen. Frevisse, taller, was able to see beyond them, to where Suffolk was gracefully bowing Alice to a place on the bench beside Queen Margaret's chair. The queen immediately turned and spoke to Alice while Suffolk, after bowing to her but not yet sitting down, leaned—gracious, smiling, confident—to say something to William Tresham and his wife on the next bench back.

Why did she distrust him so completely?

Once asked, the question had ready answer.

Because of Henow Heath.

Because of those thousands of men gathered against an army Gloucester wasn't bringing.

Because, of the several possible reasons Suffolk might have gathered them, none were good. Either he had done it by mistake, having trusted someone who badly misinformed him—deliberately or because they were too stupid to count straight—or else he had been hoping to stir fear and anger against Gloucester, to cut short questions when the accusation and arrest were made. Whichever had been the reason, neither was acceptable in a man said to have more power than anyone else in the realm. If the first, then he used bad sources who corrupted his actions. If the second, he was corrupt himself.

She wished she had better sight of King Henry. He was not likely to show much here with so many eyes to see him, but surely he must be affected somehow, whether he actually believed in this betrayal by a man who had been loyal to him all his life or if he did not.

Above the noise and talk of people, a trumpet called out high and clear from the open gallery above the screens passage. Talk cut off and every head turned toward the trumpeter standing above them there, his horn glinting in the upcast candlelight. At the same moment the servants waiting beside the candlestands along the hall put out all the candles almost as one, sweeping the hall into shadows, so that as the trumpeter flourished to an end, swung down his trumpet, and stepped back out of sight, everyone turned back toward the only light still in the hall, the candles flanking the playing place, and saw, high on Heaven's throne, Wisdom seated in all his majesty, glowing golden in the candlelight, with Lady Soul kneeling and lovely at the foot of the heavenly stairs.

Clear and fine, Wisdom's voice rang out in his opening speech. Sweet and strong, Lady Soul answered him. And against all the likelihood everything that had been slack, stumbling, and wrong this afternoon was gone. The play sang with beauty, first between Wisdom and beloved Lady Soul, then between her and her virtuous Mights, before they went away behind the curtains and Lucifer appeared out of a burst of roof-high red sparks.

More often than not, devils were played for laughter

but Joliffe had chosen smooth, warm charm, with only gradually his underdarkness breaking through in all its ugliness before the Mights returned and he set to wooing them to sin. When they were corrupted, he unleashed a set of his Devils to them for a lewd and ugly dance complete with stinking smoke from Hell. When Lady Soul returned, corrupted by her Mights' fall and companioned by two small Demons, Wisdom charged her with her wrongs to him, she and her Mights repented, Devils and Demons fled, and all ended with a prayer, and on Wisdom's last word, angel voices (of those who had been Devils a few minutes ago) rose from behind Heaven in a joyously sung *Deo gracias*, with Lady Soul and her Mights dancing with glad grace away to out of sight behind the curtains while Wisdom rose with immense dignity from his throne, descended the stairs, and followed after them.

With his going, the hall seemed suddenly far more empty than one man's leaving should have made it. But then, it was not a man but Wisdom itself that had gone, the illusion powerful enough that silence held for a long-drawn breath after the playing place was empty before well-pleased clapping broke out, led by the king.

Unwillingly released from wonder, Frevisse joined in. Clapping, too, Dame Perpetua leaned to ask in her ear, "The young man we talked with in the library this afternoon, was he Lucifer here?"

"He was."

Puzzled, maybe a little worried about it, Dame Perpetua said, "He was more . . . pleasant then."

"He can be," Frevisse granted.

A drum's cheerful roll signaled the players' return, coming in a line from either side to meet in the middle of the playing place. All the clapping doubled with the pleasure of seeing them again and they bowed or curt-

sied, depending on their garments, first to the king and
queen and Abbot Babington, then to the hall at large.
Master Wilde had not returned, a sensible choice, it being hardly seemly for Wisdom to bow to anyone, nor
did the players make the error of trying to hold too long
to what they had but, while the acclaim was at its height,
bowed one more time and disappeared the way they had
come, all except John, who ran forward to his parents.
Frevisse saw Suffolk scoop him up, laughing and
pleased. Servants were relighting the other candles, talk
was starting up all over the hall, and the crowd beginning to mill, and when Dame Perpetua asked, "Shouldn't
we go?" Frevisse was willing, abruptly aware of how
tired she was and feeling no need to take John off his
parents' hands. Let them see to him for tonight. For tonight at least she simply wanted to be done with any
duties or troubles and began to lead their way along the
wall toward the door.

They had reached the screens passage and were almost
out the door among other people leaving when rising
voices and a stir ahead of them warned something had
happened. Dame Perpetua, far less used to crowds and
beginning to be frightened, gripped her arm and asked,
"What? What is it?"

The rush of excited words reached and swept past
them from one person to another and into the hall and
Frevisse answered Dame Perpetua's fear quickly with,
"Nothing. It's all right for us," urging Dame Perpetua
onward to the door and out into the cold, torchlit night
before adding, "It's just that some of the duke of
Gloucester's men have been arrested now for treason,
too."

Chapter 14

n the hours since he had been left alone, Arteys had found that the chamber was too small for sufficient pacing to wear out his thoughts, but neither could he sit still nor hold his mind to the book he had tried to read by the gray daylight through the window. Since Bishop Pecock had left him alone, his mind would not hold still, had been squirreling up one thought, scurrying to another, going back to the first or on to others, settling nowhere because he only knew enough to worry and wasn't likely to know more until Bishop Pecock returned.

When bringing him here to St. Petronilla's yesterday, Bishop Pecock had explained him in passing to the master as an old friend's son who needed somewhere to stay until a certain trouble with his father was worked out. "Nor is that a lie," Bishop Pecock had said when he and Arteys had reached his chamber. "A misdirection of the truth perhaps and to be regretted, but we might presently have regretted outright truth more."

His chamber was a large room at the top of stairs off the hospital's cloister walk, with a small fireplace in one wall, thick-woven reed matting on the floor, a plain chair, a single joint stool, a long table untidy with books and papers, the bishop's traveling chest along one wall, and a large bed with dark red coverlet and curtains. The room's simplicity and one small window with a slight view of a thatched roof and a lean bit of sky told this was not Petronilla's best chamber. Or even second best, probably. "Which comes of being so minor a bishop as St. Asaph's," Bishop Pecock had said, "but that is all to the better, isn't it? No one pays much heed to what I do and therefore is unlikely to pay much heed to your being here."

His explanation to Master Orle, his chaplain, and Runman, his servant, was simply that Arteys would be spending at least the night and probably tomorrow, possibly longer, and was to be fed but not talked of.

They had both said, "Yes, my lord," and Runman, whose accent was deeply London, had asked, "You'll want supper for both of you here, my lord?"

"If you would, Runman."

Runman had bowed again, said, "Of course, my lord."

"They both my-lord me overmuch," Bishop Pecock had said when they were gone. "They say I tend to forget who I am if I'm not reminded. Take off your cloak. Sit."

Confused with hunger and the day's bludgeoning, Arteys had obeyed and, searching for something to say, asked, "You've no one else waiting on you?"

"Not when I can help it. Have you any thought on

how tedious it is to have people following you everywhere you go?"

Betrayed by his tiredness, Arteys said, "I know how tedious it is to follow." And came up short, hearing himself. Was it only this morning, going to meet Gloucester, he'd been thinking that?

"The same problem from a different side," Bishop Pecock answered, pouring wine. "And it's not as if I can't find my own way to places. I was a priest in London for thirteen years and went here and there and everywhere without clerks and servants and other miscellaneous folk at my heels." He handed a filled goblet to Arteys. "If I'm bishop long enough, I'll likely grow used to it but it's hardly fair for St. Asaph's to bear the expense of my hauling servants with me to no good purpose, and since I prefer not to be dogged at the heels by people I don't need there, I therefore have only Master Orle and Runman to serve me here, who have heretofore never evidenced desire to betray me or any of my business to anyone else and are unlikely to begin now, and a groom who sleeps in the stables and is probably up to no good since he's had nothing to do since we arrived."

Arteys had realized that the flow of words was deliberately meant to distract him and he let it, both then and through supper. Not until Bishop Pecock had sent Runman out to find if the play was to go on because, "If it is, I'd best go, on the chance I'll hear something to our purpose," had Arteys leaned forward on the cleared table and asked, not much hiding his fear and desperation. "What am I going to do?"

"Nothing for now. At present we know too little, and ignorance is never a good tool to work with. Why don't you go to bed?"

Exhausted by the ill-turned day and his fears, Arteys did, and had slept most of the time Bishop Pecock was gone, which was as well because after Bishop Pecock had brought back word of the arrests, he had not slept well the rest of the night. Worse, word had been all that Bishop Pecock brought back, no names or certainty of how many or anything about Gloucester at all. He had gone out this morning, taking Master Orle with him, to find out if more was being said, leaving Arteys alone except when Runman brought him a cheese-egg potage and bread for his midday dinner.

Now it was early afternoon and Arteys shoved away from the window, paced the room's length, paced it back again and, giving up, came back to the window and the useless book. He'd escaped St. Saviour's but to what good? Shut up here and doing nothing, he was as worthless as if he had stayed. More worthless, because if he had stayed, maybe there would have been something he could have done there. Here, he was doing nothing at all save too much useless thinking.

He leaned his head against the window's glass, willing the clouds to break. He was so sick of all the grayness both outside himself and in his own thoughts.

Men—several—were coming quickly up the stairs. The sudden sound of their footfall faced Arteys around to the door, hand to his dagger's hilt. If these were men come to arrest him . . . He dropped his hand away. If they were come for him, they would have more than only daggers to use against him and what would fighting serve except to make him look guilty?

But it was Bishop Pecock who came in and Joliffe with him and Arteys took a quick step toward them, asking, "Do you have anything? About Gloucester or the others?"

"Tut," said Bishop Pecock. "You've not kept the fire up. You'll take a chill."

While he went to the fireplace, Joliffe said, "Nothing

has happened beyond the arrests, so far as we know. Gloucester is still at St. Saviour's, kept under guard in his own rooms, and hasn't been seen."

"Who was arrested? How many?"

"Only five. Sir Roger Chamberlain. Sir Richard Middelton. Sir John Cheyne. Sir Robert Wer. Master Richard Needham."

"Needham!" Arteys looked sharply to Bishop Pecock, who looked around from laying kindling into the young flames he had roused from the embers to nod confirmation. "Needham?" Arteys insisted. "But he's in Parliament."

"And therefore a voice in favor of Gloucester to be taken out of the way." Joliffe pointed to the pitcher on the table and asked, "May I?" of Bishop Pecock.

"By all means. For all of us, please."

Arteys followed him to the table, a cold hopelessness tightening in his chest. "Has there been any outcry about Gloucester? Any protest?"

Joliffe handed him a filled goblet, though by rights Bishop Pecock should have been served first. "No outcries. No protests. It's all come too fast. Everyone is crouched and waiting to see what's going to happen next before they make a move of their own. Drink."

"But something . . ."

Bishop Pecock rose from the fire, saying as he took the goblet Joliffe brought him, "It's been done in the king's name, by the king's men, for the king's good. That leaves little space for anyone else to do anything without whatever they do being called treason."

"Something," Arteys repeated, from stubbornness more than hope.

Turning from the table with a filled goblet for himself, Joliffe said, "Not by us, that's sure. Not yet. I have a

way, though, that might give you chance to see Gloucester if you want."

Bishop Pecock said with surprise, "You never said as
much to me."

"Why say it twice?" Joliffe asked. His gaze on Arteys
was considering. "Or even once, if it wasn't going to
work. I wanted to see if Arteys was fallen apart yet with
fear or was maybe steady enough to try it."

"I'm steady enough and I'm ready," Arteys said. His
fear was his own business.

"I'd wait to hear what young Joliffe has planned before waxing wide with eagerness," Bishop Pecock murmured.

"I'm ready," Arteys insisted.

Still considering him, Joliffe said, "Master Grene,
presently warden of St. Saviour's, enjoys plays, and
when Master Wilde's way brings him through Bury, his
company always plays there. When word first went out
that Parliament was to be here, Master Grene bespoke
Master Wilde for some pastime for whatever lord or
lords he had for guests. By the time the chance to do
Wisdom for the king came up, it was known his grace
of Gloucester would be at St. Saviour's, and rather than
give up one for the other, Master Wilde committed to
do both. Our company is to play there tonight."

Bishop Pecock sat down on the chair. "I'm hard put
to believe that Suffolk—or Viscount Beaumont, since he
officially has Gloucester's keeping—is going to allow a
play for Gloucester's diversion."

"I would be, too, if I hadn't spent part of this morning
rehearsing for it," Joliffe answered. He hitched a hip
onto a corner of the table and somewhat sat. "Not that
we need much practice for this. It's a farce we've done
so often we could do it in our sleep and three-quarters

drunk if we had to. It might go better if we were drunk,"
he added thoughtfully. "It's by Lydgate."

"But it's actually to be allowed?" Bishop Pecock said.
"It seems Master Grene has taken a great dislike to
the use they're making of his hospital, with hardly a by-
his-leave along the way. I gather he's said that he's paid
for players to perform and, St. Saviour be his witness,
he's going to have what he paid for. Apparently there
was some hint of hellfire and damnation behind the
words because Lord Beaumont agreed to it with more
haste than grace, as the saying is."

"Tonight, you said?" Bishop Pecock asked.

"Tonight. Which isn't so bad as it seems, at least for
us. After being terribly wise one night, being a fool the
next is a respite."

"You weren't wise last night," Bishop Pecock pointed
out. "You were Lucifer."

"Lucifer is wise in his own way," Joliffe protested.
"It's worldly wisdom but wisdom nonetheless."

"If it's worldly," Bishop Pecock returned, "it's hardly
wisdom. Wisdom is an attribute of God, to which his
created creatures should aspire—note that I say 'should'
rather than 'do'—but of which they can attain only a
shadow."

"But the Devil, though admittedly created, was created among the angels and not of the world and therefore
can have some share of wisdom beyond that of lesser
created creatures."

"Possibly true, though his rebellion and fall from
grace argue he can have had little of heavenly wisdom
and surely lost that little in his Fall. But it's worldly
wisdom you contend he has."

"I might better have said he's wise in the ways of the
world. Would that suit better? Or . . ." Joliffe forestalled
Bishop Pecock's reply with a raised hand. ". . . should it

be 'knowledgeable' in the ways of the world? Would that suit better?"

"Knowledgeable to a degree, as a half-blind man is knowledgeable of what he sees only to a limited degree and no more."

Arteys, listening from one side to the other, understanding their pleasure in their game more than he understood most of what they were saying, said finally, "About tonight?"

Both men stopped and looked at him. Then Bishop Pecock, immediately contrite, said, "Your pardon, please, young Arteys. We forgot ourselves and, worse, forgot you."

Joliffe, more practical, took up the wine pitcher again but found Arteys' goblet still full and ordered, "Drink. You won't want to say afterwards that you agreed to this while you were sober."

Arteys set his goblet aside, not for the sake of sobriety but because he did not trust his inward trembling not to reach his hands. "Tell me how there's a chance I can see my father."

"Gloucester is said to have taken to his bed," Joliffe said and forestalled Arteys' instant question with a raised hand. "That's all I know. That's all that's being said. But for your purpose it's to the good because when we start the farce in St. Saviour's hall there'll likely be more interest in what we're doing than in guarding a sick man in his bed."

Arteys immediately saw the possibility there. "Leaving a chance I could slip in to see him."

"Only a chance and probably a slight one," Bishop Pecock warned.

"But better than no chance at all. I'll take it," Arteys said, because he had taken his chance to run and must needs take this chance to go back.

* * *

TheRe was more waiting to be gone through first, though, this time in the loft that was Joliffe's sleeping place above an alehouse in Whityng Street off Church-gate.

"It's not much," Joliffe had said, "but I can come and go without bother," by way of a narrow gap between the alehouse and a leatherworker's shop next door, into a back yard that smelled pleasantly of brewing and up a ladder to a short door in the house's gable end under a steep-slanted roof.

Inside, standing upright was possible only in the very center of the little space there was between the door and a wooden wall that closed off the rest of the space under the roof. Joliffe had nodded at the wall and said, "The family's bedchamber. Master Riggemen is a carrier be-tween here and Norwich mostly and often gone, but there are still Mistress Riggemen and three children and noise enough sometimes, but no babies to cry in the night, thank goodness. There's some bread and ale there." He pointed to a box on the short-legged table pushed back under one steep side of the roof. "And the bed," under the other side of the roof, where sitting sud-denly up would be perilous to the head. "Rest if you can. Eat before you leave. You're going to need your wits and strength tonight. An hour after Vespers, remem-ber."

Arteys had nodded, too stiff-jawed with cold and worry to say anything, even thanks, and Joliffe had left, bending double through the short door. They had laid their plans at Bishop Pecock's and there was nothing else to say, only the rest of the day to be gone through; but even though the days were still short here at Feb-ruary's end and the dark drawing in all the sooner with the thick overcast, the afternoon had gone on forever, without even the relief of pacing. The three cramped strides one way and three back that were all Arteys could take were of no use. That left sitting on the joint stool or the floor or else lying down. Arteys had chosen to lie down. The short-legged bed was a rough-made, rope-strung frame with straw-stuffed mattress and thick wool blankets but it was clean, no small things moving in it. Come to that, everything about the room was clean, with no sign anyone stayed there at all except for a battered box at the bedfoot, small enough to be picked up and easily carried. Arteys supposed it was Joliffe's, with maybe all that Joliffe owned in it, and he left it alone, unlocked though it seemed to be.

But if all that Joliffe owned was in that box, he still had more than Arteys presently did. He had never had much of his own—some clothing, a few books, a sword—all given him by his father and all of it likely to be forfeit if Gloucester was found guilty of treason, because Arteys had no provable claim on anything. All he could lay claim to was what he presently wore and what was in his belt pouch. Clothing but none to spare, a cloak, his sheathed dagger hanging from his belt, enough money to see him to somewhere else so long as it wasn't far, and Gloucester's white swan badge hidden in the bottom of his belt pouch.

Unable to lie still with his thoughts, Arteys rolled off the bed and went to sit on the floor beside the door. Since there was no window and he didn't want to light the candle stub on the table, setting the door slightly ajar was the only way to have light or see out and he sat there, cross-legged and wrapped in his cloak, watching the flat gray sky and nothing happening in the yard below him. There were children's voices below him in what was probably the kitchen since what warmth the room had came from there, and sometimes men's laughter burst up loud from the alehouse. Ordinary sounds of people simply living the lives they expected to live, not people waiting out a desperate time to try a desperate thing and lonely in the waiting.

When finally the abbey's bells called to Vespers, Arteys nearly started to his feet in relief but remembered the peril of the roof and stood up slowly, watchful of the rafters and his own stiffened body. Bells from the hospitals beyond the walls joined the abbey's, exciting the afternoon's end, but he had to wait until the Office had run its course of prayers and psalms and then another hour until he should be at St. Saviour's. That was still too long a time to wait and he set himself to eat and drink, as Joliffe had told him to do because, yes, he was going to need his wits and strength tonight—his wits to get him into where Gloucester was, his strength to run with if things went wrong.

He ate most of the bread, drank all the ale. The bread was heavy and the ale light, but he felt the better for having them inside him and thought briefly of leaving a coin in payment; but Joliffe was Bishop Beaufort's man; let Bishop Beaufort pay for it.

In the loft it was dark because outside the twilight was well thickened, and whatever the time, he couldn't bide here longer. He needed to be out and doing something, even if only walking toward St. Saviour's. Below him what sounded like cheerful quarreling around a supper table was going on, a woman bidding John eat and not hit his sister with that spoon, and fairly certain of going unseen, Arteys went down the ladder to the yard and along the passageway to the street. Lighted lanterns were already hung outside some doors, yellow-patching the gathering darkness, with enough people still out and about despite the growing dark and cold that he felt safe from being heeded.

He made his way back to Churchgate Street, then rightward down the slope toward the abbey, not hurrying. Bury St. Edmunds' two parish churches were at the edge of the abbey yard, their west doors opening into the town's lower marketplace. If there was a way he could tarry unsuspiciously along the market's edge until people came out from Vespers, he would know he had only an hour more until he could be at St. Saviour's; but he found as he came into the lower marketplace that he had been more patient than he thought. People were already coming out of St. James near the abbey gate and with relief—tainted by a chill tightening in his stomach that told him how badly afraid he was—he turned aside, with nothing left but to wander through Bury's streets for the while. Fewer people were about now, all cloak-huddled and hurrying home to suppers and warmth and family, Arteys supposed. Cloak-huddled, too, but without family or home or decent supper, he walked and turned from one street to another to another. Bury was not so big he had any chance of being lost and the moving kept him something like warm until finally he gave up waiting and passed through Northgate with a straggle of other late-goers, trying to hurry no more than anyone else.

He had worried he would not be able to find his way back among the houses, sheds, and fences to St. Saviour's wellyard wall, especially in the dark, but he recognized the gap between two head-tall fences when he saw it and turned from the road, remembering Juliffe's warning, "Don't look around to see if anyone is watching you. Go as if you had the right to and even if someone is looking they likely won't think twice about it." As the heavy shadows swallowed him, he slowed, hop-

ing no pits had been dug or other perils laid in the day
and a half since he had followed Joliffe through here,
and came out unscathed behind a long building where
the thumping, the steamy air, and women's loud talk the
other day had told it was a laundry fronting on the river.
Tonight everything was silent there. He could even hear
the river's murmur on the far side, peacefully about its
own business in the dark. The sound kept him company
as he leaned against the laundry's back wall beside the
board fence between it and St. Saviour's, waiting and
trying not to think. So far he had done nothing much—
had run away, hidden, let others help him—but once he
went back into St. Saviour's that would change. There
would be no one to help him, and no one but himself to
get it right or wrong.

He found he was clenched all over—hands, jaw,
shoulders, back—and he tightened more at the sudden
rattle and bang of a drum and a burst of shouting from
beyond the buildings between him and St. Saviour's
main yard. "You'll know when we're there," Joliffe had
said. "We come with noise, to jolly up our audience
before we start, usually not until we're inside but tonight
I'll see to it we start in the yard." And he had. There
was no mistaking the signal, and Arteys felt in the dark
for the board he wanted, pushed it silently aside, and
slid through the gap.

Chapter 15

 s Arteys had hoped, the wellyard was deserted at that cold, dark hour. He swung the board back into place and moved away from the fence. "Once you're in," Joliffe had said, "move as if you belong there. Try to stay out of the light, where you might be recognized, but don't skulk. Nobody looks at servants going about their business but they look at skulkers. You understand?"

Arteys had understood; had understood, too, when Joliffe added, "After you're in, how you come to Gloucester is your trouble. I don't know inside St. Saviour's well enough to give you even a guess."

"He's in the rooms he was meant to have?" Arteys had asked.

"Yes."

"Then if the guards go away, I can reach him."

If the guards went away as Joliffe had hoped *and* if nothing had been done about the outside stairs from the warden's yard to Gloucester's bedchamber.

But to find those things out, Arteys had to reach there, and remembering Joliffe's order not to skulk, he walked openly out of the wellyard, across the stableyard, and into the wider yard beyond it. No one was anywhere. A few torches were burning, fretful in the wind, but such people as might usually have been out and about were away to the hall, he guessed, just as Joliffe had said. What had seemed possible when talked of in Bishop Pecock's chamber began to seem truly probable.

His first pause came at the gate into the warden's small yard. Keeping to a patch of shadow, he stood still, listening for any sound of someone on guard at the stairs. The red glow of a firepot was reflected on the courtyard's far wall, telling somebody was or had been there, and he watched for a shadow of a pacing guard across it because the pot's small charcoal-warmth was enough to keep a man from freezing but not enough to keep him warm. Anyone there would surely, sooner or later, move, shuffle, shift, or pace; but save for an outbreak of large laughter from the hall that told him the players were at work, Arteys heard nothing and slowly he edged his head around the gateway's corner.

No one was there. He gave himself no time to think about it but rapidly crossed the yard to the stairs, into the darkness under their penticed roof meant to keep rain and snow off them but making welcome shadow tonight as he went up them to the door at the top. They were of wood but gave no betraying creak and at the top the wooden walls that porched the door on two sides to shield against wind gave him more hiding and would serve to keep any light from shining out like a beacon into the night when—if—he opened the door.

Safe from being seen but hardly feeling safe, Arteys leaned his head against the door's thick planks, listening while he opened his belt pouch and took out the key. He heard neither voices nor movement but that was assurance of nothing. Besides the door being thick, someone there might be simply quiet. With nothing for it but to be ready to run if need be, he slipped the key into the lock, turned it. The grate of metal on metal would alert anyone who was there, and with nothing to gain by waiting, Arteys pushed the door barely open, slid in, and closed it behind him all in one quick movement.

Nothing happened.

No surprised or angry voice demanded what he was doing. No guard rushed him.

Nothing.

There was laughter again from the great hall, and in the quiet after it he was aware of the fire talking to itself among the remains of logs on the hearth and that there was no sound or movement from the shadows beyond the curtains half-drawn around the bed across the room.

He had had two almost-equal fears. One was of being seen and caught. The other was that his father was already dead. The first had not yet happened and in suddenly desperate need to know the other he took the four needed strides to the bed and pulled back the nearer curtain. From the pillows Gloucester looked back at him with narrowed eyes and one hand raised, holding a book as if ready to throw it.

Fear flowed out of Arteys on a gasp. "My lord father!" he exclaimed in a whisper weak with relief and sat down on the bed's edge without being given leave.

Gloucester dropped the book, whispering gladly back,

"Arteys!" and reached with both hands to grab his. "Saint Alban be praised."

Arteys clasped his hands in return, meeting him smile for smile but noting with worry his face's pale-clay color and shrunken look as, still holding tightly to him, Gloucester sagged into his pillows, saying, "I thought you were someone come to kill me."

Despite it had been a shadow-fear behind his others, Arteys protested, "They'd not dare!"

Familiar anger, good to see, flared in Gloucester. "Who would have thought they'd dare this much, damn them." But then he squeezed his eyes suddenly shut, let go one hand from Arteys, and pressed it against the side of his head as if to dig his fingers into his skull, holding his breath in open pain.

Arteys tightened his hold, frightened. "Sir?" he asked, and when Gloucester did not answer, said, more frightened, "What is it? What's been done to you?"

Gloucester's hand fell loosely to his chest and he began to breathe again, in quick, shallow breaths now, his eyes still shut as he whispered, "I was in such a . . . rage . . . at Beaumont. At Buckingham. I was arguing and something . . . It felt like something broke. My head. It hurts and it won't stop."

"Won't they let you have a doctor? Let him give you something for the pain?"

"There's been a doctor. One of St. Saviour's. He gave me something. It made no difference."

He stirred under the blankets, restless with pain, and Arteys let go a hope he had barely had—that he might get Gloucester out and away from Bury and escape to Wales where there were places no one would easily lay hands on him again. Watching his pain, Arteys knew that wasn't going to happen and said, "You need a different doctor then. You—"

"There won't be any other. I won't have someone from outside. Not someone of Suffolk's choosing, the treacherous ape. I'm not dying by poison. Not in that kind of pain."

"Someone else then from here. They have to do that much for you."

Gloucester gave a dog grin, all teeth and no laughter. "They don't 'have to' do anything. 'In the king's name' and 'we have our orders.' That's the most I get out of them. Sir Roger argued with Beaumont over it and that's the last I saw of him."

"He was arrested," Arteys whispered.

Gloucester's face tightened with a different kind of hurt. "I was afraid he was. Anyone else?"

"Sir Richard, Sir John, Sir Robert, Master Needham."

Frowning, Gloucester spread one hand over his forehead, thumb digging into one side of his temples, fingers into the other. "That's bad. What about the duke of York?"

"York?" Arteys echoed, not following the shift of thought.

"Is he still free? Suffolk hasn't found a way at him yet?"

"No one has said anything about York."

"He'd better be damned careful." Gloucester moved his head from side to side, seeking a way away from the pain. "He'd better damn well watch his back. Tell him that if you see him. If Suffolk gets away with this, there'll be no stopping him and York is next."

"Suffolk won't get away with this," Arteys said fiercely. As if at that, laughter came loudly from the hall. In the cautious back of his mind Arteys was keeping ear to the laughter. It was his safeguard. While there was laughter, no one was likely to bother with Gloucester, and past the laughter he insisted, "When people have had time to think, he won't dare go on."

"No," Gloucester agreed grimly. "He won't. And sooner or later he'll have to bring me to trial. We'll see what happens then to Suffolk and his treason charges." He opened his eyes, still frowning, and added, quarrelous with the pain, Arteys thought, "That's why I'm risking no more doctors, no more medicines. I'm not going to die by poison for them."

"They wouldn't dare that," Arteys said past the fear lumped in him that, yes, they would.

"Wouldn't they?" Gloucester bitterly echoed his thought. "Everything would be simpler for them if I was simply dead. I don't know whose guards are outside for the world to see, but it's only Suffolk's men ever come in here, and if I die, who's to say I *didn't* die of natural causes if that's what they say?"

"People would know."

"What people know and what they can do about it are two different things. As I've found out over the years." Gloucester shifted with pain and tightened his hold on Arteys' hand where it lay on the bedclothes. He smiled. "But you. You got clean away, didn't you?"

"I shouldn't have." Arteys' shame and confusion soured in his voice. "I should have stayed."

Gloucester lightly shook his hand. "No, you should not have. Better that you're free. Better you're clean away from these bastards." His face twisted with distress momentarily more of the mind than body. "When I'd won back Henry's favor, I was going to ask him to legitimate you. Like the Beauforts were. I meant to settle lands on you then, see to it you had something of your own to live on. An income of some kind. Fool that I've always been, I've waited too long. I'm sorry, Arteys. I'm sorry, sorry . . ."

It was as much pain as anything talking in him and to quiet him Arteys said quickly, "It's no matter."

Gloucester let go his hand, fumbled at one of the three great rings he always wore, slipped off and held out his signet ring, massive and gold and used to seal in wax his documents and letters. "Here. Take this."

Arteys drew back. "I can't."

"Take it. Better it isn't here anyway, for them to use against me. Um." He flinched his head aside from pain, and held the ring out more insistently. "If I live, give it back to me. If I die, melt it down for the gold. Either way, they won't have it to use for any lies they want to." As Arteys took the signet ring, Gloucester said, "And here," pulled at a smaller ring, gold, too, but set with a rough diamond, until it came off, kissed it and clenched it tightly in his fist, saying, "My Lady Eleanor gave me this after we'd first pledged our love. If ever you see her—" his voice broke on unshed tears—"give it to her from me." He thrust it at Arteys. "Otherwise, keep it for pledge of my love for you."

"Father . . ."

But Gloucester was taking off his last ring, thick gold again and set with a garnet. "And this one. I won't have—"

Arteys shook his head, completely refusing it. "Not that one."

Gloucester pulled at it. "I won't have Suffolk . . . I won't have *any* of those mongrels . . . so much as . . . touch it." He forced it past his knuckle and held it out.

"You can't," Arteys said despairingly.

And for a moment it seemed Gloucester truly could not. With eyes shut and tears slipping from beneath his eyelids, he pressed his hand and the ring against his heart. "Thirty-four years ago," he whispered. "Thirty-four years ago. Hal saved my life at Aglncourt. There in the middle of the battle. And that night, afterwards, he gave me this. Spoil from some French lord. He gave it to me and said 'remember' and I always have. By God and all the saints, I swear I've never forgotten." Gloucester opened his eyes, unashamed of the freely flowing tears, grasped Arteys' wrist, drew his hand forward, and forced the ring into it. "You remember, too. I've told you all this enough times. Swear to me you'll remember."

"I'll remember." Arteys choked on his own tears. "I swear I'll remember."

Pain twisted Gloucester's face again and he let go of Arteys to take hold on his head again but forcing out, with eyes shut and breath short, "I swear it to the hosts of heaven I've never been anything but loyal to him. To my lord the king. To King Henry the Fifth." He put the lost sound of long-silenced trumpets into his brother's name. "And to his son." With a silent heave of his chest he began to cry openly—tears of pain and grief and weariness. "This thing is Suffolk's doing. God help me, I've failed Hal, I've failed his son, I've—"

"No!" Arteys thrust the rings into his belt pouch, forgetting them even as he did it. He grasped his father's hands and held them tightly. "You haven't failed. This isn't done."

Gloucester seemed past hearing him. "And you. I've failed you. I'm sorry, sorry."

Beyond the room's inner door there was the creak of someone heavy-footed crossing the room there.

Gloucester and Arteys both froze. Then Gloucester shoved Arteys away, ordering with a harsh whisper, "Leave. Get out."

"Father—"

"Let me have the pleasure of seeing you away. *Go.*"

Arteys went, crossed the room and eased out the way

he had come, into the dark and cold, pulling the door shut after him as he heard a key turn in the lock of the door across the room; but there he stopped. He needed to lock the door behind him and dared not turn the key until whoever was come in had gone again, and he leaned there, his ear to the small gap he had left, listening, wondering who it was. There was still laughter from the hall, louder than ever. Who had left it and why?

The bedchamber door closed. He listened to someone's heavy footfall across the room, heard Gloucester start to say something, then heard . . .

He did not know what. Something. A muffled struggle. A thudding . . .

He flung open the door and himself into the room. A thick-shouldered man was leaning over the bed, pressing a pillow down onto Gloucester's face, with Gloucester's body heaving under the blankets, his legs somehow thrashed free and beating at the mattress.

Arteys was across the room, his dagger out, almost before the man knew he was there, before he could more than straighten and start to turn from Gloucester. But only started, because Arteys drove the dagger into him with the full force of his own body behind it.

The man grunted, staggered back a step, grabbed hold on him. Arteys with his free hand grabbed him in return and shoved the dagger deeper, as far as it would go, saw the man's eyes darken with beginning anger, then go abruptly puzzled, then blank, and his legs gave way. Falling, he almost dragged the dagger from Arteys' grip but Arteys wrenched it up and out, stepping back with the force of his effort, leaving the man to slump sideways, sprawl fully down, and roll onto his face.

Not caring, Arteys spun away to the bed, reaching desperately to shove the pillow from Gloucester's face, crying out, "Father!" Only to freeze at sight of Glouces-

ter's slacked-open mouth and eyes rolled up white in his
head. But he was breathing—a harsh, shallow rasping
from high in his lungs—and Arteys slid the uncleaned
dagger back into its sheath, closed the eyelids with gentle fingers, then still gently and all the while watching
him breathe, afraid he would stop, straightened his
sprawled legs and smoothed the blankets and bedcover
over them; smoothed the bedcovers over his chest and
tucked them close around him; lifted his arms from
where they had fallen wide to his sides and folded them
so his hands lay beside each other on his chest.

That done, he laid a hand over Gloucester's and whispered, hoping, "Father?"

Only Gloucester's breathing answered him, loud in the
quiet room. The far too quiet room, where nothing
moved but the last, dying flames in the fireplace and
their low shadows flickering across the floor. A room
with no sound but Gloucester's harsh breathing and the
drub of Arteys' heart hitting against his ribs. A room
where a dead man's blood was soaking into the carpet
under him and laughter burst up from the hall below.

Arteys kept from looking at the dead man, did not
need to make certain he was dead. He had seen the life
go out of his eyes while the dagger was still in him. He
had never, until now, seen a man die because he had
killed him and he never wanted to see it again. Or, ever
again, the man to whom he had done it.

Gloucester's harsh breathing went on. From the hall
there was a louder roar of laughter and then clapping
that told Arteys the play was done and he had no more
time to be here. That had been his father's last order to
him—to get out and away—and feeling frozen to the
heart, Arteys obeyed, slipped out into the night again
and this time locked the door, no worry now about the
rasp of metal on metal as he turned the key. There was
no one in the room to hear it.

Chapter 16

The day after Gloucester's arrest went not so badly for Frevisse as she had feared it might. All the talk at night and in the morning in the guesthall dortor had been of the arrest, with Prime giving respite but afterward had come breakfast and more talk, some people dark with worry about what might come of it, others head-shaking and tut-tutting, others merely excited by the scandal of it; but to Frevisse's surprise, there was very little malice toward Gloucester. She was reminded of fish in a well-stocked fish pond when food was thrown to them—the food hit the water and the fish surfaced in a swirling mass, seething around each other as they gobbled with staring eyes and gaping mouths. At present, the duke of Gloucester was food and the

gaping, gobbling, and staring were all around her when
she parted from Dame Perpetua after Mass.

Despite it was Sunday, Dame Perpetua was bound for
the library, kept open for monks who wished to spend
their day of somewhat rest in reading. Frevisse, less happily, went on her way to Alice. The man on duty at the
head of the stairs told her before she even thought to ask
that my lord of Suffolk was already gone to the king.
Frevisse thanked him without showing how very thank-
ful she was for that and went in, passing through the two
outer rooms with her eyes lowered, catching a little of
the talk among the few men there but hearing nothing
new, only gaining the thought that, to judge by their
open, exceeding glee against Gloucester, not even a battle victory over the king of France could have set them
higher. She wished she had ignorance enough to be simply pleased at Gloucester's trouble or—better still—to
have no other than pious regret for his fall. But to want
ignorance, and for no better reason than her own comfort, was wrong and she breathed a brief prayer as she
knocked at the bedchamber door.

Admitted, she found Alice about to go out, surrounded
by a flustering of her women putting things away in the
long traveling chest and John sitting on the bed end,
drumming his heels.

"I'm late," Alice greeted her. "The queen expects me
and I'm late. Alyson, take John into the next room. All
of you. I want a moment alone with my cousin."

They went, but with the steady intent of four years
old, John asked over his shoulder as he was led away,
"Can we go see the wheel today, Dame Frevisse?"

"Possibly," she said, looking not at him but at Alice,
who after waiting with open impatience for the door to
close, gestured at herself and said fiercely, "Look at this
gown!" It was one she had worn yesterday of finest,

deep-dyed crimson wool double-woven all over into
curving, leafing patterns with enough yards of cloth in
the skirts spread around her feet and behind her to make
three cloaks for lesser women, Frevisse guessed. "I
mean, look at this!" Alice cried. "The king's uncle, a
man we've known all our lives, is under arrest for treason. King Henry won't talk about it, acts as if it hasn't
happened. Poor Margaret keeps saying, 'But of course
he should be arrested if he wanted my lord husband's
throne, yes?' What do I *say* to that?" She did not wait
for an answer but grabbed handfuls of skirt in either
hand as if hating it. "If Gloucester is guilty of treachery,
we ought to be in mourning of some kind but I'm ordered—*ordered*—to make joy over it and see to it that
so does the queen and that she brings Henry around to
public pleasure at it, too."

"Pleasure?" Frevisse repeated. Solemn thankfulness,
yes, maybe. But pleasure?

"Pleasure." Alice dropped from smothered outrage to
plea. "Frevisse, what am I to do? Despite all the times
and ways Gloucester has been a fool over the years, he's
never had it in him to be disloyal to King Henry. Something is terribly wrong and I don't know what."

With no safe answer to give, Frevisse met Alice's an-
guished stare in silence, watching helplessly as Alice
drew up her courage and said in a raw, low voice, "St.
Anne help me, Frevisse, but my husband is at the heart
of this and I don't know what to do. Time was I would
have asked and expected a true answer. Now all there
will be is a kiss on the forehead and a soothing 'Not to
worry, love, I have it in hand.' If that much."

"Why?" Frevisse asked before she could stop herself.

Alice turned and sat down on the chest beside her, the
gown's skirts heavy around her. "I don't know. No, I do
know. It's the king's marriage. Ever since Suffolk made

it, it's as if he's seen something in himself that he can't stop looking at."

"What?"

"Greatness." Alice made the word ugly, let it lie between them a moment, then went on. "To make the king's marriage, Suffolk dealt with three kings all at once—Henry of England, Charles of France, Rene of Sicily, Jerusalem, and Naples. Never mind that we're not supposed to acknowledge there's any king of France but our King Henry and that Rene of Anjou's royal title to Sicily, Naples, and Jerusalem is as empty as air. They're all of them kings and Suffolk dealt among them as almost their equal, it seemed to him, I think. He liked it. He liked having no one above him in the world but kings. He wants to go on that way and the best way he sees to do it is to hold all the power he can around King Henry."

"You've tried to talk to him about it?" Frevisse asked carefully.

"I've tried. For answer, he's cut me out of almost everything he does. We no longer lay our plans together. He *tells* me what he wants me to do. I didn't marry him to be *told* what to do."

"Alice," Frevisse said, warning her voice had risen.

Alice jerked it back down but said with no less bitter anger, "What he wants from me is to make sure Queen Margaret, poor child, turns only to me for everything. Then I'm to see to it she influences Henry the way Suffolk wants him to go."

"Alice," Frevisse said from the heart, "I'm sorry."

Alice forced a pained part of a smile. "*I'm* sorry I so badly needed to say all this to someone and there's no one else but you."

"I'll pray for you both."

"Pray for King Henry and Margaret and Gloucester,

too. We're all in need." Alice stood up, the familiar iron of her will come visibly back to her, hardening her voice. "Go on finding out what you can, please. Anything."

"I've been little use so far," Frevisse hedged.

"You can tell me what people away from Suffolk are saying about Gloucester's arrest. Are they angry or do they accept it?"

"There's no great choosing of sides yet, that I've heard. Mostly there's only talk and wondering."

Alice shook her head as if she did not understand that and gathered up her skirts. "I have to go. Will you take charge of John for this morning? I haven't the time just now to browbeat his nurse into admitting she's well."

Hoping John would be better company than her thoughts were likely to be, Frevisse agreed, and indeed he proved better refuge from thinking than church or library would have been. He wanted, first, for her to tell him how good he had been in the play last night. Then he told her what King Henry and Queen Margaret had said to him and what his father and mother had said.

"But I can't see Giles again until tomorrow. The players have to practice today. They have another play tonight and I'm not in it. Can we go see the wheel?"

They did, and Frevisse stood uncomplainingly for as long as John wanted to stare at and talk about it. When finally that palled for him, they went for a walk through the abbot's garden, having it almost to themselves this glooming day, and spent a long, chill time on the bridge to the abbey's vineyards across the river, dropping sticks into the water on the bridge's upstream side and crossing to the downstream side to watch them come out of the shadows and drift away on the dark swirling current. To the sea, she thought. Some of them would maybe go all the way to the sea. Not all of them, though. Not most of them, probably, because most things did not come to the ends dreamed for them. Neither sticks nor anything nor anyone.

They played until John complained his feet were cold—long after hers were—and that he was hungry. By then it was time for Nones, but having already forgone Sext and Tierce because a small and restless boy was not good company at prayers—and even less good company at Sunday's longer Offices—Frevisse let Nones go, too, merely took John back to Suffolk's rooms, where a servant brought them dinner. Then, because neither of the two squires left on duty in the outer room seemed to think John was to come into their charge and there was no one else around, Frevisse spent the afternoon with him by the fire, playing true-lady with marbles on a polished board until almost lamp-lighting time.

One of Alice's ladies came for John then, bringing apologies. "My lady is sorry to have left you so long. She's been with the queen and now she's sent for Lord John to come and have supper with the queen and her."

That should make Alice happier, Frevisse thought, as John asked, "May Dame Frevisse come, too?"

Quickly Frevisse said, "When queens ask for one person, they don't want to see two. You go, as your lady mother wants. Why don't you take your true-lady board with you?"

John accepted the game as reasonable substitute for her, and she helped him gather the marbles into their bag, tied its cord for him, put his cloak on him, handed him the playing board, and saw him away. Only when he was gone and she was putting on her own cloak did she have the surprised thought that she had enjoyed much of today.

The abbey bells were pealing to Vespers as she went out into the rapidly darkening twilight, barren of any sunset color. It was as bleak as her wondering if Arteys was still safe with Bishop Pecock. There was no reason he should not be, but too often in life "should" was not the way things went. At least Joliffe, if John had been right, had been in practice with the players today and would be performing tonight, with therefore small chance of him getting into trouble. Or making trouble, come to that.

There was no chance to do more than nod to Dame Perpetua in St. Nicholas' chapel before Vespers began. Only at supper in the guesthall refectory with everything they said to each other masked by the generally loud talk around them did Frevisse ask if she had seen Bishop Pecock today.

"He didn't come to the library," Dame Perpetua answered. "Or if he did, he didn't speak to me or I notice him." That latter was all too possible if she were far gone into her work, Frevisse suspicioned, while Dame Perpetua went on happily about how far she was into copying the *Boece*. "There are such things in it," she said. "Listen. 'Hope after nothing, nor dread not.' And 'If Fortune begins to dwell stable, she ceases then to be Fortune.' It's so true and finely said."

Not until they were going to Compline did she think to ask how Frevisse's day had been and only when they were readying for bed did she wonder, "That trouble with the duke of Gloucester, how has that gone?"

Glad her lack of curiosity needed no long answer, Frevisse answered, "So far as I've heard, nothing has changed."

But by morning it had.

The day began well enough. Dawn was growing golden up a clear sky when Frevisse and Dame Perpetua went from the guesthall dorter to the church for Prime and the raw edge was gone from the air, as if overnight the weather had slipped toward spring. Light poured through the abbey's colored windows, flooding the columns, paving, and altars with patterns of sapphire, ruby, topaz, and emerald, their richness lifting Frevisse's heart, which had gone heavy to bed with her and been no better when she awakened. Through Prime she let the light hold her, with the thought that, come whatever darkness men made, there was still beauty in the world and the beauties of heaven beyond it and all of them pale against God's burning love.

Not until breakfast did the day darken, inwardly if not outwardly. The meal was a mere matter of ale and bread and, this morning, cheese set out on the tables for people to help themselves as they would. They could then eat either sitting or standing, taking long or less at it, and Frevisse and Dame Perpetua were content to draw aside and stand, thick-cut bread and cheese in one hand, an ale mug in the other, making no haste. Frevisse was supposing that after Mass she would go to Alice. Another day with John was all too likely but she hoped some way during it to make chance for Joliffe to find her so they could talk. Unless he sought her out at Mass, little though she would like that.

Her thoughts running that way, she was not listening to the talk around them. There were only so many ways to exclaim over a thing and surely all the ways over Gloucester's arrest had been exclaimed yesterday, with nothing left for today but repeating it. It was Dame Perpetua who said, "Did you hear that?", turning her head to look after two women who had just passed, their own breakfasts in hand. "What they were saying? Something about the duke of Gloucester. That he's gone insensible? That he can't be wakened?"

Newly excited voices were rising all over the refectory. Jarred into listening, Frevisse picked out from the babble near her a man and woman saying the same thing that Dame Perpetua had—that sometime in the night the duke of Gloucester had slipped into a deep unknowing and could not be roused from it.

"Do you suppose it's true?" Dame Perpetua asked. "How awful if it is. The poor man. Or maybe it's a mercy, with the treason and all."

But her voice was as excited as everyone else's. And why not? Frevisse thought. What was Gloucester to her or probably anybody here? No more than a figure in the royal pageant around the king. The play of *Wisdom* had lasted perhaps an hour; the play around the king went on for always—a lifetime's worth of diversion for people to gape at.

Come to it, though, Frevisse thought, how much would she herself have cared about Gloucester's fall except she was forced to? Probably not even as much as most of these people here because it would not have particularly stirred her one way or the other.

"I have to go to Lady Alice," she said.

"Of course. If you need me, I'll be in the library after Mass. Unless you think I could be of help and should come with you?"

"There's probably nothing even I can do. Best you be useful in the library while I'm being useless around my cousin. That way one of us will do some good today."

Dame Perpetua smiled happy agreement with that and Frevisse left her, finishing her ale and bread as she went, setting the cup on a table and going out as quickly as she could among the busily talking people in her way. The guesthall yard was still deep in shadows but overhead the sky was a scoured, brilliant blue fretted with a few thin clouds, the lately risen sun's long, molten-golden rays striking at a long slant over the abbey church's high roof. It was too beautiful a day for the darkness come into it, and Frevisse's regret for that went

with her across the Great Court and up the stairs to Suffolk's rooms where men were crowded in taut-voiced
talk in the outer chamber.

She was too familiar there for anyone to pay her any
heed as she passed through with eyes down and ears
open. Suffolk himself was beside the window in the middle chamber, a tight gathering of more men around him,
mostly other lords, Frevisse guessed by their rich clothing and the intentness of their talk at Suffolk, who was
just saying forcefully, "If there's no explanation, then
there isn't. Let's . . ."

Frevisse missed the rest, her knock at the bedchamber
door immediately answered by one of Alice's ladies,
who stood aside for her to come in.

"Go out," said Alice sharply from where she stood
beside the bed, giving Frevisse pause until she realized
the order was at Alice's three ladies, not her.

They seemed more than ready to go, the sweep of
their skirts almost tangling into each other as they
crowded to be out the door. Frevisse shut it after them
and said to Alice across the room, "Not a good morning?"

"A very bad morning," Alice snapped. She was
gowned as she had been yesterday but with her fair hair
still loose down her back and an air about her of not
knowing which way she would go next. "A very bad
night, a very bad morning, and probably a very bad day
to come. You've heard about Gloucester, I suppose?"

"There's rumor running that he can't be wakened.
That's all I've heard."

"It's worse than rumor. It's true. It happened to him
sometime in the night."

Aware of something different in the room, Frevisse
asked, "Where's John?" Neither he nor any of his toys
or clothes were anywhere in sight.

"I sent him away to Wingfield at first light this morning. He's better out of this." Alice turned half around, seeming to be looking for something without being sure of what. Her voice rose. "I wish we were all out of this!"

"Alice . . ."

"When word came last night about Gloucester, my husband hoped aloud he'd die without ever waking. Frevisse, he *prayed* for it."

Had prayed for a man to die without making his soul's final peace before God's judgment came on it.

Hiding her horror at that, Frevisse crossed to take gentle hold on Alice's arm, guide her to the window seat, and order, "Sit."

Alice did, and Frevisse went to the table, finding warm, spiced wine in the silver pitcher there and pouring a goblet full while behind her Alice said in a half-whisper, the words too painful to say aloud, "Frevisse, he's pleased beyond measure about it."

Frevisse brought her the wine, offering with it the only other almost-comfort she could. "He was maybe thinking how there'll be no ugliness of a trial if Gloucester dies quietly in his sleep."

"You mean no trial where Gloucester might prove himself innocent of all the charges against him." Alice paused, then added, "No trial where maybe someone else might be proved guilty instead of him."

"Drink," Frevisse said.

Alice drank, but when she lowered the goblet, her eyes were still troubled with looking at something she did not want to see. She drank again, finishing the wine, rose sharply to her feet, and went to set the goblet back on the table, saying as she did, "God help Gloucester. What am I going to do?"

"What little you can. Your duty to the queen for one thing?" Frevisse offered.

"What am I supposed to say to her about all this? She asks questions and I don't know what to say. And there's something else." Alice returned to the window seat, sat again, and gestured Frevisse to sit with her. She had steadied, her voice level, her eyes fixed on Frevisse's face. "Last night it was Viscount Beaumont himself brought the word about Gloucester. He said it right out, for everyone in the room to hear, but afterwards he and Suffolk went aside." She pointed to a far corner of the room. "He told him something else. I don't know what but he was disturbed about it, and so was Suffolk after he'd been told whatever it was."

"Disturbed?"

"Bothered. Angry. Thrown out of balance. I don't know. That Gloucester was gone insensible was no trouble. It was whatever else Viscount Beaumont told him that Suffolk didn't like."

"But you don't know what it was?"

"They kept their voices down even while they traded sharp words over it."

"They were angry at each other?"

"Not at each other, I think. At whatever had happened. Then they seemed to agree on something and Beaumont left. When Suffolk and I were alone, I asked what it had been about and he . . ." Alice's face tightened with anger. "He patted my cheek and told me not to worry, everything was going very well. I might as well have been John being told I'd have a sweetmeat at bedtime if I were good."

"What has he said this morning?"

Coldly Alice said, "I haven't spoken to him since then."

Frevisse wondered if Suffolk had any thought of how unpleasant his life would become if Alice stayed both frightened for him and angry at him, and asked cautiously, wary of swinging Alice's anger toward her, "What are you going to do now?"

"What can I do?" Alice sounded suddenly more weary than angry. "What you said, I suppose. What little I can, beginning with going to the queen." She stood up. "Thank you for letting me talk at you. Saying it out helps."

Frevisse stood up with her, hesitated, then asked anyway, "Alice, if somehow I find out anything and it's against Suffolk, do you want to know of it?"

Alice hesitated, too, then said with hard certainty, "Yes."

Chapter 17

Frevisse had no doubt that what Alice had said, Alice meant. What she did doubt, after leaving her to her women again and going out into the sun-filled morning, was what she herself would do about it. Or to the more immediate point, what she *could* do about it. To wander, listening to people talk on the chance of overhearing something useful, seemed likely to be a waste of time and she had no way of coming to where she might hear more.

Standing on the walkway at the foot of the stairs, trying to decide what was best to do, she was suddenly impatient at Joliffe. Where was he? And what of Arteys? Did he know about his father yet? Surely Bishop Pecock would see he did as soon as might be. Then what?

Come to that, "then what" about *anything*?

At her elbow a boy said, "Please, my lady," and she looked around and down to find Giles Wilde there. "Master Giles," she said, the more welcoming because she thought he was from Joliffe. "You're out and about early enough today."

He took off his hat and made her a deep bow, better at it than many a lord she had seen, then looked up at her, earnest with hope. "Please, my lady, is Lord John up yet, do you know?"

Disappointed of her own hope, she was sorry to disappoint him in return. "Lord John was taken off to home first thing today, I fear."

Giles' face fell. "Oh."

"I doubt he's happy about it," Frevisse offered. "He was talking yesterday about seeing you today."

Giles brightened a little. "So he hadn't forgotten."

"Assuredly not. He was looking forward to it gladly." In the hope of bringing him around to saying something of Joliffe, she went on, "I heard you did another play last night. It went well?"

"We were laughed at like anything! There's talk we're maybe to do it for the king before Lent starts."

"I wish it for you." Frevisse's pleasure on their behalf was unfeigned, but it was still for Joliffe she asked, "Where did you play last night?"

"At St. Saviour's," Giles said blithely, but must have seen her face change because he immediately added, greatly earnest, "Not for the duke of Gloucester, though. He kept to his room. Or was kept. But everybody else in the place was there in the hall to see us."

"Nothing was wrong with the duke then, or there would have been more upset, I suppose." Frevisse kept her voice light.

"I suppose." Giles shrugged, not much interested. "John really won't be back, then?"

"I fear not."

Giles' face quirked all over with a sudden big smile. "I'll bet he's mad about it. I'll bet he's really mad."

Frevisse gave him a smile back. "I'll bet he is, too." With that thought—unsatisfying to her but cheering to Giles—they parted, Giles giving her another bow before skipping backward and turning to run off across the yard, dodging and disappearing among men and horses, leaving Frevisse with the worrisome thought that Joliffe had been at St. Saviour's last night. It was only happenstance, she knew, and nothing to do with Gloucester, and yet . . .

Knowing the nothing she knew, there was small use in thinking about it, and putting it firmly from her, she made up her mind that until she heard from Joliffe or Bishop Pecock, she would follow her own desire. The church and the library were the two places where Joliffe and Bishop Pecock—and Arteys, come to that—would most readily think to find her, and because she doubted she would pray well at present, she went libraryward. If nothing else, she could at least be useful to Dame Perpetua.

The aged monk was no better pleased than ever to see her but let her pass unchallenged. Dame Perpetua's welcome was better, a mixture of pleasure and happy guilt. "I've unstitched the book, you see," she whispered, openly pleased with herself. "I can put it back together without trouble when I'm done, but it's easier to copy with the pages apart. If you'll take these . . ."

Provided with Dame Perpetua's spare pens and inkpot, Frevisse took the pages and blank paper to another of the desks, hoping no one would arrive and protest her being there. She expected to settle gladly to Boethius and simply writing and for a while she did, then found herself staring out the window at the sky's clear blue, her pen unmoving and dry over the paper. When she found herself doing it a third time and looked down to see she had reached "Then evil is not among the things that ought to be desired," hardly five lines on from where she had been when last she stopped, she cleaned the pen, closed the inkpot, and went to tell Dame Perpetua they were both going for a walk in the abbot's garden.

Dame Perpetua started to protest but Frevisse said firmly, "God has given us the gift of a warm day and a clear sky. We should acccpt his gift graciously." One of the abbey bells and then another began to ring from the church's tower. "Right after Sext," she amended.

At Sext's end they returned through the passageway into the abbot's garden, but rather than toward the prior's yard and the library, they took one of the paths laid square-cornered among the ordered beds. Enclosed by a high wall on two sides and abbey buildings on two other, it was far larger than the nuns' walled garden at St. Frideswide's but also far less private, with monastery windows overlooking it on two sides. With so much of the abbot's palace presently given over to the royal household, it was lately not private at all and today the turn in the weather had brought out others besides them to walk its paths—a scattering of gentlemen walking in pairs and threes, a few ladies companioned together or with a gentleman, a few dark-clad churchmen. Frevisse and Dame Perpetua were able to keep mostly to themselves as they paced the paths much as they would have St. Frideswide's cloister walk or garden, their hands tucked into their opposite sleeves, their heads slightly lowered, exchanging only nods with those they encountered and no words between themselves, comfortable with silence.

Only when they had woven their way back and forth through the garden and were beginning to cover the same paths again, did Dame Perpetua say, "Do you know when we'll be going home?"

In honesty Frevisse could only answer, with just about truth, "With everything that's going on, I don't, I'm afraid. I gather clerks and officers and suchlike have to see the deed first and I don't know what else before it's done. You know." She ended vaguely, telling herself she must remember to ask Alice about the grant, if only to keep up the appearance that it was her reason for being here.

"Yes," Dame Perpetua murmured, sounding as unclear about it as Frevisse had deliberately been but not in the least cast down. "Then very likely I'll have time for all of *Boece!*"

"I'll try to help you more, now that Lord John is gone," Frevisse said contritely.

"He's gone?" Dame Perpetua asked in surprise. "Gone where?"

Frevisse explained that with so much happening, Alice had made things a little simpler by sending him away.

Dame Perpetua made a small tching sound of pity. "I suppose it is more troubling for her than many, with how worried her husband must be by it all. Everyone around the king must be worried. Still, if it was treason the duke had planned, this fading away might be best, both for him and everyone else."

It would certainly be best for Suffolk, Frevisse did not say.

Dame Perpetua peered forward. "Is that Bishop Pecock ahead of us?"

To Frevisse's relief, it was. He was walking toward them in company with another man who was neither

Joliffe or Arteys, merely someone she did not know, cleric-dressed in plain black with none of the signs of rank about him and therefore probably a minor priest or lesser clerk, not another bishop. Her first thought was that Bishop Pecock had deliberately made this meeting, but deep in talk with the other man, he seemed unaware of them, looking downward at the path and saying intently as they neared each other, "Simply because St. Jerome wrote a thing doesn't make it unquestionably true. He didn't hold the keys to heaven or hell, you know. He . . ."

It took a touch on his arm from the man beside him to make him aware two nuns had stepped to the side of the path to let him pass. He vaguely sketched a cross in the air in blessing toward them and would have gone on, still talking, except Frevisse said firmly, "My lord bishop."

At that he actually looked at them and said with open pleasure, as if they had just arrived unexpectedly and from far away—which, into his awareness, they had, "Dame Perpetua. Dame Frevisse. Well met." To the man with him he added, "I've spoken of meeting these nuns, I believe?" And by way of introduction added, "Master Orle, my chaplain and sometimes clerk, who attempts to keep me from wandering so far away in the fields of thought that I forget my duties."

Master Orle was a young man with a wide, clever face and sandy-brown hair whose neatly shaven tonsure showed as he took off his hat and bowed to them, while Bishop Pecock asked, "You're out to enjoy the pleasant weather while it's with us, my ladies?"

"As you are, my lord," Dame Perpetua answered.

"Not so much out for the pleasure of the day as for the pleasure of avoiding my fellow lords, I fear."

"Parliament isn't meeting today?" Frevisse said.

"Parliament is assembled, both lords and lay, but chattering away like a dray of squirrels and about as sensible."

"Squirrels may well make sense to each other," Frevisse suggested, "even if they don't to anyone else."

"Then I can assume that I am not a squirrel, I suppose, because my fellows in Parliament don't make sense to me. Or perhaps, to be fair, I should say that they do somewhat make sense but go on at too great length while doing so and in too many circles while they're at it. I stayed long enough to see that no one is willing to commit to anything regarding the duke of Gloucester until everyone knows to what the king means to commit, and then I came away. Dame Perpetua, I trust you're not going in circles with your work?"

"Indeed not, my lord. I go well forward, though more slowly than I'd like. But Dame Frevisse has said she'll perhaps be able to help me since her cousin's boy is gone home."

Bishop Pecock turned with mild interest to Frevisse. "Has he?"

"With all that's happening, Lady Alice thought it best, my lord."

"One can see why. But how are you coming with Boethius, Dame Perpetua?"

"Not nearly quickly enough but enjoying it greatly."

They shifted to the side of the path to let several ladies pass. Bishop Pecock looked around and said, "Would you care to walk farther abroad, while the day is so fair? There's a way between the prior's house and the infirmary to the monks' walk along the river."

Except Bishop Pecock suggested it, Dame Perpetua might not have gone but said when they had come out from among the cloister buildings and across the small bridge over the ditch dug to bring water to the abbey's mill into the meadow running long and narrow between there and the river, "It's so good to be out from walls. Is that a vineyard?" Pointing across the river to ordered rows upon rows of bare vines waiting for spring and summer's flourish.

Bishop Pecock confirmed they were.

Behind them, clear in the quiet morning, one bell and then another began to call to Tierce. Dame Perpetua immediately drew back a step, ready to make farewell curtsy and go back, but Bishop Pecock quickly signed the cross at them both and said, "I absolve you of the nccd to go." He was very pleased with himself. "There. There *are* advantages to being a bishop. I must remember to make use of them more often."

Master Orle rolled his eyes heavenward, as if in silent prayer.

"I saw that, John," Bishop Pecock reproved. "You'll come to no good end, mocking your bishop."

"I wasn't mocking, my lord. I was making an honest prayer to heaven for your increase in wisdom and strength. Surely that's something to be hoped for, for you and every man."

"You hope a little too fervently sometimes. And a little too often, come to that. As if heaven were insufficiently answering your prayers."

Master Orle made a small bow. "As your grace says."

They were both solemn at it, but the laughter of friends underlay their words and, "Come," said Bishop Pecock. "We look like a clustering of crows, standing here all in black and talking to each other. Let's walk on."

They did, taking the well-used path across the meadow to the river's bank, Bishop Pecock walking ahead with Dame Perpetua, talking of Boethius, leaving Frevisse to Master Orle's company. For form's sake, he and she traded a few remarks but were both more interested in the scholarly talk ahead of them. They reached the riverbank, where the path split to run upstream to the bridge where Frevisse and John had played yesterday and downstream to another bridge at the very edge of the abbey's walled grounds. It was possible, by way of the bridges, to cross from the meadow where they were to the river's far bank and around, past the vineyard, to the meadow again, which Bishop Pecock suggested, then said, "Dame Frevisse, if you'll walk with me? I would hear if you think there's anything I might do for Lady Alice."

Frevisse went forward to him, Dame Perpetua moved back to companion Master Orle, who asked as they began to walk downstream, "Tell me, do you find the shifting from prose to poetry and back again in Boethius distracts or increases your understanding?"

Bishop Pecock, as he had said he would, asked after Alice. Frevisse, watching the sunlight's gladsome sparkle over the river's rippled surface, said she did not know that Lady Alice was in need of anything but to have this business over with.

"It's said she's a good friend to the queen. Is there anyone a good friend to her?" Bishop Pecock asked.

"I hope I am," Frevisse said. As good a friend as she could be despite working against Suffolk. She gazed downriver toward where—although out of sight from here—St. Saviour's was and the duke of Gloucester was prisoner and perhaps dying. How was it with Arteys, knowing that but unable to come to him?

They were still too near Dame Perpetua and Master Orle for her to ask that, but while making careful conversation, she and Bishop Pecock both lengthened their strides, drawing a little more ahead; and when Dame Perpetua and Master Orle paused, still talking of Bo-

ethius, on the bridge to watch the flow and swirl of water
under it, Frevisse and Bishop Pecock, across and turning
to follow the path upstream, left them enough behind
that she was able to ask, "How is it with Arteys? He
knows what's happened with Gloucester?"

"By now I suppose he does. As for how he is, I can't
say. He went with Joliffe yesterday because there
seemed a way he might slip in to see Gloucester while
the players performed at St. Saviour's last night. Did you
know they were to do that?"

There was no way to help her sinking feeling but she
kept her voice even as she answered, "I heard this morning they had. *Did* Arteys see Gloucester?"

"I've had word from neither him nor Joliffe since they
left me yesterday." Bishop Pecock sounded no more
happy saying that than she was to hear it, but he added,
"Although if Arteys had come to grief, been caught in
the attempt or suchlike, surely it would be noised abroad
by this morning."

"The players' boy I spoke with didn't say anything
had gone amiss at St. Saviour's last night while they
were there at least." But something had, then or later, to
guess by what Alice had told her. That thought fingered
coldly through her while Bishop Pecock went on, "Arteys was to reach his father's room, if he could, during
the play and be out again before it was over. If naught
went amiss, then likely we merely need wait until one
of us hears from one or the other of them. Do you think
you'll be in the library all this afternoon?"

Aware that Master Orle and Dame Perpetua had left
the bridge and were following them again, Frevisse began to answer, "Very likely. I—"

Behind them Master Orle called, odd-voiced, "My
lord."

Bishop Pecock turned around and Frevisse with him,

saw Dame Perpetua and the priest had stopped on the
path and were looking down the bank into the water,
and went the little way back to join them. The river
flowed slightly less swiftly, slightly more smoothly just
there, but drifting a few feet out from the bank there was
a slightly humped darkness that, busy in talk with
Bishop Pecock, Frevisse had not noted when they went
by. Only now, with Master Orle pointing at it, did she
see it and begin to be afraid in the same moment that
Bishop Pecock ordered, his voice gone whip-sharp, "Get
him out!"

Master Orle, apparently having finally believed his
own eyes, too, was already plunging down the bank,
grabbing up the skirts of his robe to clear his legs to
wade into the water, reaching out for the darkness that
looked to be the back of a man's doublet.

"Bring help," Bishop Pecock ordered at Dame Perpetua.

Already backing away, her unbelief turning to raw
dismay, she stammered, "Yes. Yes, my lord. Yes."

"That way." He pointed upstream where the bridge
was not so near but crossed the river closer to the abbey
buildings.

"Yes, my lord," Dame Perpetua repeated, made him
a slight, unthinking curtsy, and rushed away.

"There are men there," Frevisse said, pointing to the
other bank where a pair of men were strolling down the
path toward the river.

"They'll come when they see her running," Bishop
Pecock said, starting down the bank after Master Orle,
who was thigh-deep in the water, holding on to the doublet with one hand, gripping the bank's long grass with
his other, his gown's skirts floating around him.

It was hardly a stance he could hold for long but neither could he shift from it without letting go with one

hand or the other, and Bishop Pecock with his feet braced on grassy tussocks reached out and grabbed hold on his belt. "I have you," he said, and Master Orle let go the grass to seize the man's doublet with both hands and lurch backward at the same moment Bishop Pecock pulled on him so that he stumbled against the bank, dragging with him what was all too clearly not merely a doublet but a man's body. Together, he and Bishop Pecock hauled it mostly out of the water, onto the grass, and rolled it over, looking for life although almost surely there was none. From above them on the path Frevisse saw the man's face, did not know him, and felt fear go out of her with a gasp.

"He's dead," Master Orle said pointlessly, because the staring eyes, gaping mouth, and slack-sprawled limbs already told that.

"He's been stabbed," Bishop Pecock said. "Here." Pointing to the slice through the left side of the man's doublet at heart height.

Master Orle, kneeling in the puddle spreading from the dead man's clothing and his own soaked gown, crossed himself and began to pray.

"His belt pouch is gone," Bishop Pecock added. "He was robbed before he was thrown in the river."

"Not robbed," Frevisse said. "He still has a ring on. There on his right hand, see? And look at his boots. Those are too good for a thief to leave on a dead body."

"He might have been killed where it was too dark for the thief to see the ring or note the boots," Bishop Pecock said, then added immediately, "Though to bother with robbing him at all, the thief would likely have known what he had worth stealing before going to the bother of killing him."

"Perhaps it was murder first, with robbery an after thought," Frevisse said.

"That's possible," Bishop Pecock granted. "And not long ago, whichever way it was. The body hasn't been in the water long at all."

"Or drifted very far," Frevisse said.

"No. Not considering weirs and suchlike all along the river. It would be caught on one thing or another before going far."

They both looked upstream. The arch of the bridge was wide enough for the body to have been carried through on the current, rather than caught there, but beyond that, a hundred yards and more, was the abbey's outer wall. It was arched over the river's flow, but an iron frame with bars was gridded across the gap.

"Killed here in the abbey?" Frevisse asked, as if Bishop Pecock had said aloud what she was thinking— that the body could not have drifted past that.

But he said, "The bars stop just above the water, to keep from trapping branches and suchlike when the river is in spate. A body could have drifted under."

"How do you know that?"

"I like to walk about. I like to take note of things. So he may have been killed outside the abbey and his body has floated in. Either way, he's likely to be from Bury or nearby. That means soon missed and soon known."

"Or he's come in some lord's retinue. He's plainly dressed but well enough to be of someone's household."

"There's no badge on him but that means little," Bishop Pecock agreed. "Yes, he could well have come to Bury in someone's retinue. Either way, he'll still be soon missed."

Master Orle had broken off his prayers, was looking from one to the other of them, bewildered. "How can you guess all that so quickly?" he asked.

"Not guess," Bishop Pecock said. "Judge. A drawing of conclusions from what is obvious to what is therefore probable, limited always by what is possible. Not," he repeated firmly, "guessing. Either of us."

As Bishop Pecock had foretold, the men on the other bank had gone to meet Dame Perpetua, and while she had gone on to disappear among the abbey buildings, they had come running this way, loud with questions as they neared and, upon seeing the body, exclaims. Frevisse drew aside, out of their way and away from the body, willing to leave whatever needed to be said to Bishop Pecock and Master Orle.

Chapter 18

afe out of St. Saviour's, Arteys had been back into town well before the closing of the gates at curfew, forcing himself to walk as if headed homeward in no great hurry. The Shrovetide holidaying was picking up, he guessed from the high humour of people still in the streets. He doubted he'd be remembered among them and there were lanterns and torches enough still burning beside householders' doors and outside of taverns that he found his way back to Whityng Street and the alehouse without trouble, always reminding himself to walk, just walk. Despite he felt naked and blood-covered and desperate like a hunted animal.

He slid gratefully into the narrow blackness of the shadow-filled alley beside the alehouse, groped its black length into the slightly lesser darkness of the rearyard, and climbed the ladder into the loft and hiding. With the door shut between him and the night, he felt his way through more darkness to the foot of the bed and sat down with his cloak and his arms wrapped tightly around himself, not wanting a light, rocking slowly forward and backward, holding in his desperation lest it turn to something worse.

To open grief and pain and howling aloud.

He had killed a man.

His father was going to die and he had killed a man.

And he sat there and rocked until finally Joliffe came, singing softly, slurredly, in the way of a man slightly, pleasantly drunk along the alley but surefooted on the ladder and, once inside and turned from hasping the door tightly closed, with no sign of drunkenness on him at all as he asked while setting a small, lighted lantern on the table and taking a crisp-crusted loaf of bread, a hard cheese, a fat sausage, and a brown pottery bottle from under his cloak, "How did it go?"

While Arteys told him, he divided the food into equal shares, only pausing at slicing the sausage to look up and watch Arteys tell of the man smothering Gloucester and what he'd done to him. The cold-sober lack of judgment in Joliffe's face goaded Arteys to insist at him, "Joliffe, I *killed* him. That man. He's dead."

Joliffe cocked his head slightly to one side. "Would you rather have left him alive, to finish what he was doing?"

"No!"

"Was there any other way to stop him?"

"No. Yes. I could have hit him with something. Knocked him out."

"Was there anything there you could have grabbed sufficient to do it with one blow?"

Arteys cast quickly through his memory of the room. "No. Nothing close to hand."

"And if you'd fought him bare-handed, supposing he didn't draw his dagger and do for you right off, there would have been noise and you'd have been caught. Would that have been better? Would you or Gloucester have wanted that instead?"

A little sullenly. "No."

Joliffe went back to cutting the sausage. "Then I wouldn't go grieving over having killed a man who was willing to smother a sick man in his bed."

But when Arteys told how Gloucester was when he left him, Joliffe stopped again, laid down the knife, and said, "Arteys, I'm sorry. That's hard."

"Not for him." The bitterness in his voice surprised Arteys before he realized he was bitter not at his father but at his own helplessness.

"Which is a thing you should remember. That he at least is well out of this for now. Take what comfort you can from it."

It was a rough comfort at best, but Arteys found he could eat and drink when Joliffe told him to, and afterward he slept, as far over on the bed as he could be, to give Joliffe the most of it, it being his bed.

He awoke in the morning to find Joliffe seated at the table, eating thick-cooked something from a wooden bowl. When Arteys sat up, Joliffe, his mouth full, pointed his spoon at another bowl waiting across from him.

"Um," Arteys answered, needing to gather his wits before he moved. Yellow sunlight was streaming across the floor through the open door and he said, still somewhat stupid with a sleep far heavier than he had expected to have, "The sun is shining."

"The obvious is always best at times like this," Joliffe

agreed. "Yes, we've a clear day finally. Come and eat while the stuff is still warm."

Arteys moved from the bed to the table and dragged the waiting bowl toward him, finding it full of barley gruel and a thick drizzle of honey. Around his first mouthful he said, "You've been out. What have you heard?"

"Nothing yet." Joliffe scraped the last of his gruel from the bottom of his bowl. "I only went down to fetch our breakfast up. I'm just off to find out what I can, including whether I've more rehearsal with the players. There was talk last night we might do that Lydgate's damnable Hertford farce—St. Genesius help us—for the king, rather than last night's play. You'll stay here until I come back?"

Having no thought of what else he might do, Arteys said, "Yes."

Joliffe gathered up his cloak. "There's ale left in the bottle. There'll be a boy up to empty the slops. I'll bring food when I come back, so just stay put. No matter what."

He left, Arteys finished his breakfast, and in a while a boy came and took away the covered slops bucket and the bowls and spoons. He gave Arteys a long look but neither of them spoke, and shortly he brought back the bucket, empty and washed, and after he had gone silently away again, all Arteys had for company were town sounds from the street, children sounds from the rear-yard, the sunlight's slide across the floor, and the some-time ringing out of the abbey bells. With nothing to do but wait, he was left to think and found his thoughts were not of much use, circling through the same fears and doubts over and over. Fear for his father. Fear for himself. Doubt at what he should do next. Doubt he should trust Joliffe, though it was late now to change his mind on that. Doubt that he should trust anyone, even the bishop of St. Asaph's or that nun.

But what was he to do instead? Sir Roger and anyone else most likely to help were arrested. He had nowhere to go and no one else to ask for help.

And he had killed a man.

That certainty sat sick inside him. He could justify it, that was not the trouble. It was that, just as he would have wanted to wash himself clean after handling filth, he needed to make expiation of some kind before he would feel clean of that death.

And then—under and through and around everything else—there was the grief. Grief for Gloucester who was going to die or else be imprisoned for life, and grief for himself, because without Gloucester he belonged to no one, had no one who belonged to him, and nowhere to go that was his or he was wanted.

Sitting cross-legged on the floor in the sunlight's patch, he brought out his father's rings and sat turning them to catch light, first in the garnet, then in the diamond, but putting none of them on, as if by not wearing them he somehow kept possible that Gloucester might live and take them back, might somehow rise up and throw Suffolk down.

It was later, just after Nones, when Joliffe returned. Hearing him on the ladder, Arteys stood up from the bed edge and was demanding before he was through the doorway, "My father?"

Joliffe straightened and went to the table to set out more bread, more cheese, another sausage, another pottery bottle of ale. "He's alive but still unsensible."

"He's not dead?"

"Not dead."

Arteys sat heavily down again and asked, more of his own despair than of Joliffe, "What am I going to do?"

"To begin with, eat. Then, if you've any sense, disappear. Go abroad and make your fortune. Gloucester isn't going to come out of this alive, whatever happens. Leave while the leaving is good."

"I'm not leaving. If the worst comes, I want at least to see him to his grave. I owe him that."

Joliffe regarded him steadily, then gave a curt nod, it seemed more to something he told himself than to Arteys, and said, "As you will. But come and eat anyway."

Hunger made that an easy order to obey, but around a mouthful of bread he asked, "Have there been any more arrests?"

"None."

"What's being said about the man . . ." He dropped his voice, not from caution but because the words were heavy. ". . . I killed?"

Joliffe paused from cutting off a piece of sausage, looked straightly across the table at him, and said, "What man?"

"You know what man."

Joliffe shook his head. "There's no talk of any man dead at St. Saviour's."

Arteys' voice scaled up in protest. "But I—"

Joliffe held up a hand and said, seriously enough, "Truly, there's nothing being said about any murdered man at St. Saviour's. Not a whisper. Not a word. Nothing."

"But . . ."

"On the other hand, there are questions being suddenly asked about who besides St. Saviour's warden has a key to the duke of Gloucester's chamber. Unhappily for someone's peace of mind, everyone says there isn't any other key."

"But Master Grene knows I have one. He gave it to me. Other people know it, too. I—"

"*No one* admits to there being another key. I gather from kitchen talk that neither Master Grene nor anyone else who belongs to St. Saviour's likes the use being made of their place and are all being as little help as they can with anything demanded of them. Including questions. It seems they're a very ignorant lot at St. Saviour's these days. There's something else, though. A dead man was found in the river inside the abbey walls this morning."

"The abbey? But . . . that's upriver from St. Saviour's."

"Too true."

"So it's not the man I killed."

"Seemingly not. But how many murdered men are there likely to be in a place the size of Bury St. Edmunds in one night? Here's what he looks like . . ."

"You saw him?"

"I joined the crowd and stared with the best of them while he was still laid out on the riverbank. Listen."

He described the body and its clothing and Arteys said doubtfully, "That could be him."

Glumly, Joliffe said, "I was afraid of that," and began to eat again.

"But if it's him, how did he come there?"

"A good question. Eat. Then we'll do what we can to find out."

Chapter 19

revisse lifted her head, raised her gaze from the dark red floor tiles on which she knelt, past the small-burning lamp above St. Nicholas' altar with its beautifully woven, golden-embroidered altar cloth to the window in the wall beyond it. It was a round-topped window, narrow in the thick stone wall, set mostly with blue glass that glowed sapphire when the sun struck through it in the morning but now, in early afternoon, was darkened to black-blue. Somewhat like Man's hope of salvation, Frevisse thought, with the sun of God's love ever-shining and always there but Man's life a narrowness through which he either reached God and his soul's salvation or . . . he did not.

She had been praying for the dead man's soul and for

whoever had killed him, but she was prayed out for now and signed herself with the cross and stood up slowly, wary of her knees, taking time before trusting their co-operation and turning to leave the chapel. As always during the day, the great church itself had been murmurous and rustling with people coming and going along the nave. Some were loud, some were lesser, but quiet as the quietest might be, there was always their soft foot-fall, the whisper of their clothing, and from a lifetime of churches Frevisse knew how to shut their sounds away while she prayed and therefore was unknowing she was not alone in the chapel until she turned and found Joliffe and Arteys standing there.

Her irk at not knowing how long they had been there was counterbalanced by relief at seeing Arteys. Until she took in his face. And then Joliffe's, too, as he asked, "Might we have a little of your time, my lady?"

They were as likely to be private here as anywhere and she beckoned them to come farther into the chapel as she moved toward them, asking, "Master Arteys, you're well? Were you able to see your father last night?"

"I saw him. I talked with him." The words seemed to come hard. "But no, I'm not well."

His voice failed him. He looked to Joliffe, who said, very low, "He had to kill a man who was trying to kill Gloucester."

Sharply Frevisse said, "There's been nothing said about a murder at St. Saviour's."

"We know and there should have been, because all Arteys could do was leave the body lying there." Joliffe paused. "On the other hand, there is your dead man from the river."

"On the third hand," Frevisse said, an edge to the

words, "we're upriver from St. Saviour's. The body didn't drift against the current to here."

"Very probably not." Joliffe matched her edge. "But if the dead man isn't the man from St. Saviour's, who is he? Or if he's someone else, then where's the man Arteys killed? Why's there been no outcry or any word about him? Then again, if the dead man in the river *is* Arteys', how did he come to be *here*?"

Frevisse turned to Arteys. "Tell me what happened."

He did, or enough of it, leaving out what had passed between him and his father but clear about the killing, even though he looked sick while he told it.

When he had finished and was watching her, waiting, she said slowly, considering as she went, "First, this man tried to murder Gloucester. Why? On whose order did he do it?"

"Maybe he was on his own," Joliffe suggested.

"Do you think that?" Frevisse asked.

"Not for a moment."

"Nor do I. So. Someone tried to murder Gloucester and was murdered himself. Then, either there were two murders done in Bury last night and we have one body but not the other, or else there was one murder and the body was taken away, we don't know by whom, and dumped into the river upstream from where he died, we don't know why."

"Given that Arteys says your dead man looks much like his, I rather favor there being only one murder," said Joliffe.

"As do I," Frevisse agreed. "But why the secrecy and the river?"

"To confuse things?" Joliffe offered. "Whoever gave the order for Gloucester's murder can't have been pleased to find his murderer murdered and no sign of who did it. Arteys brought his dagger away with him and locked the door after him. Gloucester was in no condition, even before, to have done anything much against an armed man, besides he had no weapon. I suppose you could try out that Gloucester had grabbed the man's dagger, stabbed him with it, cleaned the dagger, put it back in the sheath, then laid himself tidily out in bed and went insensible. It's . . . possible."

"Barely," Frevisse said dryly. "The more immediate trouble for whoever ordered Gloucester's murder was that he had the wrong man dead on his hands."

"True. What he wanted was a dead royal duke without a mark on him. What he had was an insensible but still breathing duke and a dead murderer with a dagger wound in him. Not something I'd care to try to explain to anyone."

"There was nothing to show the man meant to murder Gloucester," Frevisse said.

"No. But I'll warrant he was someone who shouldn't have been in the room at all. I'll wager that every one of the men who had been keeping watch on Gloucester were very much in the great hall watching us last night. If anyone asked why, the answer was, well, why shouldn't they be? Everyone knew Gloucester was too ill to leave his bed. At the play's end someone would return to duty, find him dead, and raise an outcry. A grievous thing, to die so unprepared and all alone, but maybe it was by God's mercy because now he need not suffer through a trial."

"With much shaking of heads, a suitable funeral, and no more questions," Frevisse said.

"Oh, there'd be questions in plenty, but none asked openly or by anyone that could do anything about it."

"But we have to do *something*," Arteys put in. "Or I have to. Before they do kill him."

With surprising gentleness, Joliffe said, "They won't

do anything more to him. They only have to wait."

Arteys went very still, fighting to steady himself, his voice very even when he finally said, "I want to know who ordered my father's murder and then I want everyone else to know."

"Yes," Joliffe said.

Still very steadily, looking him in the eyes, Arteys asked, "Why are you willing to help me in this? You're Bishop Beaufort's man. Whatever he wanted out of this is over. Gloucester is going to die."

"Gloucester is going to die because someone is playing a filthy game that will surely befoul England and King Henry before it's done. Bishop Beaufort has tried for more years of his life than not to protect both England and her king. Will it help if I say I'm not doing this for Gloucester but against whoever did it to him? Because that *is* a thing Bishop Beaufort would want of me."

Arteys looked at Frevisse. "Why are you willing to deal in this?"

"For the same reasons. And because I don't like murder." And because she had promised Alice her help, but that was not something she meant to tell either of them, and carefully putting thought of Alice aside for now, she said, "Bishop Pecock could be of use in this."

Arteys looked doubtful. "He's been kind but this is something more. This is—"

"Dangerous," said Joliffe. "Plain dangerous and probably foolish. Unfortunately, he won't be stopped by that any more than we are. He said he would be in the library this afternoon if I needed him."

"When did he say that?" Frevisse demanded.

"This morning at the dead man."

"I didn't see you there."

"You were being kindly escorted away by the

crowner's man when I followed the crowd into the garden. To spare your delicate feelings, I presumed."

Frevisse's mouth twisted wryly. "The crowner didn't seem to realize that if I'd been going to faint or shriek with horror, I'd have done it by then. He said Bishop Pecock and Master Orle's testimony would be enough and sent me away."

"You found the body in the river?" Arteys asked at her. "That's why Joliffe said 'your dead man'?"

"To be precise, Bishop Pecock's chaplain saw the body first, but Bishop Pecock and I were there, yes. That far, we're both part of this already."

"It all tangles together very prettily, doesn't it?" Joliffe said. "I have to join Master Wilde and the others in about an hour. Shall we to the bishop while we can?"

That they not be seen all together, Frevisse went first to the library, exchanged nods with the deaf monk at the door, spoke briefly to Dame Perpetua, slipped into her stall, and sat down to wait, twirling a quill pen between her fingers for the short while until Joliffe and Arteys unhurriedly entered.

"Haven't you found that play yet?" the monk demanded at Joliffe.

"I found it but Brother Lydgate and the playmaster are quarreling and I have to find another."

"Foolishness and nonsense," the monk barked.

"Like much of life," Joliffe replied.

The monk, already bending back to the book in front of him, did not hear him. Frevisse did but did not look up when he and Arteys passed her. With effort, she made herself wait more before she rose and went to join them, in time to hear Arteys say, "I came away then, went back to Joliffe's. I didn't know what else to do."

"You did rightly." Bishop Pecock was seated but turned away from the desk and the book there, with Arteys standing in front of him and Joliffe leaning against the shelves beyond him. He looked up at Frevisse with a welcoming nod, then asked Joliffe, "Have you learned anything?"

"Only that Arteys thinks from what I told him the dead man in the river is the man he killed."

Bishop Pecock considered that before he looked to Frevisse again. "Have you learned anything else, my lady, or mayhap thought of something since this morning?"

"Nothing."

"Well, then." Bishop Pecock looked down at his hands folded in his lap, considered for another moment, then looked up and said, "Until a few moments ago, I had no hesitation in leaving the problem of the man in the river to the crowner. Now it would seem to be ours after all. Do you agree, Joliffe?"

"I have to, I'm afraid."

"It isn't," Arteys said back at both of them. "My lord, I've no claim on your help. I've followed Joliffe in coming to you but why would you—"

Bishop Pecock held up a hand, stopping him. "The why is very simple. The duke of Gloucester is presently heir to the throne. Accused of treason or not, guilty or not, he is still heir. Someone tried to murder him. That is, in effect, an attack but one step removed from the king himself. Someone bold enough to do that is more than a little dangerous."

"The someone who did it is also dead," Joliffe said.

"Don't make digression, Joliffe. None of us think it much likely the dead man attempted the murder all on his own. Someone ordered him to it. Given that, the would-be murderer, in himself, is not the important point. Only in so far as he may help us to learn who set him on is he important, the important matter being, you

see, to determine who is behind this attack on Gloucester. What we want is the person who is, in effect though
not in actual deed, responsible for—"

"Sir," Joliffe interrupted. "You're going on."

Bishop Pecock paused, considered that, then granted,
"I am. I ask your pardon. To the point, then. Why we
are all willing to involve ourselves in this? Whoever
ordered Gloucester's death is dangerous. He—I say 'he'
in the general sense of mankind, you understand, there
being nothing to preclude a woman giving such an order
if she held the power and the desire to do so—he is
someone with likewise probably a great profit to gain
from Gloucester's death. Or a profit that seems great to
him. Therefore, this man is a grave danger not only to
Gloucester but to anyone whom he sees to be in his way,
and he must be stopped."

For most people, their thinking was done as by-the-
way as breathing, but Frevisse was coming to understand
that for Bishop Pecock thinking was a tool to be used
deliberately toward determined ends and, moreover, a
tool he took pleasure in using. He *enjoyed* thinking.

"Toward stopping this man," he was going on, "our
first question must be—" He stopped and looked to Joliffe, like a teacher seeking a student's answer.

"Who stands to gain from the duke of Gloucester's
death," Joliffe answered like the obedient student Frevisse doubted he had ever been.

"Suffolk," Arteys said immediately.

"The marquis of Suffolk first and foremost, I fear,"
Bishop Pecock agreed. "There are others, of course, who
would benefit by Gloucester's removal. The duke of
York for one. He would become the king's immediate
heir in place of Gloucester. However, since York is hardly more in favor than Gloucester, to be put more to the
fore in matters would, at present, hardly serve him well,

would in fact likely serve him ill, and since nothing I've heard of him shows him to be foolish—"

"My lord," Joliffe interrupted again. "The point?"

Bishop Pecock drew a deep breath and said, "Dorset and Buckingham are among the more powerful lords around the king and not to be forgotten but, yes, I think it's reasonable to consider Suffolk before everyone."

"He has the most to gain by Gloucester's death," Joliffe offered.

"He does indeed. While Gloucester lives, it's always possible King Henry will return him to favor. Suffolk would see that as an ill thing. He openly wants his desires and the government to be the same thing. As who does not. But the more reasonable among us see what an ill thing it would be and therefore let it go."

"Or let it go because we can see we're wasting our time to want it," Joliffe said.

"Another portion of the truth, yes, but not one Suffolk sees, I fear. He believes it possible and is willing to do grievous things to get it."

"But how do we prove he's tried to kill my father?" Arteys broke in.

"Or prove that he did not," Bishop Pecock said. "That, too, remains a possibility. Nonetheless, at present, things standing as they are, it's against him we'll seek what evidence there may be."

"How?" Arteys insisted.

Bishop Pecock looked at Joliffe again like a teacher expecting a favored student to take up a problem.

Joliffe pulled a face at him but answered, "We have to link him to the man who tried to kill Gloucester last night."

Now Frevisse asked, "How? Thus far, we aren't certain that the man in the river is the man Arteys killed,

and besides that, so far as I've heard, no one has yet
named the man from the river."

Joliffe shrugged. "I'm willing to lay odds it's the same
man."

"So am I," Frevisse returned. "But it will take more
than having Arteys see and identify him. How do we
link him to Suffolk?" Then, beginning to see the way,
she answered her own question. "By finding how his
body came from St. Saviour's to where we found it. That
might well give a link to Suffolk. Someone moved it.
Several someones probably, and probably with a cart,
rather than carrying it openly through Bury St. Edmunds."

"And if from St. Saviour's, then very probably with
a cart from there," Joliffe said. "I wonder if they bothered to return it when they'd done? I wouldn't. I'd get
away from it as soon as possible and leave people to
think it had simply been stolen."

"How do we find out if a cart is missing from St.
Saviour's? Or else that a cart has been found abandoned?" Frevisse asked.

"That's what servants are for," Bishop Pecock said
serenely. "I don't see that questions can safely be asked
at St. Saviour's itself, but I'll set Runman to looking
elsewhere for an abandoned cart."

"My guess would be they'd not risk bringing the body
through Bury at all," said Joliffe. "They'd either circle
around the west side or else cross at the Eastgate bridge
to go upriver to where there are fewer houses. But not
too far upriver or the body would have been caught up
on a weir or some other thing before it reached the abbey."

"That's something Dame Frevisse and I had considered already," Bishop Pecock said. "Yes, that will limit

the search. You, I think, are needed with the players this afternoon?"

"And this evening, I'm afraid. We're to put on one of Lydgate's farces for the king on Shrove Tuesday and Lydgate is making changes in it."

"It won't help," said Frevisse, aloud but enough to herself that the others ignored her, Bishop Pecock going on, "For my own part, I'll go to St. Saviour's this afternoon, to see what can be learned there."

"On what grounds?" Joliffe asked.

"On the grounds that I wish to pray over the duke of Gloucester. No one else is, so far as I know, except probably a priest of the hospital itself." He laid a hand over his heart and said with great dignity, "I am a bishop and therefore, humble though I am, my prayers are more worthy of a duke than a mere priest's are." He dropped his hand and his pose and said soberly to Arteys, "It will give me a chance to see your father and tell you how he does. I'll also, for courtesy's sake, of course, spend time in talk with Master Grene while I'm there and learn what I can from him about last night and today. Dame Frevisse, may we ask you to be in Lady Alice's company, to listen, talk, and subtly question, to learn what you can?"

Frevisse bent her head in silent acceptance, having expected it.

Arteys shifted restlessly. "What do I do while all this goes on?"

"Keep out of sight," Joliffe said.

"Stay here," said Frevisse. "Favor me by doing the copying I've promised Dame Perpetua I'd do."

"That would serve very well," said Bishop Pecock, "and occupy your mind with other than worries."

Doubtful, Arteys said, "I don't write a good hand."

"It's only a rough copy," Frevisse said. "It won't matter."

"Shall we plan to meet here again not long ere Vespers?" Bishop Pecock asked. "To share what we've all learned?"

With that agreed on, he and Joliffe left together. Frevisse gave over her work and workplace to Arteys, paused to tell Dame Perpetua she had left a young man of Bishop Pecock's to do her work, and with a silent nod to the monk, went out of the library in her turn.

Joliffe was waiting for her on the stairs.

Somewhat curtly she asked, "What is it?"

He made one of his half-mocking bows. "Our good bishop asked me to stay and give you a message."

"Yes?"

"He says to be careful to make no one suspicious of you." Joliffe paused, then added, "I say it, too."

It was Frevisse's turn to pause, before she said, all edge gone from her voice, "I hope you'll take your own advice."

"Oh, I always take my own advice."

"Ever anyone else's?"

"Oddly enough, no. Well, Bishop Pecock's sometimes. And Bishop Beaufort's when he chooses to give it."

"You keep exalted company."

"Or they do, as it may be."

His mockery was back and to it she said, "Bishop Pecock's bishopric isn't a powerful one but it's a bishopric nonetheless. If he slides into trouble with this, he can't retreat into a monastery the way I will into St. Frideswide's, or disappear the way I suppose you will. He won't be able to either hide or run, and much though he likes to think and sharp though his mind is, I wonder if he's thought of a saying my mother was fond of."

"You mean," said Joliffe, catching up to her in the disturbing way he sometimes had, "'don't be so sharp you cut yourself'?"

"That one, yes."

"I don't know about *his* mother . . ." Joliffe started away from her, down the stairs. ". . . but I warrant *your* mother said it often enough."

Chapter 20

The sun, fiercely red-orange, was sliding from sight, the day draining after it out of a sky still clear of clouds, when Frevisse returned to the library. A younger monk was on watch this time, ready to challenge her anew, but Bishop Pecock said from a nearby table spread with books, "I'm expecting her."

The monk did not seem pleased about that but let her pass on a bishop's word. For his part, Bishop Pecock greeted her with merely a nod, picked up one of the books from the table, and led her toward his stall at the room's far end. Dame Perpetua was still at her desk, scribbling rapidly, bent closer to the paper as the light failed, not looking up as they passed.

Piled papers on the desk where Frevisse had left Arteys showed he had made use of his time but he was waiting in Bishop Pecock's study stall and stood up abruptly from the chair there, tense with a patience that must be wearing galls in him, Frevisse thought as she asked, "Where's Joliffe?"

"He's been and gone, Master Arteys says, but said he will find me out later to hear what we've learned. It seems Brother Lydgate is being very troublesome over his play. A petty man who seems to have confused 'prolixity' with 'competent,' from what I've read of his work."

To be difficult, Frevisse said, "He's very highly thought of."

"And by no one more highly than himself," Bishop Pecock returned.

To be tart over someone else's failings was relief at the end of a day such as today had been but, "Did you learn anything new?" Arteys asked.

"On my own part," said Bishop Pecock, "mostly only what rumors are running, but those can be useful, the source sometimes revealing more than the rumor itself."

"What's being said?" Arteys demanded.

"Of Gloucester, a number of things. That he cried out horribly in the night and then was found insensible in his bed. Or on the floor. Or in a chair. Or everything was silent as the grave all through the night and he was found in the morning, quiet in his bed but unwakable. Or he was found—either in the night or in the morning, depending on the story—sprawled among his twisted bedclothes as if he had writhed in agony."

"If he awoke after I left and . . ." Arteys said with pain.

"He didn't," Frevisse said quickly. "Not from what's being said by those most likely to know."

"And they would be?" Bishop Pecock immediately asked.

Frevisse had known this would come but liked it none the better for that. Too many people were presently trusting her, all for different reasons and to different ends. At what point did serving one person's trust betray another's? She didn't know but she was too far in for going back, saw nowhere yet to turn aside, and said firmly, hiding her reluctance, "My cousin. And the queen."

Arteys drew a deep, startled breath. More steadily Bishop Pecock asked, "How did that come about?"

"My cousin was attendant on her grace today. I went to the queen's hall and asked to see my cousin, pretending I was in distress over finding the body in the river."

"As well you might be," Bishop Pecock said. His voice was mild but his eyes sharp, watching her.

"Not as much as I claimed to be. My hope was Alice would come talk to me and I might learn what she had heard about Gloucester, but my lie served better than I thought it would. I'd given my excuse to the servant who went for her. Lady Alice came out almost immediately, told me she had had to tell the queen why she was leaving, and Queen Margaret had bade her bring me to her."

"She wants to hear about it from someone who was there," Alice had said. "Instead of only tittle-tattle. She says everything happens around her and she never knows anything. It will divert her."

Repelled at the thought of using a man's death for someone else's diversion, Frevisse had momentarily pulled back. "Nothing happened. We found him and he was dead, that's all."

Alice had already been turning to go back past the guards flanking the doorway, saying as she went, "There's always more to it than that. Come."

Frevisse had gone, following Alice into the queen's

bedchamber. The room looked to have been the abbot's; the walls were hung with tapestries of St. Edmund's crown of kingship and the arrows of his martyrdom worked in gold on bright blue, alternating with other tapestries of green woven with a pattern of vines. The wide bed with its elaborately carved posts was hung with curtains that matched the green tapestries. A tall window with traceried stonework and painted shutters set open from the glass that was clear below but painted above with doves and white lilies looked out over the abbot's garden, with bright-embroidered cushions on the seat below it. Underfoot was a thick carpet woven in Flemish patterns of bold reds and greens and blues.

Queen Margaret had sat as if enthroned on the padded top of a chest at the foot of the bed, with her half-dozen ladies gathered around the room on floor cushions or the window seat, and when Frevisse had sunk into a deep curtsy to the queen, Alice had gracefully made Frevisse known to her, and Queen Margaret had gestured one of the women to bring forward the room's only chair for her, her smile girlishly eager as she leaned forward to say, her English words lightened by her French accent, "I pray you, tell me all. How you saw the body and what happened after that. Everything."

Frevisse could speak French and Alice knew it, but Queen Margaret had spoken in English, so she did, too, telling not all but enough about finding the dead man to draw murmurs and soft exclaims from the women. The queen had been disappointed to hear there was no blood because it had been washed away in the river, as if Frevisse had failed to give her something she wanted to have, and Frevisse had offered, "His doublet, though, was terribly stained with his blood. It was soaked through, all over his side." It had also been so darkened as to have been almost anything but she had not said so. Queen

Margaret had been too pleased at being horrified and afterward had made some slight talk with her about why she was at Bury St. Edmunds and promised to have her charter shortly sealed. "As soon as this present unpleasantness is done, you shall have it."

Frevisse had taken her chance then, saying with the same light eagerness as Queen Margaret had asked after the dead man's blood, "If it please your grace, there are so many things being said about the duke of Gloucester and how he is. What's the truth of it?"

Queen Margaret had thrown her hands up. "Pah! The duke of Gloucester. I shall like it when he's dead and we don't talk about him again. My Lady Alice, what did my lord of Buckingham say when he was here? When I had him tell me all?"

"He said there were many stories running but he had questioned people at St. Saviour's—from the servant who found Gloucester last night, to the doctor and priest who came to see him then, to the master himself and on down to scullions from the kitchen—and from all they said, it seems Gloucester simply slipped from sleep into his present deep senselessness. The bedclothes were smooth over him. There was no outcry nor any sign he had been distressed in any way."

"A blessing from merciful God." Queen Margaret had crossed herself and, while everyone around her did likewise, added, "You will have much to tell at your nunnery when you go home, madam, will you not?"

She had dismissed Frevisse to Alice's care after that and called one of her ladies to play at dice with her. Drawn aside with Alice, Frevisse had asked, "How likely is the duke of Buckingham's report to be true, rather than convenient?"

"Buckingham's best quality as a royal councillor is that he doesn't have the wit to be convenient. He's thorough at what he does and you can be certain he believes what he says. His report of Gloucester is as true as he can make it." Alice had paused before adding, "In other words, it's true so far as he sees anything."

For Arteys and Bishop Pecock, Frevisse told only what the queen had said about Gloucester and Alice's judgment of Buckingham, to which Bishop Pecock nodded agreement before asking, "But there was nothing about a man found dead in the duke of Gloucester's chamber?"

"Nothing." Frevisse hesitated before adding, "My cousin says Suffolk is badly unsettled over something other than Gloucester. She doesn't know what but it's grievous enough she's worried over his worry."

"Then, unless there are more troubles in hand than we have even glimmer of, very probably Suffolk's worry is about how the man sent to kill Gloucester came to be killed instead," said Bishop Pecock.

"Because it means someone else was there," Frevisse agreed. "That someone else knows Gloucester was meant to be murdered."

"And Suffolk does not know who it is or to whom this person may speak about it."

Fiercely Arteys put in, "It also means it was Suffolk who ordered my father's murder."

Bishop Pecock looked at him with kind sadness. "I'm afraid it does suggest that." He raised a warning hand. "Mind you, it doesn't prove. It may be that Suffolk knows who did order it and fears he will be involved if they are accused. Or he may not know at all why the man was there or anything else about him. The mere fact he was there and dead, without Suffolk knew why, would be troubling enough. There are always other possibilities to be considered in any matter."

"It was Suffolk," Arteys said. "Nobody else would dare."

With unwonted brevity, Bishop Pecock granted, "I fear so."

"What I wish," said Frevisse, "is that we knew for a certainty what happened when the man was found dead. Rather than raising an outcry, whoever found him either went to someone for instructions or else made decisions themselves. But someone had to have helped move the body, whatever was done with it then."

"The cart has been found," Bishop Pecock said. "Or *a* cart has been found with the hospital's badge painted on the side and much where Joliffe thought it would be if it had been used to the purpose we've supposed."

"That's good!" Arteys said.

"It's a small cart, meant for a single horse to pull. Runman pulled it himself back to St. Saviour's. He was given twopence reward for his trouble."

"No one wondered why a bishop's servant was troubling with a cart?" Frevisse asked.

"I didn't send him out wearing my livery or badge," Bishop Pecock said reproachfully. "Particularly since I told him to return the cart if he found it and was able to do so, and to find what would be said about it being gone, such as when and how long and so forth. It might have been a cart innocent of any wrong use, after all, merely gone astray."

"Was it?" Frevisse asked.

"Innocent? I think not. The steward at St. Saviour's complained at length about the business. The cart was indeed taken last night and by someone of the hospital itself, because there's no question but that the gates into St. Saviour's yard were properly barred this morning when someone went to unbar them for the day."

"Which means whoever took the cart returned to St.

Saviour's," Frevisse said, "and barred the gates after coming in."

"So it would seem."

"Unless it was someone who knew the same way in and out that I used," Arteys said. "They could have taken the cart out, gone back in, barred the gate, and gone around and out the way I did."

"Possibly," Bishop Pecock agreed. "But that begins to confuse the matter past any hope of solving it. I think we should hold to the hope that whoever saw to moving the body is someone who stayed at St. Saviour's last night."

He looked to Frevisse, who nodded agreement but said, "Which nonetheless solves nothing since we have no way to find them out."

"Yet," said Bishop Pecock.

"Did you see the duke of Gloucester as you purposed?" Frevisse asked.

"I did, with no trouble." He glanced at Arteys. "I told Arteys of him already but you'd like to hear, too?"

"If it please you, my lord." Lest she become so drawn into the tangle of questions and seeking out of answers that she forgot there was a yet-living man at the heart of it all.

"There's little to tell. He still sleeps and seems at ease in it. Or ease enough, though his breathing is labored. I prayed by him a goodly while and noted no change. He never stirred, save for his breathing."

"Everything else was as it should be? No sign of blood on the floor, so slight it could be overlooked if not looked for directly?" Frevisse asked.

"None. I made careful note of the floor beside the bed while I knelt there. Nor, curiously, was there even sign it had been particularly scrubbed within the day. The man must not have bled much." The bishop frowned slightly over that. "Given the wound, I should think he would have. Perhaps he fell face upward. Did he, Master Arteys?"

"He didn't. He . . ." Arteys stopped. "The floor? There was a carpet there. He fell on a carpet."

Bishop Pecock's look sharpened. "There was no carpet in the room. There were bare, albeit well-polished, floorboards. Nothing else."

"There was a carpet. Patterned in mostly red, with greens and cream."

"And he fell on it downward, bleeding, you say? Blood would be difficult to clean out of a carpet sufficient to their need of there being nothing suspicious in that room." He turned a look nigh to triumphant on Frevisse. "And the carpet that should be there is gone."

With equally rising hope, Frevisse asked, "How large was the carpet?"

"About three feet by five?" Arteys said uncertainly. "I'm not certain."

"But a large one, as such things go?" Frevisse asked.

"Yes."

"Not something to be merely thrown out," Bishop Pecock said, "because if found, there might be questions why something of such worth was cast away."

"Especially if it had a large bloodstain on it," Frevisse said dryly.

Bishop Pecock dismissed that briskly. "They would have scrubbed the blood away as much as might be, enough that it would serve elsewhere but not there, where they can afford no suspicions of any kind to arise."

"They could have carried it away with the body," Frevisse said. "On the cart."

"And thrown it in the river, too," Arteys said in despair. "Rolled and tied, it would sink."

"That wouldn't serve," Bishop Pecock protested. "It might still be found. That's not an idle river. It's constantly in use. A fishing line or some other thing might all too easily snag it, and a carpet in a river would be too suspicious a thing to be ignored, nor do I doubt but that Master Grene or someone else of St. Saviour's would be able to identify it if questions were asked widely enough."

"It had to disappear," Frevisse said, more to herself than either of them. "Burying wouldn't suit. It would take too much time and the digging would leave plain signs. Nor would burning it be possible. They had neither time nor place to do it. Not drown, bury, or burn. Hide in some way, then."

"Not in St. Saviour's," Bishop Pecock said. "Just getting the body out must have been difficult enough without then wandering about seeking somewhere to hide a carpet."

"Under the bed?" Arteys suggested. "For a while at least?"

"Possibly," Bishop Pecock granted, "but I think they were moving in hurried fear and would want anything that linked violence and the duke of Gloucester far apart from one another. If they were shifting the body out, why not take the carpet, too? But do what with it?"

"Sell it," said Frevisse. "Scrub the blood out as best they could, roll it up, take it with the body out of St. Saviour's, dispose of the body last night, and this morning someone take the carpet to a regrater who sells used goods."

"With a large wet spot still on it?" Arteys asked.

"It's the sort of thing that makes something into used goods, nor are some regraters known for asking close questions. I could make a tale right now that would satisfy. A displeased housewife wanting the thing out of her house for one furious reason or another and sending a servant to get rid of it, or—"

"Yes," Bishop Pecock said. "That would serve very well to be rid of the thing. Arteys, could you describe this carpet in some detail to Master Orle? He can go tomorrow morning to such shops as seem likely. It's too late today."

Indeed, the library was so in shadows that Dame Perpetua had no business still to be writing, though it seemed she was because the young monk was saying to her, "It's time to stop, Dame. I'm not instructed to allow lamps. It's nearly time for Vespers anyway."

"We are about to be discovered," Bishop Pecock said, sat down at the desk, raised a magisterial hand with pointing forefinger, and launched into, "But if you grant that this is true, then you must also see the difficulty in disobeying them . . ."

The young monk came into sight at the corner of the stall, hesitated, and finally said, "My lord?"

". . . though they are in error." Bishop Pecock broke off and asked, not unkindly, "Yes?" Then said, before the monk could answer, "Ah, the hour. Of course. We know your charge and will obey, brother." He stood up as if dismissing a class. "Until tomorrow, shall we say? About eleven of the clock? You raised an interesting point, dame, and I'd like to discuss it further." Adding to Arteys, as Frevisse made a slight, accepting curtsy to that, "Would you care to come to dinner with me, sir?"

Faintly, Arteys said he would and Bishop Pecock took him by the arm and walked him away. Hoping that meant Arteys was seen to for the night, Frevisse bent her head slightly to the monk and went to Dame Perpetua, just finished with tidying away her ink and pen, as the bells began to ring to Vespers.

Chapter 21

That night was too short on sleep for Frevisse. Not even able to toss and turn in bed because Dame Perpetua was sleeping soundly beside her, she lay staring into the dorter's darkness, listening to the even breathing and soft snoring of everyone around her, broken only by an occasional snort and shift of some sleeper, and wishing she was sleeping, too. She told her mind that although she could weave what facts she so far had into some sort of sense, nothing could be done with them until she knew more and therefore she might as well sleep as lie there pointlessly thinking. Not impressed, her thoughts went on, turning around and around on themselves, circling through worry for Alice, her life tied to Suffolk who very probably had ordered

233

murder, to curiosity at how Joliffe had come to be Bishop Beaufort's man, to worry at what would become of Arteys at the end of all of this. Come to that, what would become of all of them, including her? Because whatever they learned about the dead man and who had ordered Gloucester's death, there was almost surely nothing they would be able to do except live with the knowledge, and what good would that be to anyone?

Finally, aching with tiredness and the annoy of being here and part of it at all, she opened her eyes to the darkness and silently, defiantly told herself she was going to stay awake as long as she possibly could and not close her eyes while she did.

She shortly thereafter went deeply to sleep.

But her thoughts were waiting for her in the morning, like a patient dog waiting at his mistress' bedside. Distracted in them, she was up and dressed and adjusting her wimple around her face before she noted that the usual morning groans and murmurs of the other awakening and rising women were laced with laughter and gay talk so at variance with her own feelings that she almost asked Dame Perpetua why everyone was so happy out of the ordinary. Then she remembered and felt foolish and a little angry that with all that was happening she had let the knowing slip to a side part of her mind. It was Shrove Tuesday, with its burst of last great feasting and merriment before tomorrow when Lent began its fasting and penance through winter's end and spring's beginning to Easter.

Contrite at so grievous a neglect, she crossed herself and said aloud, remembering something else, "Confession. We have to make confession today."

Dame Perpetua, pinning on her veil, sighed. "Along with all the royal court and parliament. The lines will go on forever. I won't go far with Boethius today, I fear."

"Bishop Pecock," Frevisse said. "He means to be in the library again today. He might take our confessions."

Dame Perpetua brightened. "He might indeed. He's very kind."

Together, they pulled up and straightened the bedding, and were bent over, smoothing it, when Dame Perpetua said, low-voiced and not looking at her, "If you need me to know what's going on, I suppose you'll tell me. Please know I'll help. If I can. Even if it's only by going on pretending I don't know anything is going on."

Frevisse kept steadily at the bedmaking for a silent moment before saying, very quietly, "Thank you."

In that quiet they went to Prime. The church was fuller than usual for the dawn Office and murmurs ran that the king was present though Frevisse did not see him. For the while of Prime she kept her mind to the psalms and prayers, taking most deeply to her heart today, *"Et sit splendor Domini Dei nostri super nos . . . et opus manuum nostrarum dirige."* And let the brightness of our Lord God be over us . . . and guide the work of our hands. Because she was much in need of being guided.

At breakfast in the guesthall refectory there was laughter and talk and readiness all around for pleasure; and when she and Dame Perpetua went out of doors on their way back to the church for Mass, they caught through the gateway into the Great Court a brief view of the busy setting-up of food stalls and over the wall heard the rattle of a drum and happily roused voices already about the day's pastimes. Nor did everyone who left the guesthall turn toward the church for Mass.

Because the Mass—that sacred gathering of power where the Divine and Man met most closely together—was one of the great pleasures and treasure of her life,

Frevisse took her mind away from everything else, set herself to lose herself in its mystery and wonder, and succeeded. Only when the last prayer had risen toward the high roof and faded to silence did she stir, to find her body had weight, her mind had thoughts, and her heart wished it could go back into that wonder and away from here. But one of life's more unyielding lessons was that back was not possible. There was only forward, and all around her people were surging into talk and movement. Unused to crowds, Dame Perpetua moved to put her back against the wide base of the pillar beside her rather than be swept along. Frevisse joined her, willing to wait for the nave's emptying before trying to go anywhere else.

The question was, where should she go? To Alice, who would be taken up with whatever merrymaking was Queen Margaret's pleasure today? She hardly had excuse to do that. Nor was she minded to spend time with the holidaying crowds in the Great Court in the vastly unlikely hope of overhearing or seeing something useful. Better she actually *be* useful, while waiting to see if anything had been found out by Bishop Pecock, Arteys, or Joliffe.

When she and Dame Perpetua left the church and passed through the gateway into the Great Court, they found a loud, colorful array of food and ale stalls, foodsellers crying their wares of pies or cakes or roasted meat, jugglers, tumblers, bearwards, minstrels, games of chance, and a great many people openly set on having a good time among it all. Helping everyone's high spirits were the eased weather and mild sunshine though they were edged with a wind that flapped cloaks and women's veils and the canvas sides and roofs of the booths and snapped the many-colored pennons flying over some of them.

Dame Perpetua stopped, staring. She probably had not
seen the like since she became a nun even longer ago
than Frevisse had. In St. Frideswide's, Shrovetide was
nothing more than a day of ease and somewhat better
eating, and Frevisse asked, kindly, "Do you want to
wander awhile and look?"

"Oh, my," said Dame Perpetua; and then, "Oh, no. I
think I'd rather not."

"Not?" Frevisse asked, surprised.

"No." Dame Perpetua made a small move of her hands
at everything. "All these people and the noise and busyness and crowding. No, I don't like it. Unless you want
to stay awhile," she added.

"No," Frevisse answered. "I've no great urge to it."

"To the library and Boethius then?"

"To the library and Boethius."

"And please," said Dame Perpetua, "do you think we
could forgo at least Sext and Tierce today, instead of
coming back through all of this? We can pray at our
desks instead?"

"I think that would be well," Frevisse said and Dame
Perpetua sighed with relief.

The elderly monk was on duty again and traded no
words with them as they passed. Through the morning,
bursts of jollity were sometimes carried on the wind for
them to hear but never enough to disturb Frevisse's
copying once she was set to the work. Arteys had made
good progress yesterday; there was little left to do, and
interrupted only by praying the brief Offices allowed
when necessary, she was writing the book's final
words—". . . you work and do before the eye of the
judge that sees and knows all things."—when the monk
said, "Your grace," to someone coming in.

While she closed her ink, Bishop Pecock followed by
Arteys passed her without a word. When her pen was

clean, she left her desk and joined them in the last stall and was relieved to see that neither of them looked as if anything desperate had happened since yesterday. If anything, Bishop Pecock had something of the cat in the cream about him that made her ask instantly, with hope, "What is it?"

"Master Orle found the carpet. As we thought, it was sold as used goods."

"You're certain it's the same one?" Frevisse asked.

"Certain," said Arteys.

"Master Orle outdid himself, I think. We planned he was to say he wanted to buy a carpet but not one that had been sitting around forever, growing moldy. That way he would be shown only what had lately come in."

"There can't be that many carpets going used, can there?" Frevisse asked.

"Not ones worth having on one's floor, I should imagine, unless bought from needy heirs selling off an estate or suchlike. This shop had only the one, anyway, and just come in yesterday, the shopkeeper assured him. Master Orle said doubtfully he'd look at it, and when it was unrolled for him, he ran his hands all over it and found . . ." Bishop Pecock paused, beaming.

"A wet place as if something had been recently cleaned from it?" Frevisse said.

"Exactly so. I suspect that if we examine it deeply, we'll find blood still in the threads, blood not being something easily removed, especially by someone in haste. With it in hand, we can show, if nothing else, that something violent happened in the duke of Gloucester's bedchamber."

"Suffolk can claim that it was only a spill of blood from a basin when Gloucester was bled." A common way of balancing an ill man's humours.

"Gloucester has not been bled. That was among the

things that came out of my talk with Master Grene, who was unhappy about it."

Frevisse passed over the thought that a poor man in St. Saviour's hospital hall would have had more done for him than Gloucester had and said, "Now, more than ever, we need to know without doubt the body in the river is the man you killed, Arteys."

"And then?" Arteys asked bleakly. "If I accuse Suffolk, my word that the man was trying to kill my father will be set against Suffolk's protest that I'm lying. It won't be Suffolk who'll find the weight of law going against him then, that's sure."

"Before we come to that," Bishop Pecock said, "remember we don't know he was Suffolk's man. For all we're certain of, we may be aimed at the wrong lord. He might have been Dorset's man. Or Viscount Beaumont could have sent him, acting under orders from someone else."

"Or he could have been York's," Frevisse said.

Bishop Pecock's eyebrows rose. "Why his grace of York?"

"Why not? He has more wealth and more possibility of power than anyone in the kingdom except for the king himself."

Bishop Pecock shifted his eyebrows upward again and waited.

Frevisse listened over to what she had said, and said, "Oh."

Bishop Pecock nodded. "You see. He has wealth. He has power. He's close in blood to the king. Just like Gloucester, whom those about the king are in the process of destroying. Would you, if you had any wits at all about you and things being as they are, want to remove the one man there is between you and their attentions?"

"Rather than remove him, I'd keep very still, with my

back to the nearest wall, and hope nobody remembered I was alive."

Bishop Pecock beamed with approval. "You have it in full. And yet, because of his wealth and power and place, York must attend on the king, must show himself to the world, hopefully in such a way that lies and rumors against him won't stick, while dealing with men who would just as soon he were dead and he knows it. Not, on the whole, a goodly way to live."

"Suffolk," Arteys said bitterly. "It has to be Suffolk."

"He remains most likely, yes," Bishop Pecock granted. "The problem remains how do we find out beyond doubt. No one has come forward to name the dead man. In fact, he has somewhat disappeared. I was unable to learn where the body presently is and that is suspicious in itself."

"My cousin will know or can find out," Frevisse said. "She might help us put name to him, too."

"She'd help in this?" Arteys asked.

Frevisse hesitated over how much of Alice's fears to give away, before saying, "She's worried over what's been happening and angry at being told nothing by Suffolk. She wants the truth of it."

"Does she?" Bishop Pecock asked gently. "Or does she only think she does?"

"She's openly afraid of the truth but wants it anyway."

Bishop Pecock accepted that with a sober nod. "How would you proceed, then?"

"I'll tell her the dead man might be someone of her household and ask her to view the body and take me and Arteys with her when she does."

"She may know me," Arteys said.

"That shouldn't matter," Frevisse replied. "No more moves have been made against any of Gloucester's men, no orders for arrests or anything. There's no reason she can't have dealings with you. If the dead man was in Suffolk's employ, she may well know him. If nothing else, you'll have chance to see him."

"If he is the man I killed, what can we do with the knowing?"

"I don't know," Frevisse said with level honesty.

"But knowledge is ever a better weapon to wield than ignorance," Bishop Pecock offered, "having the sharper edge and therefore able to cut more deeply to the heart of things."

"A weapon has to hit your foe to have effect," Frevisse returned. "We're hardly close to hitting Suffolk. Or anyone else."

"A point well made. But even with weapon in hand, a warrior can only advance step by step toward the battle." He laid a hand on Arteys' shoulder. "We have our weapon and are taking our steps. When can you speak with your cousin?"

Chapter 22

An abbey bell began to call for some Office. Arteys realized he did not know which one, the past few days had become so disjointed, but Dame Frevisse stood still a moment, her head raised to the sound, before she gave herself a small shake and said, "Abbot Babington is feasting the king and some of the royal court today, with the players' farce to come at its end. Lady Alice will be with the queen now and then at the abbot's feast. At its end will be my soonest chance to reach her."

"Haste may make waste," Bishop Pecock said. "This might better be done later, rather than in the midst of everything today."

"The longer we wait, the more chance there is we'll lose the chance altogether."

"Too true," he granted. "Arteys, best you wait here until Dame Frevisse sends for you then."

"No." Arteys had had enough of waiting these past days to last him the rest of his life. "I'll go with her."

"You risk being seen and known," Bishop Pecock warned.

"She said the sooner done the better. Besides, who would she send for me?"

"Points well taken." Though Bishop Pecock looked as if he would rather not take them.

The other nun appeared at the stall's open end, gave them all a quick look, but asked of Dame Frevisse, "Nones?"

"Dame Perpetua." Dame Frevisse sounded as if she had forgotten her, then said, "Bishop Pecock, we wondered if you'd hear our confessions."

Confession. Arteys had not been thinking of this as Shrove Tuesday but, yes, he wanted confession, to purge his soul and be given penance for his sins before Lent began, and maybe Bishop Pecock, looking at him just then, saw that in his face because his momentary hesitation at Dame Frevisse's request went away and he said, "Of course. If you wish it. And here is as good a confessional as any."

He heard Dame Perpetua first, then Dame Frevisse, while Arteys waited, seated at one of the tables, gathering up his sins, as it were, to have them ready. When his turn came, he went willingly to kneel in front of Bishop Pecock seated at his desk, put his hands between the bishop's, and with bowed head and closed eyes said the ritual words, "Forgive me, Father, for I have sinned."

He first confessed things that, four days ago, would

have seemed heavy to him—that since he last confessed he had fallen into anger, been sometimes slothful at his duties, once been envious, once been gluttonous over candied ginger . . .

He trailed to silence.

Bishop Pecock waited a moment, then asked, "And?", knowing as well as Arteys did what else there was to say.

Softly Arteys said, "I killed a man."

"Of purpose and in anger?"

"Of purpose. But not in anger." Arteys stopped. Could that be right? Slowly, working his way through the thought, he said, "There wasn't time for anger. I wanted to stop him, that was all."

"Tell me about it."

Arteys almost said, "I already did." But Bishop Pecock was plainly not one of those priests who simply took a confession as it came and gave penance by rote. He was one of those who probed, wanting to know what the sinner understood about his sin, the better to help him clear his soul, and with head still lowered and eyes still shut, Arteys obediently told the killing over again, careful at the words, wanting them right both in his head and aloud.

When he had finished, Bishop Pecock asked very gently, "Is the pain lessened?"

Arteys held silent a moment before raising his head to look at the bishop's quiet face. "Yes. That's wrong of me, isn't it?"

"No. That's right of you. The purpose of penance is to heal, not to keep the soul's wounds open."

"I haven't done penance yet."

"Did you enjoy telling me how you killed him?"

"*No.*"

"Nor did I think you would. The telling was a penance

in itself, then. And each telling puts more words between
you and the act, setting it further off from you.
Therefore, your telling served both as penance and a
beginning of healing."

"I'll never be healed." He hadn't let himself know that
fear until now.

"Not of the knowledge of what you did, no, but of its
weight on your soul, yes." Bishop Pecock laid a hand
on the top of Arteys' head. "Remember that. Confession
and penance are to free you from guilt's weight, lest the
burden bear you down and twist you from your rightful
shape. Now, for the rest of your penance."

Afterward, feeling raw inside but cleaner, Arteys left
the library with Dame Frevisse. He thought that, as always, life would soon sully him again but for this little
while, whatever happened next, he was cleansed and
lightened and he held to that feeling as they came out
of the passageway's cool half-darkness into the windy
sunlight and happily noisy crowd filling the Great Court.
The King's Hall was only a little aside from there along
the walk, its doorway flanked by half a dozen guards,
some of them in Suffolk's livery. Silent until then, Dame
Frevisse said, "Wait here," went, and spoke to one of
the guards just as trumpets sang out from inside the hall,
only a little muted by stone walls.

She returned to say, "They're beginning the second
remove already. There'll be a third remove and then Joliffe's farce before they're done. What about our own
dinner in the meanwhile? We should eat at least one
pancake today, shouldn't we?"

She tried a smile that looked as stiff as Arteys' own
face felt as he tried a smile back to her. Too many things
were twisted together inside him, and in her, too, he
guessed, for easy smiling. But pancakes were a tradition
on Shrove Tuesday, a way to use up the fats and eggs

forbidden during Lent, and he said, "We should."

Among the foodsellers in the Great Court there were choices of pancakes a-plenty. Pan-cooked and soft; fat-fried and crisp; thin; thick; plain battered or dyed green or red or saffron; alone or wrapped around spiced meat. Dame Frevisse chose and bought, and with a warm, meat-filled pancake in his hand, Arteys found he was hungry. They walked together through the crowd and booths and merriment while they ate and even stopped awhile among all else there was to see to watch a man beating a small drum slung from his belt while piping on a triple whistle and dancing for a delighted knot of children. Dame Frevisse dropped a coin into his waiting cap when they moved on toward a stall selling crisp cakes.

"Let me pay this," said Arteys.

"Let Bishop Beaufort. This is his money I'm using."

Arteys liked that thought enough that he let her, and her smile and his were slightly easier as she handed him one of the thin cakes, saying as they walked on, "It's surprising the weight that the small, good things of life have against life's great troubles."

That was true, Arteys found as he thought about it. He had been—he was—heart-deep afraid through these past several days but now, because he was out in a merry crowd and sunlight and was eating a crisp cake that tasted good, he could remember—and almost feel— what easy happiness was like.

But they came back finally to the King's Hall, where an outburst of laughter from inside brought Dame Frevisse to say, "The play is on. I'd best go in, to be ready when it ends. Wait here."

He wanted to. He also wanted, almost as much, to walk away from it all, to leave and pretend there was nothing he could hope to do. But he owed his father better than that, owed Suffolk more than that, and said, clenching silence around his fear, "I'd rather go in. I want to see them." Suffolk and the lords who were making all this happen.

Dame Frevisse gave a long look into his face before saying, "Come then."

Because the guards in Suffolk's livery both knew her, she was let in without trouble, and because Arteys was with her, so was he. Inside, the wide doorway from the screens passage into the great hall was crowded with servants watching whatever was happening in the hall and laughing aloud. Damc Frevisse moved through them with a firmly murmured, "Clear, please. Clear," and they did, both for her and for Arteys at her heels, but once into the hall, there was no going onward. With tables, trestles, and benches removed, the whole middle length of the hall had been given over to the players, everyone else drawn back to stand along the walls save at the far end where King Henry, Queen Margaret, Abbot Babington, Suffolk, Lady Alice, York, Buckingham, Dorset, several high churchmen, and other lords and ladies were seated on the dais. The best Dame Frevisse could do was ease sideways along the wall just inside the doorway, making a small place for herself and Arteys to stand.

He had no way to tell what the play was about, except there seemed to be several pairs of husbands and wives in improbably colorful peasant garments, apparently hilariously quarreling with each other. It took him a few moments to find out Joliffe, looking particularly strange in a tattered yellow and green tunic, his hair greased to stand out from his head. He was paired with a big-bosomed, large-bottomed, loud-voiced woman whom Arteys only barely recognized as the young man who had been Lady Soul, while the man who had been Wisdom was to one side, rat-tatting madly on a drum whenever some wilder moment of the play needed it.

Whatever was going on, their audience was almost helpless with laughter, and Arteys' anger that these past days had been almost all at Suffolk jerked sickeningly in him as he watched King Henry wiping laughter-tears away. How could he sit there laughing, no sign of grief about him at all? How could he leave Gloucester to die without a word, without anything, even the comfort of his own people around him? For Suffolk, Gloucester had never been anything to him except someone in his way. But how could King Henry truly believe Gloucester had turned traitor to him after all this time and be so cold about it?

If, in that moment, Arteys had had to choose between his blood-cousin the king and the hound Gelert back in Wales, it would not have been King Henry he chose.

The play ended with a rat-tatting of the drum and the players mock-fighting at each other for better places as they made a line below the dais, their deep bows marred by elbows jerking sideways into other people's rib and elbows jerking back, all while they tried to keep a most earnest dignity. Laughing hard, King Henry motioned one of the squires standing attendance behind him to take a small purse to Master Wilde, who stepped forward and received it with a bow so low his head nearly touched the floor. Queen Margaret, wiping her eyes with one hand, pointed one of her waiting ladies to give a like purse to Joliffe, who made great show of being too weak in the knees with shyness to step forward until rudely pushed by his fellows on either side. He matched Master Wilde's bow but stumbled over his own feet when he made to step back to his place so that he lurched against the player next to him, who gave him a hard push into the man on Joliffe's other side, who shoved back as Joliffe shoved the first man, then turned to shove him, the whole line instantly in chaos and the players making a running retreat down the hall in a flurry of colors and noise and the onlookers' laughing and clapping, the servants parting to let them into the screens passage and away.

Low in Arteys' ear, Dame Frevisse said, "I'm going to try to reach Lady Alice now. Go to the dark end of the screens passage and wait for me."

The crowd was spreading out across the hall and servants were bringing trays of drinks and sweets to serve to the king and queen and others on the dais, everyone still loud with pleasure from the play. Arteys had no trouble slipping out and to the passage's far end from the door, taking with him the sudden hurt that this was how today would have been for Gloucester, for him, for all of them—an ordinary holiday among ordinary other days—except Suffolk had darkly twisted everything out of shape and out of hope.

A few people were leaving the hall, most going the other way from where he stood but not many past him to the stairs, mostly servants and no one particularly noting him standing very still in a corner until Dame Frevisse came out of the hall, Lady Alice with her, one of her ladies following. Lady Alice bade the woman stop before they reached him, came on with Dame Frevisse, and said as he made a low bow to her, "Arteys. I remember you. You came sometimes with your father to court. I'm sorry beyond measure for all that's happening."

Her warm voice and courtesy confused him. "Yes, my lady," he said, making himself think of her as Dame Frevisse's cousin, not Suffolk's wife.

"Dame Frevisse wants me to view this dead man, to see if maybe I know him. You want to go with me, I gather, to see him, too. Yes?"

"Yes, my lady."

"That's all she's told me and I gather she would rather I didn't ask more, so I won't. There's something I'd ask of you, though. Ask me yourself, in your own words, for my help in seeing this man. Then, if there's trouble about it later, I can honestly say you asked me and maybe not have to bring Dame Frevisse into it."

"Alice?" Dame Frevisse asked, openly surprised.

Lady Alice looked at her. "I'm afraid. I've told you that. Nothing feels safe anymore. I'm not putting you at risk if I can help it." She looked to Arteys again. "Sir?"

"My lady, will it please you to help me have sight of the man who was found dead in the river?" he asked.

Lady Alice granted that with a gracious inclination of her head. "Now ask Dame Frevisse to speak to me on your behalf. That way, if she's brought into it after all, I can say you asked for her help in speaking to me and that, so far as I know, that's her only part in this. Because, so far as I know, it is her only part."

"Alice, if you think this is all that unsafe—" Dame Frevisse began.

"Dame Frevisse," Arteys said before she could say more, "would you aid me to speak to your cousin, Lady Alice of Suffolk?"

Her mouth a tight-shut line, Dame Frevisse nodded that she would. "Thank you," said Lady Alice. "Now all we need do is find where this body is." She beckoned her waiting lady to her. The woman came readily, making a curtsy to Lady Alice and Dame Frevisse while giving a slight smile and upward look through her lashes at Arteys. "He's comely, yes," Lady Alice said crisply, "but leave off your looking for now, Madelayn. This dead man who was found in the river. I've heard you and the others talking about it. Has anyone named him yet?"

"No, my lady. Rafe says no one has even been able to see him since he was brought up from the river."

"Not even a priest?"

"He's been prayed over, I suppose, surely," Madelayn said. "But he's not in church or chapel or anything like that, you see."

"Where is he then?"

"In the prior's garden, my lady."

"In the prior's garden? Your Rafe has been telling you stories."

"No," the woman protested. "There's a shed there. The body was put in there."

"Why in a shed in the prior's garden?" Lady Alice demanded.

Madelayn looked doubtful. "To have it out of the way while the holidaying goes on?" She brightened a little. "But it's to be moved. Rafe had the dawn watch on it this morning and says there's talk it's going to be."

Guard on a dead body? Arteys wondered, while Lady Alice asked, "Where's this garden?"

"I know it," Dame Frevisse said. "If it's walled and on the other side of the prior's courtyard from the library."

"That's it," said Madelayn.

"Good," said Lady Alice. She gathered her full skirts forward from where they trailed behind her, draped them over her arm, and started for the outer door.

"My lady, you'll need a cloak," Madelayn protested.

"Have mine," said Arteys, beginning to unclasp it.

"Thank you. Madelayn, fetch me my own from wherever it is and bring it after me."

The woman made quick curtsy and hurried away. Arteys laid his cloak around Lady Alice's fashionably bare shoulders and moved ahead to clear the way for her and Dame Frevisse. Outside, they turned along the walkway, not making open haste but moving quickly to the passageway through to the abbot's garden.

"You'll be missed from the hall," Dame Frevisse said.

"Waiting on the queen does not excuse one from bodily needs. If we do this quickly, no one will ask where I've been," Lady Alice answered. "And quickly is how we want to do this, I think?"

In the abbot's garden the sounds of the fair were distant beyond the buildings and there were few people to be seen. The prior's courtyard was empty of anyone and even quieter. Only at the gateway through the head-high wall around the prior's garden were they able to see the lone man in plain brown doublet and hosen sitting on a bench beside the door to a shed in the far corner, his head back against the wall, his legs stretched out in front of him, an axe-headed halberd leaning against the wall beside him. Arteys tried the gate but the latch did not lift and the man on the bench stood up, fumbling up his halberd as he called, "No one's to come in. Go away."

Arteys stepped aside, giving way to Lady Alice, who moved forward and said back, "Simmon, I'm coming in. Open this gate."

Simmon's pause was barely there before he leaned the halberd against the wall again and came hurrying. The garden was small—four squared plots with paths between and turf benches along the walls. The guard had the gate open in hardly a moment, trying to explain something, but Lady Alice swept past him toward the trellised shed, saying, "We've come to see the body found in the river."

Left with the choice of hurrying ahead of her to open the door, or not, Simmon chose to hurry and grabbed it out of her way barely before she would have had to stop or walk into it. As it was, Lady Alice stopped and ordered, "Go in and open the shutter. It's too dark to see anything. Why is the body here instead of a chapel or the church? Do you know?"

"I don't know anything, my lady," the guard said, scurrying inside to unlatch and push aside the one window's shutter. "I wasn't told anything but not to let anyone in. That's all I was told."

"Why aren't you in livery?"

"I was told not to be, my lady."

"Then you were told two things. What about a priest? This man died badly. Has there been a priest to pray by him?"

"I don't know." Desperate to know something, he said, "I was told there'd be a cart come to take him away this afternoon."

"To where?"

"I . . . I don't know, my lady."

She flicked a hand at him, wordlessly bidding him to come out and go aside. He did and she went in, followed by Dame Frevisse and Arteys, last. The shed was low-roofed and narrow but cleanly kept, the gardener's tools hung up or sitting orderly against the walls. In the room's middle, the dead man was laid out, wrapped in a length of rough canvas, on boards held up on two trestles.

"Not even a proper shroud," Lady Alice said. Despite her voice was low and even, her anger showed.

Dame Frevisse went forward, found a loose edge of the canvas, and pulled back a fold to uncover the man's face. "This is who we found, yes," she said quietly and stepped aside for Arteys to have clear look at him.

Arteys went closer. He had seen the man's face only in the instant of killing him but, with one brief look, knew him again beyond any doubt.

"Arteys?" Dame Frevisse asked.

He stepped back, swallowing hard. "It's him."

"Lady Alice?" she asked.

Not needing to come closer, her voice cold, Lady Alice said, "He's Edward Griggs. He's . . . he was one of our yeoman of the hall." Meaning he had been immediate and in the middle of Suffolk's household, known to any number of people. "Now I'm going to have to find out why he's lying here unacknowledged and all but abandoned."

She did not sound as if she expected she would like the answer.

Arteys turned, went out of the shed, and stood staring at the garden's quietness until Dame Frevisse and Lady Alice joined him a moment later. Dame Frevisse stopped beside him, briefly touched his arm. He looked at her and, to her silent asking how he was, made a bleak half-smile and shrugged one shoulder, helpless to find words. He had thought to feel more—horror perhaps, or sick shame, or even a deepening of his guilt despite of Bishop Pecock, but he seemed to feel nothing much at all, and that, in its way, was worse.

They left the garden, Simmons shutting and locking the gate behind them, and were midway across the courtyard when Lady Alice's lady-in-waiting came hurriedly around the corner of the library with Lady Alice's fur-lined cloak in her arms. Arteys took back his cloak and Lady Alice put on her own and around the same corner of the library Suffolk came into sight, two squires behind him.

If he was there by chance, it was a bad chance. Or it was maybe not chance at all; Arteys saw Lady Alice give one hard glance at her woman before she asked, bright-voiced, "My lord, what do you here?"

"I came seeking you, my lady," he said. His voice was light but he was looking past her, straight at Arteys who, looking straight back at him, saw recognition harden in his eyes and his brows begin to draw down into a scowl of displeasure.

Rather than wait to see what Suffolk would decide to do with his displeasure, Arteys took a step close to Dame Frevisse, said, "Thank you, my lady," made a short, sharp bow to her and Lady Alice both, and before anyone could speak to him, swung around and made at a long-strided walk for a roofed passageway running from the courtyard into the cloister buildings.

The back of his neck was crawling with expectation Suffolk would call him back or send the two squires after him but he reached the passage's far end and turned the corner rightward, deeper into the cloister, without either happening, and once out of sight he walked faster. He did not know where he was going. Out of the cloister, into the confusion in the Great Court, out of the abbey, into Bury. That far he could see but not farther, except he knew he would not go back to Bishop Pecock. Nor to Joliffe. Nor to Dame Frevisse. Suffolk had seen him, there of all places, and recognized him. Lady Alice's carefully prepared excuse would keep her and Dame Frevisse clear but Suffolk would ask why he had been there and Lady Alice would tell him and Suffolk would guess more. How many reasons could there be for wanting to see the man who had been killed instead of Gloucester?

So no going to anyone for help anymore.

What he would do instead, he didn't know.

Chapter 23

uffolk turned from frowning after Arteys, but before he could begin another question, Alice said, "I'll see you later, Dame Frevisse. Yes?"

"Of course, my lady," Frevisse said, quickly made a courtesy toward Suffolk sufficient to satisfy him of her humility, and went away across the yard opposite from where Arteys had gone, to the library. Once out of sight, she went up the stairs as if going to sanctuary, wishing she was, but at least it was quiet and somewhere to think. More than thinking, she needed to find Bishop Pecock and Joliffe, or have them find her.

The young monk was on duty at the door and openly unhappy about it, giving her a look that said it was her fault. Dame Perpetua gave better welcome, looked up smiling from her copying to whisper, "I've nearly finished." She laid a hand on a pile of papers beside her. "Here's what you and the young man did. I hope you don't mind I brought it here."

Frevisse assured her she did not and went on along the desks, hoping Bishop Pecock might be in his study stall, but he was not and Frevisse sat down at his desk and found she was trembling—not outwardly but with a fine inward shuddering. Finding for certain how twisted a way Suffolk was moving against Gloucester had unsteadied her more than she had expected. Then to come face to face with Suffolk himself . . . that had not been good. Alice might well convince him that she and Frevisse were innocent of anything but everything would show Arteys was not.

Elbows on desk and face in hands, she sat long enough to steady herself. Suffolk and Alice should have left the yard by now, she supposed, and although she was still unsure what she would do, she could sit no longer, rose, and left the library, only to find Joliffe coming up the stairs. He was in his own clothes, his hair sleek from washing out whatever had been in it and looking so much himself after so lately looking so completely someone else that she said, unguarded with relief, "You did better by Lydgate's play than I would have thought possible. You were excellently the fool."

"You saw it?" Joliffe seemed far more pleased at that than Frevisse would have expected had she thought about it.

"Arteys and I were both there for the last part."

"Is he here? And Bishop Pecock?"

"Neither of them. I don't know where Bishop Pecock is. Arteys . . ." She found she was not as steady as she had hoped she was. She paused to draw breath, made sure of her voice, and told Joliffe what they had found out and what had happened.

"That's bad," said Joliffe at the end. "Every way, it's bad. We can be all but certain Suffolk gave the order for Gloucester to be murdered and now he'll be suspecting it was Arteys killed his man."

"And that therefore Arteys knows about the intended murder," Frevisse said. "Worse is that there's nothing we can do against Suffolk, even though we know."

"That's worse, yes, but worst will be if Suffolk decides to move against Arteys. Will you stay while I go look for him? One of us should be here if he or our good bishop comes, and I can look farther and more quickly than you can."

Because that was all true, Frevisse said, "I'll stay," despite she wanted to *do* something more than that, watched Joliffe leave, and went back to the library. She did not offer Dame Perpetua more help, doubting the worth of anything she might try to do just now, but brought Aelred of Rievaulx's *Speculum Caritatis* she had noted another day to a table from where she could see the door and tried to read. Unfortunately she was more aware of the sunlight's shifting slant through the high windows, telling the afternoon was slipping away, than she was of holy Aelred and her last pretense of patience was nearly gone when Joliffe appeared briefly in the doorway, saw her see him, and slipped out of sight again.

Frevisse closed the book, left it lying, and went out, to find Joliffe waiting at the stairfoot. Judging by his face, she did not want to hear what he was going to say but asked at him sharply anyway, "Did you find them?"

"Not Arteys. I'd just found Bishop Pecock, was telling him about Arteys, when someone from St. Saviour's came for him, said he was wanted to give the duke of Gloucester last rites, and took him away."

Frevisse made the sign of the cross for Gloucester's soul even as she asked, "Why Bishop Pecock? There are bishops in plenty in Bury St. Edmunds just now."

"I'd guess because somebody felt more than a plain priest should be there for a duke's dying and that Pecock is so minor a bishop and not known to be on one side or another that he was 'safe' to go, that he'll be believed if he says there's no wrong in Gloucester's death."

"The lords know how this all looks, then?"

"If they're listening, they've heard what people are starting to say and it's not to their favor. They don't care—or Suffolk doesn't—so long as they're rid of Gloucester."

"What's going to happen to Arteys when his father's dead?"

"I don't know. Will you still stay here longer?"

"Until Vespers."

Joliffe accepted that with a curt nod. "If he does come, tell him to go to my place and wait for me. Just wait, not do anything. If I find him . . . You'll be where you were before in the church?"

"Yes."

"I'll come there after Vespers, to tell you how things are, whichever way."

Left to wait again as best she could, Frevisse returned to Aelred of Rievaulx, found him no more comforting company than he had been but did not bother to find something else because nothing would be any better, her mind taken up with uneasy awareness that soon, if not already, the duke of Gloucester would draw his last breath, alone among enemies. It was a bitter end for anybody, and if the thought of it hurt her, how much worse it must be for Arteys?

But when Gloucester was done with earthly troubles, Arteys wouldn't be.

Nor would Alice.

What had passed between her and Suffolk? She had answers ready for his questions, but would she ask questions of her own or ask him nothing, questions being useless when she would not trust his answers?

Frevisse welcomed the bells' calling to Vespers. This being Lent's eve, there was a greater gathering of people in the church and she and Dame Perpetua had to thread their way among them to St. Nicholas's chapel, glad of its quiet when they reached it and, almost, Frevisse was able to give herself up to the Office's prayers and psalms but today she heard more deeply than usual their grief. *Domine, miserere nostri . . . multum satiati est anima nostra irrisione abundantium, despectione superborum.* Lord, pity us . . . our souls are glutted with the mockery of the rich, with the contempt of the proud.

Joliffe was not there when the Office ended and she asked Dame Perpetua, "I need to wait here awhile. Will you stay? And please, no questions?"

"Of course," Dame Perpetua agreed mildly and sat down on the low stone bench along the wall. Frevisse joined her, listening to the throb of voices and shuffle of feet over stone as the crowd of other worshipers left the church, going out to whatever feasting and pleasures they could cram into the few hours before midnight. The church had nearly emptied, was falling silent, before Joliffe came, and as Frevisse moved to meet him, away from Dame Perpetua, she knew that whatever news he brought was bad.

"Gloucester's dead?" she asked, low-voiced.

What she did not know was that he was angry until he said, "I don't know." So furious he could hardly say the words. "It's Arteys. He's been arrested. Arteys and, from what I saw, everyone else who came with Gloucester."

"You're certain?" she asked, wanting him to deny it.

"I saw it. I'd finally found him. Had seen him anyway. He was ahead of me along a street and it looked like he'd met up with someone he knew, another of Gloucester's men. While I was going toward him, they went into a tavern there. I followed them in, was making my way toward him, when half a dozen men with the king's badge crowded through the door and one big-mouth ordered everybody to stand and line up along the walls. Then he demanded if any of them were the duke of Gloucester's men and Arteys and three others stepped forward. Not that it would have been any use to not. Everyone who didn't step forward was asked who they were, and if they answered with a Welsh flavor to their words, into the bag they went."

"Arteys doesn't sound Welsh."

"No, but it wouldn't have mattered with him. Hell's foul breath, they had someone with them who looked at everyone, and when he came to Arteys, he gave him a hard, long look, pulled him forward, and said, 'This is the one. Keep him and this man with him apart from the rest.' "

Frevisse drew a sharp breath. "They were looking for him."

"They were, and there wasn't a damned or undamned thing I could do to help. Worse, as they were being herded out, he saw me and all I could do was look back at him and do nothing. *Nothing.*"

"He saw you?"

"He saw me, and oh, my lady, he was afraid. He knew what trouble he's surely in and he was afraid."

"It's my doing. It's because Suffolk saw him."

"Probably," Joliffe agreed uncomfortingly. "Saw him,

found out he knew about the dead man, and not knowing how much or how little Arteys knows, he's settled for supposing he knows too much and means to shut him up."

Frevisse stepped back from him. "You shouldn't be talking to me. Even if Arteys keeps silent about where he's been, Suffolk saw him with me. If you're seen with me, Suffolk could turn on you next."

"Too true, unless your cousin convinced him you and she were innocent in this."

"How do I undo this? What am I going to do?"

"You're going to do nothing except go back to your nunnery," Joliffe said. "As soon as possible."

"I can't just leave, not after making this trouble."

"You didn't make it. Suffolk made it. We have to keep him from making more. And by we, I mean myself, Bishop Beaufort, and even Bishop Pecock if he chooses. Not you."

"Or you either, Master Joliffe, if I may say so," Bishop Pecock said from the chapel's open end.

Both Joliffe and Frevisse startled, and Joliffe started, "I—"

"You," said Bishop Pecock sternly, "forgot to watch your back or you'd have seen me here." He entered the chapel, making his bow to the altar while saying, "I, on the other hand, have left Master Orle outside with instruction to cough if anyone at all approaches into hearing."

Dame Perpetua, forgotten and silent until then, stood up from the bench. "I'll join him, if I may. All this is something I shouldn't hear, isn't it?"

"Very probably, yes," Bishop Pecock granted before either Frevisse or Joliffe could. "And Master Orle will welcome your company." He and Joliffe bowed her away before he turned back to Joliffe and said, "Now, it's advisable you remove yourself from this matter because you are far more easily assailed than is Dame Frevisse. If Suffolk should learn of your help to Arteys and decide to deal with you, it would probably be done and over with before Bishop Beaufort could move to save you. Of the three of us, I not only have the most power to act but, as a bishop, am the least easily assailed should things go wrong."

"Remember Becket," said Joliffe. An archbishop of Canterbury murdered on a king's orders three hundred years ago.

"Saint Thomas Becket was a great and holy man who worked long and hard to have his martyrdom. My ambitions do not lie that way. I'm merely being practical. I am better placed than either of you to go against Suffolk. Why make it harder by getting either of you into trouble if you need not?"

"But if you do fall into trouble," Frevisse said, "you can't disappear as Joliffe and I can."

"Being a bishop, I don't need to disappear, merely withdraw with dignity to my bishopric. Besides, I don't see anything any of us can do at present anyway. Myself or either of you."

"You could tell the king that Suffolk ordered the duke of Gloucester's murder," Joliffe said.

"With what proof?"

"Arteys. He saw the man you found in the river. He says it's the man he killed."

"Which will serve to get Arteys into deep trouble and prove nothing against Suffolk, who can deny any knowledge of it. Which, for all we know, may be true."

Joliffe threw up his hands impatiently. "Yes. I know. There's no proof."

"And rather than make things worse for Arteys," Frevisse said slowly, "you advise we wait quietly for . . . what?"

"For what comes. For what I may find out. For whatever mistake Suffolk may make or someone else may make on his behalf. We wait to see what happens and do the best with it we can. For one thing, I doubt these treason charges against Gloucester's men will ever come to anything, not now that Gloucester is dead, God keep his soul."

He said that sadly and crossed himself. Frevisse and Joliffe copied him but Joliffe asked while he did, "When?"

"About three of the clock this afternoon. Not long after I reached him."

"It was a quiet death?"

"As deaths go, yes."

"No sign of poison or anything else amiss?"

"Nothing."

Not that that proved anything, Frevisse thought. Poisoning could be done with sufficient subtlety to leave no sign. But even Bishop Pecock forebore to point that out in the long moment they stood silent, before Joliffe said heavily, "You're in the right. Everything being as it is, the best we can do is wait."

"But will you?" Bishop Pecock asked.

He and Joliffe exchanged a long, mutually assessing look before Joliffe bent his head slightly toward him and said with only faint mockery, "I will."

"Until we find something we can do usefully, rather than foolishly," Bishop Pecock said.

Joliffe bent his head again. "Until then."

The pity was, Frevisse thought, that waiting would likely be, of almost all things, the hardest.

*   *   *

She found out all too soon how hard it was. A message sent that evening to Alice, asking to see her, brought no answer, leaving her to a night restless with circling thoughts and too little sleep. In the morning the church draped in the mourning purples of Ash Wednesday and the beginning of Lent did nothing to help. Even the weather was gone gray again. The only comfort was that the air still had a mild edge, giving hope for spring; and at the end of Prime one of Alice's ladies found her, to say Alice would see her in the Lady Chapel after Mass if Frevisse would be so good. Frevisse sent back her thanks and word that she would be there.

It was by force of will that Frevisse held her mind to the Mass but, after it, parted from Dame Perpetua with a willingness she hoped did not show and crossed the church to the north transept and the Lady Chapel. It was newer than most of the church, all pale stone and painted statues below tall windows and a blue-painted, golden-ribbed ceiling, with a carpet woven mostly in the Virgin Mary's blues on the altar steps.

Knowing she would fail, Frevisse did not try to pray but simply waited until soon—not soon enough—Alice came. Gowned in deep purple except for the wide curve of her high, gold-and-pearl-trimmed headdress and the pale gray yards of fine silk trailing from it, she left a gray-gowned lady-in-waiting behind her at the doorway and came, the long train of her gown whispering across the chapel's tiled floor, to where Frevisse waited. Without greeting, she held out two folded pieces of parchment, each with a large red wax seal hung from it by a ribbon and said, "Your deed. Confirmed and sealed with the king's own signet. You should have no trouble with it. And a grant from the queen after I reminded her of her promise to you. A small property of her own to St. Frideswide's."

Both taken aback with surprise and greatly pleased, Frevisse took the parchments, thanking Alice and asking that she thank the queen, too, on the priory's behalf.

Alice waved that aside, saying bitterly, "What she gave you cost her nothing but a clerk's effort and some ink, paper, and wax. She's hardly had the property in her hands to know she's given it away. It's come from what they started grabbing from Gloucester before he was even dead and they'll be taking more." The bitterness deepened. "It's like watching carrion crows on a corpse."

"Alice . . ."

"There's a jest running among them, too, that yet again Gloucester has taken the easy way out of trouble. 'Took it lying down, too,' that idiot Bart Halley said and they all laughed. King Henry has even ordered there's to be no mourning. What's the matter with him? With them all?"

"What happened yesterday after I left you?"

"Yesterday." Alice circled back through her thoughts as if going a long way and said no less bitterly, "I told Suffolk the 'truth' we'd prepared of how we came to there. I said I knew no more than you did why Gloucester's son wanted to see the body. That's true, you know. You must know something about it but I know nothing and therefore know 'no more' than you do. Though Suffolk didn't hear it that way nor did I mean him to. Then I asked him why, since the dead man was one of our people, he hadn't been seen to properly. Suffolk laid his hand on my shoulder and told me it wasn't something I need concern myself about." Darkly, she added, "He's going to do that once too often."

And when he did, he was going to be sorry, Frevisse thought, but she only asked, "Did he say why he'd kept the man unknown?"

Alice's voice and face closed over some hurt so inward that it was past anger. "He didn't. Even when I asked. He didn't say anything at all. He just walked away."

"You know Gloucester's men are all being arrested?"

"Yes. Has Arteys been taken, do you know?"

"He was among the first, I think," Frevisse said quietly. "Can you find out what's to be done with him, with them?"

"From what I hear, they're being sent to a number of places, to be held until matters are 'sorted out.' I think Suffolk and the others are using them to show there was reason for Gloucester's arrest. They'll be held a time, then they'll be freed. There won't be a trial or even investigation worth the name."

"There won't be?"

"How could they risk something that might show there was no treason? There wasn't, was there? So they won't dare bring any of them to trial."

That made good sense. Frevisse wished she believed that Suffolk had good sense, but there was no point in saying so and Alice, drawing a sharp, deep breath, was shifted to brisk business, saying, "You'll want to be away to St. Frideswide's as soon as may be, now you have your grants safe. If you can be ready by midday, I've given order for some of our men to go with you then. You can be a goodly number of miles on your way before dark." Tears were suddenly in the way of her smile as she held out a hand to Frevisse. "I shall miss you."

Her own smile as unsuccessful, Frevisse took her hand and said all the things that should be said for courtesy's sake and not the thing they both knew—that she was being sent away as deliberately as young John had been, for her own good and to have her out of the way. There being no point to objecting, she did not but asked, because she had to, "Alice, do you want to know why it mattered for Arteys see the body?"

Alice's hold on her hand tightened. "No. I know I said I wanted the truth but now I don't. I can't. Not if I'm to go on." A moment longer she stood looking into Frevisse's face before, with her tears beginning to slide free, she let go and turned away, with nothing Frevisse could do but let her go.

Chapter 24

hen she and Dame Perpetua rode into St. Frideswide's yard at the end of a few days' easy journey, there were glad cries and then much talk. Even removed as the nunnery was into northern Oxfordshire, they had had some tangled word of the duke of Gloucester's arrest but nothing after that and there had to be much telling of things seen and heard, with Dame Perpetua all too often saying, "But Dame Frevisse saw more than I did," and questions turned her way. That meant several drawn-out days of balancing along a line of what she could truthfully tell among all the things she must not say, until finally the questions and talk wore out and the nunnery's familiar quiet and familiar days closed around her.

They should have been like balm to a hurt and, a little, they were, but the hurt did not heal. She had her duties again, and the welcome hours of prayer and all the usual small troubles and small pleasures of ten women sharing cloistered life, but behind it all, under it all, around it all, there was the waiting, just as she had known and dreaded there would be.

She had thought it would be as much as a few weeks of waiting, but the weeks went on through all of Lent, past Easter, past the end of spring, into summer. From such travelers as came their way and servants' talk brought back from Banbury, there was word of Gloucester's body carried in barren procession to St. Alban's abbey in Hertfordshire for its burial, of Parliament's uneventful end, of Bishop Beaufort of Winchester's death in April, with of course talk of how he and his life-long rival Gloucester had come at the end to die so nearly together. A packman on his way from London told there was a general rumbling there against the marquis of Suffolk, both over Gloucester's death and the way the French truce was going, but everything that came as far as St. Frideswide's was thinned and made uncertain by distance, with nothing about Gloucester's arrested men beyond a passing mention that some had been freed, uncharged and untried.

Waiting became a hollowness in Frevisse, so familiar after a time that she hardly knew how she had felt before it. Midsummer came with its hot days and the haying was done and sheep shearing finished before finally word came and even then it told her nothing, was not even directly to her. In a letter to Domina Elisabeth, Alice asked that Frevisse be allowed to come to her in London, not bothering with a reason, simply asking it, knowing Domina Elisabeth would not refuse. She had even sent two men with the messenger for escort, and the next morning Frevisse rode out with them and Sister Amicia, who could barely believe her good fortune at Domina Elisabeth having chosen her to go not only out into the world but to *London.*

Sister Amicia would not have been Frevisse's first choice but her talk and exclaims and—after their first two days of riding—complaints at being stiff and sore kept a little at bay Frevisse's worries and wondering about why Alice had summoned her; and at night when her thoughts might have closed in on her, the weariness of having ridden from first light until long into dusk drew her quickly down into almost dreamless sleep. That the men were pressing hard to be back to London was clear but no questions Frevisse asked brought answer why, nor did they talk much among themselves for her to overhear, until finally—not understanding but accepting it—she stopped asking anything of them.

They came in sight of London in the fourth day's midafternoon. Frevisse made them draw rein on Hampstead hill and wait while Sister Amicia, silenced at last, stared her fill across the fields at the city stretched along the broad Thames, its several scores of church spires needled toward the clear sky above the dark crowd of roofs, with the great spire of St. Paul's thrusting highest of all, gold glinting at its point, while ship masts forested the river and away to the right Westminster Abbey rose like a cream-pale cliff against the distant Surrey hills.

Even for those used to seeing it, it was a sight worth looking at, and only when Sister Amicia caught up to her wonder and began to exclaim again did Frevisse nod at the men to ride on. They did, down from the hills into the valley, with Frevisse obliged to tell Sister Amicia that they would not be going into London yet. Sister Amicia protested that and Frevisse left it to one of the men to explain, "We're for Holborn, my lady. Or nigh

St. Giles-in-the-Fields out Holborn way. That's where my lord of Suffolk has his place."

"But London!" Sister Amicia wailed.

"We'll likely have chance to see it before we leave," Frevisse said, careful to make that a hope, not a promise, then padded it with telling what little she knew about lately built Suffolk Place.

Like everywhere near London, the village around St. Giles-in-the-Fields church had grown since Frevisse had last been there. Suffolk was not the only lord to have come to where St. Martin's Lane on its way north crossed the ways to Reading and Uxbridge out of London, near both to the city and the king's court at Westminster but without the crowded streets and overbuilt Strand along the Thames. Their halls and houses gleamed with newness among the fields, their gardens spread around and behind them. Frevisse knew Suffolk Place by the blue banner with its gold leopard heads lifting on the afternoon's slight breeze above the gateway even before they turned from the road to ride into the broad, cobbled yard enclosed on two sides by walls, on a third by a low run of buildings, on the fourth by the great hall with a roof-tall, stone-traceried oriel window thrust out from its side into the yard.

While Sister Amicia exclaimed at the sight of it all, the ungracious thought crossed Frevisse's mind that Suffolk had clearly built to match his own opinion of his importance.

At the foot of the broad, roofed stairway up to the hall's stone-arched doorway their escort gave her and Sister Amicia over to the liveried servant who descended to meet them. The man even took their two small bags to carry and said when he had led them up the stairs and into the wide screens passage, "I'd see you to your room first and send to tell my lady you're here, but she's given order . . ."

". . . that she would see her cousin as soon as she arrives," said Joliffe, coming out of the great hall into their way. Frevisse's eyes were still half-blinded in the shadowed passage after the bright out-of-doors but she knew his voice as he went lightly, easily on, "If you want to see this other good lady to their room, I'll see Dame Frevisse to Lady Alice, if you like."

Despite Sister Amicia dithered a little at parting from her, Frevisse sent her on her way without pity or compunction; but as the servant led Sister Amicia off, Joliffe gave no chance for questions, only bowed briefly and started away, leaving Frevisse to follow him into the great hall where servants were setting up the tables for supper. In the better light there she saw, though hardly believed, that he was in the Suffolk livery of buff and blue, which gave her to hard, silent wondering as they left the hall, passed through several rooms, down other stairs, and through another door to outside again, onto a graveled walkway bordered by a low green hedge with gardens lying beyond it. They looked to be as perfect and new as the house, laid out with patterned beds and paths, trellised and arbored and with a fountain's soft sound from somewhere. Ignoring all that, Frevisse demanded at Joliffe's back, "What are you doing here? Who are you now?"

Joliffe turned around, wholly feigned innocence on his face. "My lady? I'm Master Noreys, of course, here because I'm master of pastimes to my lord and lady of Suffolk."

"Bishop Beaufort is dead."

"He is indeed, leaving me in need of honest work. Hence, here I am."

"Why haven't you sent me some word of what's happened?"

Joliffe's lightness instantly disappeared. "Because there hasn't been word to send until now, and now it's bad enough that Lady Alice needed you to be here and quickly."

He turned and started away again into the gardens. Frevisse followed, asking, "Does she know about you?"

Joliffe looked back. "She knows enough. Bishop Beaufort recommended me to her."

"And Suffolk? Does he know?"

"No."

She was not used to so little laughter in him and asked, more sharply than she meant, "And now? What's happened that Alice wants me here?"

"Better that she tell you."

He turned through a gap in a high, square-clipped yew hedge into the small garden it enclosed, a square of greensward dotted with tiny white daisies in the grass around the double-tiered, stone-built fountain Frevisse had been hearing. Three ladies were seated with their sewing there on a turf-topped brick bench while a fourth, on a cushion on the grass, played lightly on a lute. They all paused to greet Master Noreys by name, smiling, and he bowed to them with a polite, "My fair ladies," that for some reason set them giggling as he led Frevisse across the garden to the head-high brick wall that made its far side and through the gateway there into a yet smaller garden, enclosed all around by the wall, its grass likewise starred with daisies, with a turf-topped brick bench along one side. But here there was trellis-work lightly covered by young vines on three sides and a climbing pink rose on the fourth and Alice was seated on the bench, gowned in green as summer-rich as the close-trimmed grass, with only the lightest of white veils over a small, jeweled, padded roll to cover her hair.

With a book open on her lap, she looked perfectly the gracious, wealthy lady at repose, but by the spasmed way she shut and laid the book aside, Frevisse doubted she had been anything like at repose or even reading, and while Joliffe closed the gate, she came to take Frevisse tightly by both hands, saying, "You've come. Thank St. Anne," and drew to the bench to sit down without letting go of her. "It was a good ride? Everything went well? You're well? Did Dame Perpetua come with you again?"

The questions were all what the moment called for but they came in a rush, driven rather than given, and Frevisse, taking back her hands, answered steadily that the ride had gone well, that she was well, that Sister Amicia—"whom I think you've never met"—had come with her, not Dame Perpetua.

Joliffe had followed them across the grass. Not invited to sit, he stood beside them and Frevisse could feel his waiting, as taut as Alice's graciousness, and she asked, going to the point, "What's the matter? Why have you sent for me?"

Alice looked up at Joliffe. "You didn't say anything?"

He made her a slight bow. "I thought it was for you to do, my lady."

Alice looked back to her. "You've heard nothing? Not anything?"

"Nothing about anything," Frevisse said. "Not from"— she cast a glance at Joliffe—"Master Noreys. Not from your men while we rode together."

Alice looked down at her hands gripping each other in her lap. "I told them they weren't to say anything. I never thought they'd hold so well to it." She lifted her eyes to Frevisse, took a deep, unsteady breath, and said, "I sent for you because I was afraid of what Suffolk was going to do. Now he's done it. He's going to murder five men tomorrow, including Gloucester's son."

For a long moment Frevisse sat utterly still, until with rigid effort she could hold her voice level before she asked, "Where? How?"

"At Tyburn. They're to be executed. As traitors."

Meaning they would be hung by the neck until insensible but not dead, then be taken down, brought conscious, and gutted—sliced open by the executioner's knife and their entrails lifted out—alive long enough to know what was being done to them before they died in pain, ugliness, stench, and blood.

Sickened, Frevisse was barely able to breathe to ask, "How . . . did this happen?"

Alice turned her gaze helplessly to Joliffe who said, "Yesterday Suffolk, in the king's name, sat in judgment on them as traitors complicit in Gloucester's alleged plot against the king. The lawyers pretended to trade arguments. The accused were found guilty and sentenced to death."

"On what proof?"

"Proof?" Joliffe returned, as if dismayed at the thought of it. "Suffolk named the charge against them, was their judge, and gave the sentence. What did proof have to do with it?"

Alice softly moaned. Frevisse pressed a hand over hers without looking away from Joliffe and asked, "Who besides Arteys is to die?"

"Two of Gloucester's knights and two of his squires, all arrested at Bury."

"The others that were arrested there?"

"Quietly let go."

"Then might there be mercy for Arteys and the others?" she asked and followed Joliffe's gaze as he shifted it to Alice, who whispered, "No."

"Suffolk needs them guilty," Joliffe said. "There's been constant outcry and talk against him ever since Gloucester's death, especially here in London. People refuse to believe Gloucester was a traitor. They say he was murdered and that it was Suffolk's doing. Suffolk means to show he's in the right by claiming that Gloucester *was* treasonous because, look, five of his men are going to die for it."

Frevisse turned her look to Alice, wanting her denial.

"Yes," said Alice. "I think that's what he's thinking."

"But I think he also wants, more particularly, to be rid of Arteys, who—besides being of royal blood and don't think that doesn't enter into Suffolk's consideration—knows too much," Joliffe said. At Frevisse's glance at Alice, he added, "She knows. Bishop Peacock told her."

That was who was missing in this. "Where is he? Hasn't he been able to do anything?" Though what, she did not know.

As if it were a particularly bitter jest, Joliffe answered, "Our good bishop is in disgrace for a sermon he shouldn't have preached at St. Paul's Cross"—London's most public place for sermons and other speaking out— "and has been sent to his bishopric in Wales to think things over. Or at least wait out the outrage."

"What did he preach that could bring on all that?"

"About other bishops and some points of theology he wanted to make clear. Unfortunately, he made them clear enough for people to be angry about it and the archbishop suggested he should leave for a time. Hence, he's not here."

"Even if he was, he couldn't help," Alice said. "Suffolk means for Arteys to be dead to keep him from ever telling about the murder attempt."

"Why didn't Arteys tell it at the trial?" Frevisse asked.
"What was there to lose then?"

"Tell what?" Joliffe asked back. "That he'd killed a
man who was trying to kill Gloucester? There's the dead
man to prove Arteys killed him, but where's proof the
man tried to kill Gloucester? We believe Arteys because
we tracked down some proofs to what he said, but do
you think Suffolk would ever allow those proofs? He'd
deny everything and Arteys would be left with a confession of murder and die for that if not the other."

"But—"

"Personally," Joliffe went on, "rather than be dishon-
estly killed for something I'd done, I'd rather go to the
gallows honestly declaring I was innocent of what I was
being executed for." In the same level voice he added,
"We've been trading letters with Bishop Pecock, though.
It's useful to be the lady of Suffolk with messengers to
send to bishops and for nuns."

"And because Bishop Pecock can't come, you've
brought me instead?" Frevisse asked sharply. "For what?
To be here when Arteys is killed?"

"No." Joliffe met her anger quietly. "To stop him being killed. Him and the others."

"How?" She turned on Alice. "Just how am I supposed to do that? If anyone can change Suffolk's mind,
it would be you."

Alice moved her head stiffly from side to side, de-
nying that. "He won't hear me. He won't heed me.
There's been far more trouble than he thought there'd
be for Gloucester's death. Far more anger than he expected and all of it at him. He's . . ." She paused over
the word, then said it. ". . . frightened."

"And if we're to stop what he means to do to Arteys
and the others," Joliffe said, "he has to be made more
frightened."

Wariness overtook Frevisse's anger as she looked back and forth between him and Alice. "That's what you've brought me here to do?"

"I can't let my husband do this to himself," said Alice. "If he executes those men like this, it's murder. I can't let him put that sin on his soul."

Suffolk's soul was not high among Frevisse's concerns just now but Arteys and the men condemned with him were. She looked back to Joliffe. "What is it I'm going to do?"

Joliffe smiled for the first time she had seen today. A wide, warm smile of deepest pleasure as he said, "What you're going to do is lie as you've never lied before."

Chapter 25

The day's long end was a warm rose across the western sky above the vanished sun's fading trail of gold. The gardens of Suffolk Place were already softening in a blue twilight that would be darkness soon, and the couples and few other people who had gone out to walk in them were drifting back toward the house as the evening damp came on. Standing high above them, at the window in the solar off Alice's bedchamber, Frevisse watched them and the sunset's fading and thought how far in more than miles she was from the winter-bare gardens at St. Edmund's Abbey.

She had gone to Bury St. Edmunds to serve Bishop Beaufort's purposes because, even dying, he could not let go of worldly matters. Now, because of Suffolk's worldly ambitions, she was here to keep five men alive. If she failed, Arteys would die. If she fell into trouble, there was no one who could help her in her turn. Not Joliffe, surely. He could be smashed by Suffolk as easily as Arteys had been. Nor Bishop Pecock. What slight place and power his bishopric gave were forfeit for the present and had never been enough for him to go openly against Suffolk anyway, in this or any other matter.

And Alice? She was as bound to helplessness as any of them. She was married to Suffolk and, come good or ill, would go on being married to him, with too much to be lost—including her children—if she crossed him too openly, too deeply.

Waiting there at the window, watching the day's end, Frevisse looked straight at the plain fact that there was no one but herself to do what needed to be done and no one to save Arteys—or her—if she failed. For her it would be a powerful man's displeasure and probably being shut away into an unfamiliar nunnery under strict discipline among strangers for the rest of her life. For Arteys it would be death.

She was praying for courage and strength when, behind her, the door across the room opened. Folding her hands with feigned quiet into her opposite sleeves and settling her face deliberately to show rather than hide her strain and deep-grown unease, she turned around.

The hope had been that Alice could persuade Suffolk to see her cousin the nun alone and Alice had succeeded. He stood in the doorway with no one in sight behind him as he looked around the chamber and said, "There's no light. I'll send for one."

He started to turn away to whoever was in the other room but Frevisse said quickly, pitching her voice a little high and unsteady, "Please, no. I'd rather . . ." She let her voice falter. "Please . . . it's better this way."

Suffolk hesitated, shrugged, and came in, only half-closing the door as courtesy to her, that no one be able to say she had been shut away alone with a man. Still unsteadily, Frevisse said, "It would be better closed. Please."

Suffolk's look at her was harder this time. There was still sunset light enough through the window for her to see he did not like that. But he probably disliked being here at all. Alice had said, "I'll persuade him to it by saying it's for no more than a quarter hour. I'll ask it as a favor to me, for my cousin who's distressed at something, I don't know what. He'll give me a quarter hour." Now here he was and impatient to have it done with, whatever it was. In the shorter doublet that was coming into fashion, high on the leg, with wide-puffed shoulders but tightly nipped in at wrists and waist—his present one in saffron yellow velvet trimmed with black at throat and hem—he was a goodly-looking man in his full prime of life but somewhat gone to flesh in the few months since Frevisse had last seen him. From gorging on ambitions and power, Frevisse thought, and oddly that made her fear slip aside, not leaving her but letting her anger come to the fore.

Carried by her anger, she sank toward the floor in a deep curtsy and stayed there, her head bowed in seemingly utter humility.

Suffolk crossed the room, took her by the elbow, and raised her up, saying, "There's hardly need for that, dame. We're kin by marriage, after all."

But he liked her humility before him. His voice showed how much he liked it and the chance it gave him to show his graciousness and Frevisse kept her eyes down as she said, trying to sound overwhelmed by his goodness, "You're very kind, my lord."

"If you will remember me in your prayers, then all is even between us."

"You are remembered in them, my lord." And that was true; she always prayed for Alice "and all those dear to her," which Suffolk was or Alice would not be in such pain for him.

"Then there we are. What is it you'd ask of me?" His graciousness had not reached to asking her to sit. She supposed he saw it was enough he was a great lord condescending to her humble need and probably remained on his feet to remind her to be quick about her business, that he had more important matters in hand than her. That suited Frevisse very well and she raised her head, looked him directly in the face, and said, "I've come about the late duke of Gloucester's will."

His momentary silence betrayed he had not been ready for anything like that. She watched a quick shifting in his eyes before he said evenly, "I'm afraid the duke left no will, dame. I promise you it's been a source of trouble to us all."

The first part of that was probably a lie. The second part surely was. Without a will and with no legitimate heir of his body, everything that had been Gloucester's— his fine manor at Eltham, every castle and piece of property he owned, all his offices from greatest to least, and any other wealth he had had, in whatever form—was left fair game for the taking by king, queen, lords, and anyone else able to jam a hand into the feeding trough before it emptied. The *lack* of a will had been no trouble.

The claim was that there never had been a will but Alice said there surely had. She had heard Gloucester speak of it herself a few years back at some court gathering when there had been talk of books and he had said his many, well-loved books were mostly willed to the university at Oxford. Closer yet, the abbot of St. Albans

Abbey, where Gloucester's body had been taken for burial, was asking for the money he claimed Gloucester had willed for his chantry there, for prayers and Masses for his soul forever.

"There was a will someplace, at some time," Alice had said this afternoon in the garden.

"But there isn't one now," said Joliffe, "and Suffolk doubtless wants to keep it that way. That's what brought Bishop Pecock to think of this chance."

And in the room's deepening twilight, with her back to the window so she could see Suffolk's face better than he could see hers, Frevisse said stiffly, "Of course the duke left a will and I know where there's a copy of it."

Suffolk started what looked to be a sharp denial but stopped himself, paused, then said very gracefully, very firmly, "That seems unlikely, dame."

Looking straight into his eyes, she said, "I know there is because I have it. Signed by his grace's own hand and sealed with his own seal."

Suffolk gave a short, ungracious bark of laughter. "There are easier ways to persuade me to give your nunnery a gift than by extortion."

That his first thought was of extortion betrayed a great deal about him, but evenly—surprisingly evenly, considering how tightly she was holding in her anger—Frevisse said back at him, "This isn't for my nunnery. It's for me."

Suffolk looked less gracious now. "Why would *you* have a copy of the duke of Gloucester's will?"

"Because his grace knew no one would look for it in my keeping."

"It's at your nunnery?"

"It's elsewhere, of course." Let him understand she was not stupid, that he was not the only well-witted one here. "And there are papers with it that explain everything, should anything unexpected happen to me."

An old bluff, Joliffe had said, but ever a good one. She could see Suffolk assessing it before he said, "That doesn't explain why you have it."

Meeting his angry gaze with feigned defiance mingled with equally feigned shame, Frevisse gave the lie on which everything depended. "I have Gloucester's will because I was his mistress. And mother of his son."

She had the satisfaction of seeing Suffolk's jaw fall, and just as Joliffe had schooled her, she waited three beats before going on, hardening her voice a little, "My lord wanted me to be assured our son was well provided for. Arteys. One of the men you mean to kill tomorrow."

Suffolk sputtered into laughter, choked on it, and shook his head, protesting, "You? My wife's most-holy cousin? The blessed nun? You're the bastard's mother?"

For a heart-dropping moment Frevisse thought the lie had failed but, laughing, Suffolk demanded, "Does she know? Does Alice know what you are?"

"What I was," Frevisse said stiffly. "Years ago."

"Yes." Suffolk eyed her assessingly. "I'd suppose so." He laughed again. "Gloucester's mistress. A nun. Who would have thought it?"

His scorn was hardly suitable, considering he had never made secret his own bastard daughter was by a nun he had seduced in France. Coldly Frevisse said, "About the will. And about a pardon for my son in exchange for my keeping it secret."

Suffolk's laughter vanished, a dark anger taking its place. "Yes," he said coldly back at her. "About this will."

Chapter 26

Brought last out of the prison into the walled yard, with time to wait while they finished strapping down Sir Roger, Arteys turned his face up to the sunlight, wanting to feel its warmth against his flesh rather than the cold terror cramped in his stomach or the weight of the wide iron manacles at his wrists and ankles, the drag of chains, and the screaming at the back of his mind that this wasn't happening, wasn't happening, wasn't . . .

Eyes desperately closed against the courtyard full of staring people, he tilted his head back to the summer-morning sky and willed himself to feel only the sunlight, think only the sunlight.

The clop of hoofs and the scrape of wood on cobbles

told him Sir Roger was being dragged forward and he opened his eyes as the guards on either side of him took him by the upper arms and pushed him the little distance to the hurdle being horse-drawn to place in front of him. Everything was come down to that, he thought. To little and to last. To a last summer's morning. A last few steps. A little while until he was dead.

He pulled his mind off from that. Think of something else, he told himself. Think of here and now and what. Not the guard fumbling at the manacles around his ankles. The horse-drawn hurdle waiting in front of him. See it. Think about it. A willow-woven piece of fencing a few feet wide and a little longer than a man was tall. Hurdles were made that way, light-weight for easy shifting around pastures but this one had a wood frame under it to give somewhere to attach the horse's harness and to give it strength, to keep it from falling apart while being dragged through London. With him on it.

The guard pulled one manacle off his ankle, laid it aside, set to work on the other one.

Think small things, Arteys told himself. Think little things. Cram them into the chinks in the wall across his mind that kept the terror from spilling through into his rigid calm. His mind lurched, trying to break free, but he thought desperately, Look at the horses. His was a bay, flicking its dark tail against the morning's flies. The other four waiting in a line from here to the gateway with their burdened hurdles behind them were a black, two more bays, a dull-coated chestnut. The black was Sir Roger's. Sir Richard and Tom had the bays. Master Needham . . .

Arteys' chest heaved, struggling to breathe against the smothering rise of his fear. It didn't *matter* who had what horses. It only mattered that they were good ones, able to go strongly, get it over with, not take overlong on the way to Tyburn because why spend more time humiliating the condemned than necessary? People had their lives to get on with . . .

The thought of other people's lives turned to bile in Arteys' throat as the guard loosed the second manacle from around his ankle, rattled the pair of them and their chain aside onto the cobbles, and stood up to help his fellow turn Arteys around, his hands still manacled so that together they had to lay him down, on his back on the hurdle. For half a breath, as the willow withies pressed into his back, he nearly gave way, nearly struggled against going tamely to his death, but one of the guards must have read his body because he said, rough-voiced, "Don't."

And he didn't, not because of the guard's order but because there would be no use to it. Not with his hands still chained, in a walled yard full of armed men and no help for him anywhere. He willed his body to be still and held up his arms for the guards to fasten the leather strap that would hold him to the hurdle over his chest. A wide, thick, leather strap with a heavy buckle and a padlock to hold it closed against any fumbling a desperate man might try. Maybe because he did not struggle, the guards did not pull it tight enough over his ribs to hurt. For what small use there was to that, Arteys thought, when in an hour's time or so he, Sir Roger, Sir Richard, Tom, and Master Needham would all be hung, gutted alive and, when finally dead, their bodies cut into pieces and piked up for people to stare at.

Hung, drawn, quartered.

Terror heaved up from Arteys' stomach, clamped on his heart, rose into his throat, as it had every time the thought of it came into his mind since Suffolk, seated in judgment after that farce of a trial, had stared above their heads, refusing even to look them in the face as he sentenced them to die as traitors.

And again, as he had every time so far, Arteys fought the terror down, knowing that if ever he gave way to it, he would go to his death screaming and sobbing. For his own sake and for what pride of blood he owed his father and to refuse that extra sport to everyone who came to watch him die, he meant to go on fighting it, not to give way until he had to, not begin to scream until the knife was in his belly and the pain more than he could hold against.

He supposed that by then he'd be past caring what sport he was for anyone.

The guards were pulling his feet to either side now, to the straps waiting for them at the hurdle's lower corners. He closed his eyes again. Yesterday he had said farewell to his last sunset, such of its gold and rose as he could see through the high slit of window in his cell. Had made farewell to his last night and to his last dawn before the guards had come, roused—not wakened, they had none of them slept—the five of them to go to a room where they had been allowed to wash themselves—not shave; not given anything that could be a weapon—and dress in the clothing they had worn to their trial. Clean hosen and shirts and good doublets that Sir Roger's wife had brought them. Arteys' was dark blue. That was a small, pointless thing to be pleased with but he had been. He had found himself these past days trying very hard to be pleased with small things. There were, after all, no great things left in his life. Except death.

That they were to go clean and clothed to their deaths, rather than dirty, bare-legged and in prison shirts, might have been seen as a favor, but Sir Roger had said while they dressed themselves, "Suffolk doesn't want anyone's pity on us. He wants everyone to remember it's Gloucester's 'treason' we're dying for. That's why he's letting us go grand to our dying."

Close to his ear someone said, "Master Arteys."

He flinched his eyes open and turned his head to find a priest kneeling beside the hurdle. For a moment that was all he saw, then said uncertainly, "Master Orle?"

"Master Orle," the priest agreed. "Bishop Pecock sends his regret at not being here himself."

"I heard he was in trouble," Arteys said, surprised at how his voice croaked.

"He is indeed." Master Orle fumbled under his scapular and brought out a leather bottle. "Otherwise he'd be here. But we found a way for me to be assigned with the other priests to this." He held the bottle to Arteys' mouth. "Wine," he said.

"Drugged?" Arteys asked, half-hopefully. He wouldn't mind not being altogether here for any of what was to come.

"I fear not."

Arteys drank gratefully anyway when Master Orle held the bottle to his mouth, the slant of the hurdle enough that swallowing was only difficult, not impossible. He had not known how thirsty he was. Breakfast had been only a little ale and a piece of dry bread, with something said about a full stomach making matters harder for the hangman.

"Thank you," he said as Master Orle took the bottle away.

"You all made confession last night, I understand. Everything else was seen to this morning?"

"Yes." Arteys shut his eyes against the memory of how terrible it had been to have the last rites said over him when he was neither ill nor wounded and yet assured he would be dead before the morning was done.

There was the scrape of the first hurdle beginning to

move across the courtyard paving and Arteys opened his eyes, seeking for Master Orle's face, for something good in the midst of nightmare. Master Orle, putting the bottle quickly away, brought out a gold cross, perhaps a hand's length long and plainly made but beautiful. "Bishop Pecock sent you this. It's his own."

Arteys reached out and took it between his manacled hands, grateful for it.

The priest touched his shoulder. "I'll walk beside you if you want. It's allowed."

"Yes," Arteys said. "Yes." Then, "Oh, God," as his own hurdle lurched forward, jarring him against the straps. Laid out as he was, he could not brace himself, only endure the jouncing across the cobbles and through the first of the gateways from the Tower of London onto the causeway into the city itself. They were to be killed at Tyburn, far out London's other side, meaning they were to be dragged the length of the city, first by way of Tower Street, then up to Cheapside, broad enough for the crowds to gather at their thickest and on west past St. Paul's Cathedral to go out at Newgate onto the Holburn road. Coming and going with Gloucester, Arteys had ridden that way often enough to know it. Had more than once ridden past Tyburn and seen the bodies hanging and never thought . . .

The hurdle bumped over a rougher patch of pavement, jarring his thoughts along with his body. They were into London now, the street narrow here, the crowds of lookers-on close on both sides of him and people leaning out of the overhanging houses' windows, staring, talking, pointing. Arteys stared straight up, past the faces, refusing to see them, trying to sink into his mind. If he could just not see, not think, not hear even Master Orle walking near the hurdle's end, praying aloud. If he could just know nothing from here to the end . . .

How could the sky be so piercingly, purely blue when he was going to die?

Ahead, one of the other men cried out to God, his voice so shrill with fear that Arteys did not know who it was. Not Sir Roger or Sir Richard, surely. Master Needham? Tom?

It was his fault that Tom was here at all. That last day in Bury, when Suffolk had seen him and he had run, he should have gone on running but he hadn't. He'd left the abbey, lost himself in the crowds, wandered while trying to know what to do, unable to make up his mind. He'd happened on Tom, been so grateful to see him that he had gone with him into a tavern to get warm, to gather his wits, to be with someone he knew instead of alone. Suffolk's men had found him there, and because Tom had been with him, Tom was here and going to die.

Arteys would have vowed to Suffolk or anyone who asked that Tom was no part of anything that Arteys knew or had done but no one ever asked him. He had not even seen Suffolk from that day in Bury until faced by him as their judge two days ago and by then he had known there was no point in avowing or disavowing anything. Suffolk was going to have him and the others dead and nothing would change it.

The hurdle scraped onto more even pavement and the street widened, the houses farther away to either side. "Cheapside," Master Orle said. Arteys heard himself groan, hurting from the jouncing, from being strapped down and helplessly sprawled out. But that was the point of all this miserable dragging through the heart of London. He was supposed to be hurt and humiliated before the agony of rope and knife and, far too late, death.

"Do you hear them?" Master Orle asked. "Are you listening to them?"

Arteys shook his head the little that he could. He'd kept the crowd noise around him to a half-heard, meaningless surf sound, not wanting to hear people cheerful for his death.

"They're angry," Master Orle said. "Listen."

Arteys listened. Master Orle was right. The crowd was angry, but not at him or the others. It wasn't the cheerful jeers that usually kept traitors company on their way to die but a growling displeasure and voices calling out, "God bless you! God keep you!" and once and again and another time, "Down with Suffolk!"

For the first time Arteys swallowed a sob. They knew. They knew it was Suffolk who was a traitor, not him and the others. And suddenly rage scalded up in him— rage at the stupidity of having to die because Suffolk was a fool—and he lifted up his hands, lifted up the cross, and cried out, "We're guiltless! Pray for us! We're guiltless!"

Ahead of him Sir Roger and the others took up the cry. "We're guiltless! Pray for us!"

The crowd's cries rose in answer to them, with women's sobs mixed loudly in. A half-hope of rescue stirred in Arteys. If they all rushed the line of guards . . .

But there was no rush, though the crowd at Newgate had to be cleared before the horses and hurdles could pass through, and once outside the city, Master Orle said, "They're coming with us. They're following."

Arteys pulled his head up long enough to see people were pushing through Newgate to join the throng already along the road here, bringing their anger with them. Arteys let his head drop back. The road was worse here, jarring his breath away, and it wasn't the crowd that mattered anymore but how much farther there was to go and how much longer.

The sun was well up the sky now. He turned his head

aside from it. To both sides the crowd was calling out to him and the others and cursing Suffolk. Master Orle tried to give him more wine but the guards wouldn't stop the horse and more spilled down his chin than reached his throat. And there at last came the jeers—shouts and hissing and cries of "Traitors!"—and Master Orle said angrily, "We're passing Suffolk's place. Those are his people, no one else."

From the crowd, people jeered back and stones flew. A rush from the guards stopped that but there was no more jeering.

"St. Giles's church," Master Orle said quietly.

Meaning not far to Tyburn. Arteys shut his eyes, there was nothing more he wanted to see, and finally the hurdle bumped off the road, thudded across hummocky ground, and came to a stop in welcome shade under trees. Elm trees, Arteys saw when he opened his eyes. Tyburn's tall elms.

Bruised and aching, Arteys was almost grateful.

All went quickly after that. Master Orle had just time to give him a last gulp of the wine and take the cross from him before being put aside by the guards, who knew their business and wasted no time at it. Two guards to a man, they unstrapped the prisoners and hauled them upright, unmanacled their wrists, and stripped off their doublets to leave them in their shirts and hosen. Their arms were pulled behind them and tied at wrists and elbows with rough rope. More guards were around them, keeping the crowd back and a way clear to the scaffold, Arteys saw as he was jerked around and shoved forward with the others. It was new-made of raw wood and high enough for everyone to have good view not only of the noosed ropes hanging ready from the crossbeam above one side of it but the boards where the slaughter would be done, slanted up on trestles to give the crowd better sight of the killing.

At the foot of the scaffold's ladder there was delay. Unable to help themselves up the ladder with their bound hands, the five of them had to climb with their feet while the guards braced their backs until the men waiting above could grab them and haul them the rest of the way.

Arteys was last, with chance to see the others clearly one last time as they went ahead of him. Master Needham stiff-backed and blank-faced. Tom tight-mouthed and wide-eyed, holding in dry, heaving gasps of terror. Sir Roger and Sir Richard staring into the distance, grimly showing nothing.

His own turn came to be shoved up the ladder, grabbed, and set roughly on the platform. He had time to see there were five hangmen waiting, each with a helper standing behind him, and an array of knives on stools beside each of the five boards waiting for the butchering. Unlike the scaffold, the butchering boards were of old wood, used before, dark-smeared with other men's dried blood. But at least it seemed he and the others were to die all at once, rather than one at a time with the last one having to watch and hear all the others die before him. Something to be grateful for, he vaguely thought before he was grabbed again and pushed toward the last waiting noose. The hangmen's helpers, well-practiced, moved with him, one to each man, quick-tying rope around their ankles to keep their legs from thrashing when the time came. Arteys, without time for being ready, gasped at the sudden pain as the rope was jerked tight, but the hangman was already there, putting the noose around his neck. They weren't even going to be allowed last words, Arteys realized, and then the noose tightened on him, closed off his air as behind him someone hauled up on the rope. He had told himself he would not struggle but he did, his body demanding against his brain's knowing it would make no difference if his toes touched the scaffold a broken second longer. He struggled but was swinging and there was red darkness in his eyes, red roaring in his ears . . . *pain* . . .

He didn't feel himself fall but found himself lying with his face against wood planking and someone taking the noose from around his neck, stripping the rope from his elbows, wrists, ankles. He was still gasping for air as someone turned him over but relief went from him with the return of the terrible knowing that it wasn't ended. That worse was coming . . .

But it didn't. It was Master Orle who was there, not the executioners or guards, not dragging him to his feet and to one of the waiting slaughter boards but helping him to sit up with an arm around his shoulders, saying in his ear, "It's over. You're pardoned. You're not going to die. It's over."

"Sir Roger. Tom," Arteys croaked.

"They're pardoned. You're all pardoned. You're going to live."

Arteys' shaking hands could not hold the bottle Master Orle held to his mouth but he drank despite the swallowing hurt. Around him there was a glad babble of other voices, and when Master Orle lowered the bottle, he turned his head to find the scaffold was crowded with laughing people. He glimpsed Tom being held by his brother, both of them choking on tears; could hear Sir Richard praying aloud and fervently to seemingly every saint he could think of; saw Sir Roger and Master Needham being helped away . . .

The hangmen and their helpers and the guards were all gone.

"You're pardoned," Master Orle insisted. "Do you understand?"

Arteys nodded, although somewhere in him a voice was crying out that he couldn't be pardoned for a thing he hadn't done. But more of him was sobbing with thankfulness that he was alive. Alive and not in pain. Not dying. But it was an inward sobbing, he realized. Outwardly he seemed only frozen, unable to help himself as Master Orle and another man, a stranger, helped him to his feet and to the scaffold's edge opposite to where the others were being helped down the ladder into the cheering crowd.

"How?" he asked of Master Orle. "How are we still alive?"

"Suffolk was here. He had your pardons ready. From the king. You're free. Go on. With these men. Go with them."

Arteys tried to ask, "Where . . ." but Master Orle and the man with him were urging him off the scaffold's edge. There was no ladder here but two men were waiting below with hands raised to take him. He didn't know either of them but let them lower him to the ground, let them hold him up when his legs tried to buckle while the other man he did not know swung down from the scaffold, leaving Master Orle behind. One of the men was pulling a doublet up Arteys' arms and around him, vaguely fastening it as all three of them began making a way for him through the crowd with elbows and shoulders. Some people close to hand were cheering him— for what? for not being dead?—and reaching to touch him, but most were surging away around the scaffold to where the others were being led away among more cheering. The three men guiding Arteys went sideways through the surge, then turned around and went backward, letting the crowd flow around and away from them, losing themselves and Arteys until there, in the midst of everyone, no one around them knew who he was; and when they came clear of the crowd, the men hurried him away among the trees.

Four horses were waiting there, held by a fourth man. One of the men with Arteys took a horse's reins from him and mounted. The other two moved to help Arteys up behind him, one of them saying, "We didn't think you'd be fit to ride alone. Can you hold on, though?"

"Yes," Arteys croaked. "Where am I going?"

"Away from here."

"Whose men . . ." are you? he wanted to ask but the words wouldn't come from his aching throat.

The man answered anyway. "The duke of York's."

Chapter 27

utside another long summer's evening was gold behind London's rooftops but the hour was past for guests to be received in St. Helen's nunnery, Bishopsgate. Only because she was wife to the marquis of Suffolk had Alice been allowed in and Frevisse allowed to see her after Compline, but the parlor's shutters were closed and barred and only by the light of the small-cupped oil lamp on the table beside them were they able to see each other's faces.

With no one else to hear them and no need of other greeting between them, Frevisse asked, "He's safe?"

"He's safe. York's men had him away within minutes. He was at York's house long enough to be fed and re-clothed and seen by a doctor. He's said to be unharmed."

Frevisse could only hope that was fully true; but there were harms that went beyond the body, harms that went deep into the heart and mind.

"Yes," Alice agreed, though Frevisse had not said it. "But bodily is something, considering."

Frevisse granted that with a small gesture. "And then?"

"By now he's with a few of York's household knights somewhere well away up the Thames in the duke's own twelve-oared barge. They'll take to horse at Abingdon or Oxford. Arteys will be in Wales within a week."

And as safe as they could hope to have him.

"And Joliffe?" Frevisse asked.

"Gone as soon as he brought me that word. I don't know where."

Yesterday, after Frevisse had agreed to the lies she was to tell, Alice had written a brief message to the duke of York, asking him to give heed to the bearer of it. That night, after Frevisse had won her ugly bargaining with Suffolk—promising that, in return for Arteys and the others being pardoned and set free, no one would ever see Gloucester's will by her doing—Joliffe had gone with the message to the duke.

"Tell him," Frevisse had said before he went, "that the pardon won't come until they're on the scaffold. That's what Suffolk swore. That he'd have that much out of it."

Suffolk had sworn other things, too, mostly at her, and given his promise angrily, grudgingly, ungraciously. He had threatened her, too, although Frevisse told neither Alice nor Joliffe that. She did not tell them, either, how black-angry at him she had grown in return, so that at the end she had been viciously glad to drag the promise out of him and wished she could have rubbed his face with it afterward. He had attempted Gloucester's murder,

was attempting five more, and all he felt was anger at
being thwarted of them. Nor was he ever likely, this side
of his own death, to be called to account for any of it
so long as he held the king's favor.

She, on the other hand, had penance ahead of her, both
for lying and her anger, but what had been worse burden
then was having to go to bed not knowing how Joliffe
had fared with York. Only in the morning had she been
able to meet him briefly in the garden, with him saying
without greeting, "York will do it."

"What did you say to move him to it?"

"York knows Suffolk well enough he needed little
convincing that even with the pardon Arteys won't be
safe, being Gloucester's son."

"How did you explain the pardons?"

"I said someone showed Suffolk he had more to lose
by killing Gloucester's men than letting them live."

"That was enough for York?"

Joliffe's smile had been grimly humoured. "I told
you—he knows Suffolk."

She had given way then to another fear that had come
to her and asked, "And you. What if Suffolk finds out
your part in this?"

Joliffe's smile had deepened. "I doubt I'll wait around
to find out if he finds out. When he has time to think all
this over, he may come to be suspicious and especially
suspicious if he learns by household spies that Master
Noreys was in close talk with Lady Alice and her de-
praved cousin in the afternoon and at the duke of York's
at an odd hour of that night. I'll stay until Arteys is safe.
Then I'm gone."

Because she might never have other chance to ask
him, she had said, "Why are you risking all this? Arteys
was no friend of yours before now, was he?"

"At Bury he trusted me. Worse, without telling me,

he left three rings that must have been his father's hidden among my things. For safekeeping, I suppose, if anything happened to him. Which it did. I found them later and . . . I hate being trusted."

He was so grim about it that Frevisse said, deliberately to irk him, "You know I trust you."

He had given her a hard look and half a smile and said, "I know. I try not to hold it against you." Then he had left.

Frevisse had wished she could leave, too, but until this was over she could not, the fear unspoken between her and Alice that Suffolk might be treacherous at the last. He had gone off the night before—to the king to get the pardons, he had said—and not returned. With no way to know his mind or how he meant to play the day, she and Alice had withdrawn to the walled garden to wait, no one with them but order given that any news about the executions should be brought immediately. For too long they sat, they paced, they hardly spoke, and heard the crowd on the road before a servant came running, excited with word the prisoners were being dragged past and could be seen from an upper window if Lady Alice hurried.

Alice had sent him away and they had sat side by side, silent, staring at the grass in front of them, listening, while the crowd passed; and when it was quiet again, Alice had whispered, "Tell me again that he promised."

"He promised," Frevisse had said back. But there had been no way to get word to Arteys of it. Which might be as well. If Suffolk went back on his promise, it would be more merciful that Arteys had not been betrayed into hope.

Alice had bowed her head into her hands and wept and it was forever until another servant brought word of how Suffolk had kept his promise. How he had been at Tyburn, waiting, when the prisoners were dragged up. How he had sat his horse at the rear edge of the crowd while they were made ready and brought to the scaffold. How he had waited while the nooses were put around their necks and the strangling began and how only then he had finally ridden forward into the crowd, holding up the pardons and calling out to let the prisoners down, they were freed by the king's good mercy.

"They're alive?" Alice had demanded at the man.

"They're alive, my lady. They're free."

Alice had waved him away. Not until he was gone did she say with the same cold rage that Frevisse felt, "Damn Suffolk. *Damn* him."

Frevisse and Sister Amicia had left within the hour, removing to St. Helen's nunnery because, Frevisse told her, they would be better out of the way with so much happening in Suffolk's household. Sister Amicia had been enjoying all that was happening but been too happy at going into London to question it; but it meant Frevisse had had to leave without knowing whether Arteys was safely away to York or not, and so Alice was come this evening to tell her, it not being a message to trust to anyone else now Joliffe was gone.

Knowing all else was well, Frevisse asked, half wanting not to, "How is it with Suffolk?"

"I saw him only briefly before he was away to Greenwich and the king. He looks to be keeping a good face to the world, but when there was only me to see it, he was raging."

"At you?"

"No. At the crowd. At all of London. He actually thought . . ." Alice faltered, then started over, holding out her right hand, palm upward. "On the one hand, he really thought the crowd would believe Gloucester's men were traitors and hate them for it." She held out her other hand, as if making the other side of a balance scale. "On the other hand, he thought the crowd—stinking-bodied idiots, he calls them—would see him as a hero for bringing out the men's pardons at the last possible of moments." She dropped her hands. "He's furious that London was on the men's side instead of believing him. He's furious at the men for being alive when he wanted them dead. He's furious at the crowd for being mad at him for waiting so long to give the pardons. Everything wrong is everybody else's fault."

"And mine," Frevisse said ruefully.

"Oh, his fury at you is all but lost under his fury at everyone else. He doesn't see what he tried to do was murder. He doesn't see . . . anything." Even the soft glow of lamplight, kind with shadows, could not gentle the pain in Alice's face. "Frevisse, I swear he wasn't like this when I married him. It's a thing that's grown on him with time. With the power that's come to him. It's as if what I best loved in him has shriveled while his ambition grew. It's as if . . ." Alice turned away, pressing her hands to the sides of her face as if to hold in the force of her grief. "It's as if his ambition is the most real thing in the world to him. Everything else barely matters, is hardly real." She turned around. "Is that possible? Can it really be like that for him?"

Frevisse tried to find words that would not hurt. That she could not, could only shake her head in helpless silence, was answer enough.

Alice drew a deep breath, put her grief out of sight again, and said, "Well. Things are as they are and we must do what we must do, as Father used to say. Do you need anything? Will you want to go back to St. Frideswide's soon?"

"We'll stay a few days. For Sister Amicia's sake and

while I purchase things from Domina Elisabeth's list. Will his grace allow you to give us escort back when the time comes?"

"I'll pay for that out of my own accounts. If he even thinks of it, it's not his concern. I'll pay your guest gift to St. Helen's, too, and something to St. Frideswide's."

Frevisse said quickly, "Alice, there's no need. I came because I wanted to, needed to."

"But the need came because of my husband."

And if he could neither see his fault nor make recompense for it, then Alice would, if only to mitigate her own pain, Frevisse saw, and she accepted all Alice wanted to give with a small bow of her head.

But, "There's something else," Alice said. "Suffolk has sworn you're never to come near us or ours again. He's ordered that I should never have aught to do with you anymore. I . . ." She gestured helplessly. "I don't know what to do."

Frevisse took hold of her hand. "Give him that much, for now at least. It doesn't matter."

"It *does* matter. It—"

"It's no more, on your side and mine, than a well-timed retreat." Frevisse smiled. "Like Joliffe's."

Half-unwillingly, Alice smiled back—a faint smile that faded as she said, "But the things you had to say. The lies about yourself. If anyone asks Suffolk for it, your reputation is gone."

Frevisse, smiling more, said lightly, "Do you know, I find I don't greatly care."

Nor did she. Not so long as, in her mind's eye, she could see Arteys riding away, alive and free under the summer sky.

Author's Note

Parliament and the downfall of Humphrey, duke of Gloucester, did take place in Bury St. Edmunds in February 1447. Contemporary chronicles have, as usual, slightly differing versions of the exact course of events, and choices between versions were sometimes necessary but nothing was altered for convenience's sake. *The Bastard's Tale* is built around what is known, rather than what is known being altered to fit the story.

At the time, those who had Gloucester under arrest claimed his death was from natural causes. That it was murder was the widespread belief among everyone else. Nothing can be proved at this remove in time but I wish to thank Dr. Carol Manning for her consideration of what few medical details are available. Mention of Arteys, bastard son of the duke of Gloucester, is scant in the records. He steps into history only at his father's death and disappears from it off the scaffold at Tyburn. As Kenneth H. Vickers says in the biography *Humphrey, Duke of Gloucester*, "One wonders what was [his] subsequent life?" But as Rudyard Kipling might say, that's another story. Recent historians sometimes corrupt his name to "Arthur" but he was condemned to death under the name "Arteys de Curteys" so Arteys he is in the story.

Events in London and at Tyburn, including the marquis (formerly earl, later duke) of Suffolk's part in them, are taken directly from the chronicles. Tyburn, a place of executions for hundreds of years, isn't to be found on a map of modern London, but Tyburn Way by Marble Arch is approximately there, though the plaque commemorating the site tends to move around the area.

Reynold Pecock, bishop of St. Asaph's and later bishop of Chichester, is historical, as is his sermon at St. Paul's that made him unavailable for the end of this story. It was only one of his many clashes with authority that eventually led to his trial for heresy. He was a profound scholar and prolific writer who believed it was better to convert heretics by reason rather than burning, and I owe great thanks to Stephen E. Lahey of LeMoyne College and Brent Moberley of Indiana University for rousing my interest in him, and to Dr. Lahey and Dr. Kate Forhan for the chance to present a paper on him at Siena College's Convivium in October 2000. There are various scholarly studies of his life and work, and some of his writings in Middle English are available.

Of the great abbey at Bury St. Edmunds almost nothing remains, and of St. Saviour's hospital even less, but there are numerous books and studies, and the town of Bury St. Edmunds and the lovely park around the broken remains of the abbey are well worth a visit. For more specific details about St. Saviour's see "The Medieval Hospitals of Bury St. Edmunds," by Joy Rowe, in *Medical History*, vol. 2 (1958).

The Play of Wisdom, edited by Milla Cozart Riggio, was my source of the elaborate play performed for the king, though what appears in the book should be considered an Ur-version of it, and the translations into modern English are my own. Particular admiration is due Gail McMurray Gibson, whose *The Theater of Devotion* and other work on East Anglian theater inspired me to create Master Wilde's company. Master Wilde and his players are imagined, but about forty years earlier a Master Wilde and his company were active in the vicinity.

Boethius' *Consolation of Philosophy* was a best-seller throughout Christendom for over a thousand years and is still available in a number of translations. Geoffrey Chaucer's *Boece* has not fared quite so well, popularly speaking. Again, the translations from it are mine.

Some apology is owed to scholars and fans of John Lydgate's works. My opinion (and Frevisse's) of his writings is purely personal. Most of his works are readily available in university libraries and his masque mentioned here was lately published as *Lydgate's Disguising at Hertford Castle* in a translation and study by Derek Forbes.

And again, and inadequately, my great, great thanks and appreciation to Sarah J. Mason and Bill Welland for photos, footwork, books, and a grand friendship.